IN THE
DAYS OF DREAD

Anton Marks

The
X
Press

Published by
The X Press
PO Box 25694
London, N17 6FP
Tel: 020 8801 2100
Fax: 020 8885 1322
E-mail: vibes@xpress.co.uk
Web site: www.xpress.co.uk

Printed by Cox & Wyman, Reading, UK

Distributed in UK by Turnaround Distribution
Unit 3, Olympia Trading Estate, Coburg Road, London N22 6TZ
Tel: 020 8829 3000
Fax: 020 8881 5088

ISBN 1-902934-20-2

This book is dedicated to the memory of my father
Evelyn Leopold Hewitt.
He taught me the fun in curiosity and the ethos of hard work.
Love always.

Acknowledgements

There are so many people and organisations I need to thank for their inspiration and encouragement. Here goes:

To my Family in Jamaica - Miss Hewitt and the Brown family

In England - Yvonne, Akil, Omel, Sabrina, Bones, Charmaine. You make it all worthwhile.

To all the readers of my first novel 'Dancehall' (especially my loyal female fans), I love you.

For reggae music and its musical heroes - Bob Marley, Luciano, Anthony 'B', Junior 'Gong', Junior Reid, Burning Spear, Marcia Griffith, Buju Banton, Sizzla, Coco Tea, Macka 'B', Culture, Freddie MacGregor, Capleton, Judy Mowatt, Vincent Knapp and many more.

Superhack Norman Gentles, for his unceasing promotion of my work.

Katherine Shewell, Patsy Antoine Isles, Suzanne Couch, Malorie Blackman. Just four of the strong women I deeply admire.

Merton Library - for your hospitality.

Sylvester's and Dilligence Barbers and the crew - EASY!

My lasting gratitude to the posse at The X Press.

Peter Kalu - fellow author and lover of the fantastic, friend and inspiration for 'In the Days of Dread'.

Victor Headley, Patrick Augustus, Marcia Williams, Diran Adebayo and Ricardo Allison - for their example and belief.

Desmond Spencer, George Frimpong, Louis Paya, Devon Montieth and Clay Maclean. My brothers who were always there when I needed support and first hand knowledge.

David Rodigan and Jazzy 'B' - my respects to you gentlemen.

Choice FM, Kiss FM and BBC 1Xtra and to all the pirate stations including Unique, Roots - keep up the 'riddims'.

Jet Star. The Voice, New Nation, The Gleaner, Pride, Nine, Untold and Vibe.

To friends at Heathrow Express - plenty a love.

To Mr. Seymour McLean and his unceasing efforts to have priceless artifacts seized from an Ethiopian church by British troops in 1868, returned - nuff respect boss!

And last, but by no means least to the world Rasta faith, for challenging what we all took for granted, for far too long.

The prophecies of Redemption as revealed unto
the prophet, Leonard Howell, one of the founding fathers
of the Rastafari faith.
Bellevue Mental Asylum, Kingston, Jamaica 1936.

It came to me in a vision of glory, I have seen the golden city in a place called Shashemane, Ethiopia. Jah-Jah, the God of Abraham took me and pointed to the place and told me a home of splendour will rise from the dust and it will be an example to the world. A man will come forth, a prophet who will lead us to this glory. He will take his rightful place as Negusa Negas elect of The King of Kings.

Jah, the father, burnt a message on a stone tablet like he did for the prophet Moses and beckoned me to read them and bring it back to his flock.

The words from the Almighty's hand read:

When Ethiopia cleaves with the nation of Ras and Africa begins its long struggle toward unity, the prophet will come. Known as the Peacemaker, he will end the war and lead the people to the golden city.

Who have eyes to see will see and who have ears to hear will hear. Selassie I!

> *Weep not: Behold the Lion of the tribe of Judah,*
> *the root of David, has prevailed to open the book*
> *and to loose the seven seals thereof.*
> **Revelation's 5:v5**

Centuries after these words were set down in the Bible, Ras Tafari was crowned Emperor of Ethiopia, taking the name Haile Selassie I, King of Kings, Lord of Lords, Conquering Lion of the tribe of Judah. He became the 225th ruler of the 2000-year-old Solomonic Dynasty.

In faraway Jamaica religious men saw the crowning of a black king in Africa as significant and in interpreting the scriptures, they realised the coronation was the fulfilment of a Biblical prophecy. Soon they would take the name of Rastafari - which in Amharic means 'Head Creator'. Over the new century their power and influence would be felt worldwide.

> *All the days of the vow of his separation, there shall be no razor come*
> *upon his head: until the days be fulfilled in which he separateth himself unto*
> *the Lord, he shall be holy and shall let the locks of his hair of his head grow.*
> **Numbers 6:v5**

COCKPIT COUNTRY, JAMAICA. SOMETIME SOON.

It came as it always did with no warning.

An explosion like a blast furnace of heat and sound.

As always, he found himself on his hands and knees, lifting his pounding head, his world upside down.

Everywhere he looked, there was death.

He saw men with guns moving purposefully through the confusion, killing indiscriminately. He saw bombs detonating leaving nothing more than limbs and gory splashes of crimson pulp.

Tears streaked down his cheeks.

He would die here, wherever here was.

Far from home, from his family.

He cowered beside a smooth cold pillar his throat scorched from the acrid smoke, ears ringing from every explosion.

Protect an guide mi father!

He wanted to close his eyes, to deny what he was witnessing but he was here for a purpose.

Dreadlocks!

Wails of agony grew louder around him but only one voice stood out from the swell.

Dreadlocks!

Only one voice was calling to him, pleading with him.

Dreadlocks

The only voice he could hear.

Stumbling over human remains, swaying , fighting against the fumes, the nausea, the Dread made his way to the voice.

But with every step the call of his name became fainter.

Every step fainter. Until it was barely a whisper and he was standing in front of a shattered podium.

A man lay crumpled there, bleeding. The Dread tended to him without a thought. He sat and placed the wounded man's head on his lap. He stared into those pitiful eyes and his blood chilled. The man's face was a horrific quilt work of cuts and lacerations. But it was the lines of his forehead, his nose, his cheekbones, that were significant.

Familiar.

The old man kept staring, unable to tear his eyes away.

Then he knew...

The prophet, Marcus Mosiah Garvey, spoke to him.

"She mustn't dead, mi breddah, yuh hear?" he pleaded. "Dem want her dead but yuh must look out feh her. Yuh daughter is deh future. We need her, we need her, Joshua."

"Why dem want her dead," he asked. "She is all mi have?"

But that anguished question had no answer. The figure in his arms was no longer the prophet. The once beautiful face of his only child ad replaced it, now blistered and torn. Her breath wheezed through her swollen lips and she convulsed like an epileptic.

"Mi baby!" he screamed.

He wouldn't let her die. She was the reason he never lost faith, the reason for everything.

He cradled her, gently rocking to and fro, frantic prayers spitting from his mouth.

She stiffened, convulsing wildly then went limp.

The last breath whispered from her lips. Looking down in disbelief, he held her head in trembling hands.

The evil wanted no part of his grieving, taking the corpse back to earth. The waxen flesh of her body riddled with vermin. Her skin curled and blackened, peeling away to tendon and sinew.

The old man screamed as the body of his daughter crumbled to dust. Dust that was twirling now out of control, clouding his eyes, streaming into his nose, filling his mouth and gagging him.

Choking. The Dreadlocks awoke gripping his covers, screaming.

******

HARLESDEN, WEST LONDON

Although she found it funny, a part of Yasmeen Beyene couldn't help thinking about what her star charts had predicted for her.

Your soul mate will finally walk into your life with no fanfare, no ceremony just a helping hand to put all your pressing worries into perspective.

She'd be lucky.

Her fingers kept busy over the blackboard.

"Mith!" The voice was squeaky and urgent. "Mith Beyene," the young boy lisped.

With her back to the class, Yasmeen continued what she was doing without a pause unawares she had been spoken to. Most of her class was deep in concentration, content with what they had come to know as home, for four hours on a Saturday morning. Nestled away in an North West London neighbourhood, the community centre acted as a focal point for the children living around it.

It was an austere cube with tables, chairs and a blackboard. Manned by underfunded and underpaid teachers. Volunteers to all intents and purposes. Still, Haile Selassie Saturday Class housed a group of kids with the highest aptitude test results in the borough, a proud fact she reminded them of at every opportunity.

Her brows knitted with concentration, a mess of other thoughts disturbed her mind.

The children noticed nothing. They were all focused on taking down the important notes.

Kofi wasn't to be ignored. He cleared his throat awkwardly, his brows rising into high arches. That having no effect, he started waving his arms for attention.

Finally, deciding to dispense with the niceties, he stood up and projected his nine-year-old voice on tip toes.

"They didn't sign the African Economic Accord on that date, Miss," he said.

The question produced a reaction. Yasmeen hesitated for a moment, then completed the sentence she was working on and stopped. Turning slowly, she looked at Kofi and smiled remotely.

Whatever thoughts that had begun to force their way into her mind started to fade.

Her eyes regained their intensity and she smiled.

"That's right!" She shuffled in her seat, her distant gaze departing. "Well-spotted, Kofi. I thought no one would pick up on the inconsistencies in the dates." She shielded her eyes like a sailor and glared at the rest of the class. "So some of you are actually awake."

The class laughed out and like a practised comic routine they all leaned forward, widening their eyes and pouting their lips in exaggerated concentration.

Yasmeen stepped back in playful shock at the young faces and they all giggled again.

As she resumed the lesson an eager silence descended.

"The Accord was signed three days earlier than thought by conventional history books because of an attempt on President Mbeki's life. Being the Chairperson of the Commonwealth of Democratic African States and the first leader to put their signature to the African Concorde Agreement, she was always in the spotlight. At home in New South Africa she had her own problems. Although the war raged on in many regions of the continent New South Africa didn't have to deal with any direct conflicts on its borders but there was adequate internal strife. The President became the target of many terrorist groups for her views." Yasmeen lowered her voice and leaned forward conspiratorially. Unconsciously the class reacted by mimicking the action. She stifled a smile, scanning their eager faces quickly and looked over her shoulders with mock suspicion.

"It was said that the Dread warned President Mbeki through a dream. She had known of him and his travels around the continent, speaking of unity and peace, she knew of how he had led the Nation of Ras Tafari from what it was in the past to the force it is today but more importantly she knew of his gift of the third sight. His vision saved her from a terrorist bomb and ended any possibility of a white homeland being re-established in New South Africa."

Sitting back up, she left the children staring open-mouthed. Her brow rose mysteriously.

"I'll leave it to your judgement, whether you believe that story or not. What you should know is that, even in today's world, details are hard things to come by especially for us historians. Nevertheless, as I've always told you never stop questioning the facts if it seems inconsistent, use your initiative and keep searching. Remember the truth is out there, somewhere."

The class burst into fits of laughter.

"Does that make sense?" Yasmeen asked.

Kofi's brows wrinkled with a question mark. "I think so, Mith."

He grinned and so did she.

Her enthusiasm was short lived. Those thoughts she was unsuccessfully trying to ignore became more insistent:

Why, do you stay in a Saturday school program that isn't sufficiently funded or work in a building that is desperate for renovation? No heat, no running water, health and safety rulings conveniently flaunted.

Why do you keep bothering with these kids, when most of the parents either don't care for education or are too busy keeping a roof over their heads to be aware of their children's progress?

Why, why, why?

With a dispassionate shake of her head, Yasmeen filled the chalkboard with the remainder of her notes.

A half hour later, she wrapped up the lesson, made sure the class had their notes stored in their memory pads and dismissed them before they started to get too boisterous. She watched them as they left. The usual certainty of being back with them next week was bathed in a dirty pool of doubt.

Yasmeen felt like a traitor. She had to make a choice. The children or her career.

Attaining her Masters in Ancient History and now taking the helm of a flagship museum had taken its toll. Regret didn't fit into that complicated equation, though. After all, wasn't high achievement what she strives for.

Sweeping away as best she could any feelings of guilt, Yasmeen looked forward to the silence of deep Itations with the sisters and the love of a community she had not shared her time with for over a year.

Ambition or commitment?

Only Jah-Jah could help her resolve the turmoil in her mind.

DOWNTOWN JOHANNESBURG, NEW SOUTH AFRICA.

There was a blinding flash from the gun's muzzle, followed by a deep roar, as the relic from a less sophisticated era bucked in his hand, violently shattering the silence.

"Yuh ramping, boss!" Asim Marshall growled at himself, his tone as hollow as his surroundings. "If that had been flesh an blood, turf bwoy, he would be down but not out." He squinted, playing in his mind the gruesome effects his bullet would have on the human body. "Yuh hurt him bad, but the fucker should be dead."

An involuntary shudder ran the length of his spine.

A slip like that in the field, ru'bwoy, and you'll never see your daughter again.

Stiffly, he stood up and inadvertently caught a reflection of himself in a dirty mirror to his left, it made him stop and pay attention.

Asim didn't deserve to look fit after all he'd been through.

He was supplely built and deceptively agile for six-foot one. Bald headed with hair only on his eyebrows - he could never grow facial hair and was always considered to be younger than he really was - with his almost oriental shaped eyes - a legacy from a great, great-grandmother who was half Chinese and half African-Jamaican. And then crowning those thin lids was the part of him he hated the most and women found most attractive - his long and effeminate eye lashes.

A smile crept up to the corners of his lips.

Just the thought that he would be leaving this endless war,

going back to his family and a pleasantly mundane life, was making him loosen up.

All he needed to do was stay alive to prove himself right.

Four years of active duty in the terrorist hot spots of the continent had created his controlled paranoia. The United States of Europe, in its role of aiding the nations of the African Concorde Agreement established foreign internal defence programs to keep the Commonwealth of Democratic African States intact from the inside. It had also provided Asim with a reason to abandon his family and call it duty.

Slowly, he stretched his neck left and then right, the bones of his vertebrae snapping into place.

"Forget everything else." He told himself. "My only concern is keeping my edge and staying alive. Going back to London in a body bag won't help to raise a yout."

He chuckled humourlessly.

Terrorist violence had gripped Jo'burg again. Unfortunately, Asim's unit was in the forefront. But what was most important to him was getting home in one piece.

He crouched forward again and squeezed the trigger twice. The rounds punched through the target's abdomen. His two-handed grip on the weapon was unwavering, his concentration intense.

He waited.

Deep thought and target practice somehow did not go hand in hand. He stood upright and slowly holstered the weapon and turned away from the target, his bald head gleaming under the artificial light.

Usually he was never able to take root in any one country because his kind of work could take him anywhere in Africa at a moment's notice. New South Africa became the exception.

It was an old fashioned shooting gallery, but he liked it that way. Nowadays you could do all your target practice from the comfort of your living room. Technology had the tendency to hastily sweep everything which did not meet up to its strict rules of efficiency into obscurity. Result, a world full of lazy minds and lazier bodies which had no appreciation for the solid practicalities of the past.

Just like the gallery, like his vintage guns - his 9mm Glock, the Bushmaster and the Uzi were all museum pieces - and his attitude, he was old fashioned and somewhat predictable.

He didn't like surprises and felt always more at home with the past. He knew what to expect, what had been done. The present was less clear and the future...

He peered through the small telescopic sight mounted in front of him, and confirmed his aim had been slightly off target.

A centimetre away from the bull's eye.

Like his life, maybe.

Suddenly he stood up and stepped forward. Whipping his gun from his shoulder holster, he aimed and pulled the trigger rapidly in one fluid motion.

The report was awesome, his fingers were tired, the magazine was nearly empty and his unprotected ears were ringing.

Again he checked the shattered target. This time he was pleased to see the interior circles peppered with evenly spaced punctures. Yet the muscles at one side of his fleshy lips twitched upwards irritably. Or was it a pleased smile. It was hard to tell with Asim.

Finally, from all the pain in his life a clear picture was forming of what he needed to do.

His only child.

Suddenly it had dawned on him with such force that he had to hold himself upright.

Nothing else mattered but surviving two more weeks on this dangerous mission.

The zeal for his duty had evaporated, a soldier with no cause was a liability. His career was over. The authorities just didn't realise it yet.

A short sharp, vibration. The pager in his belt, buzzed for his attention again.

Central command.

Dem just won't let me rest to raas.

He smiled thinly.

What a time to start caring about whether he lived or died.

In a moment he was gone.

******

The sun had disappeared behind the cityscape when Yasmeen came out of the secure parking facility and made her way tentatively along Mandela Street. She would have preferred arriving here earlier but had been overtaken by other things. Now, as the oppressive architecture bared down on her, a growing sense of threat accompanied the darkening shadows.

It's just your imagination, she told herself, keep walking.

The Tabernacle had been her place of worship and her spiritual home ever since she came to England from East Africa with her mother.

The Nation of Ras Tafari was much more than a way of life. It had taught her pride in herself and her heritage. She couldn't enter the house of Jah and act as if she wasn't thankful. And on the world stage it was not the novelty it used to be, but a powerful force for change. Some day she could probably give much more of herself to it. Some day. Right now she had more work to do.

Her appointment from Resident Historian, to Assistant Curator of the Hall of Ethiopia was a dream she kept alive and relevant. Long-standing traditions had been broken by her appointment and that in itself required recognition if not celebration.

The first woman ever to step into that position, the first of African descent and the first Rasta.

Miriam would have been so proud.

She had been a mother and sister to her.

Now she could only draw strength from the memories.

I wish you were here now.

Her eyes adjusted to the artificial street lights as they flickered to life, replacing the dimness of the disappearing sun. The junkies came into their habitat and this part of North West London suddenly became unpredictable again.

London was a city of paradox.

To the world, London was the Millennium city. Environmentally it stood head and shoulders above its peers in the United States of Europe. Working solutions for the problems of pollution, housing and urbanisation were tackled swiftly. The government's determination to see these changes take place bordered on hysterical. London was now like a new city. The historical and the contemporary mingled seamlessly. Biotechnology rejuvenated the Thames. Pockets of artificially maintained 'natural areas' broke up miles of steel and glass. Whatever did not fit into its shiny new image was border-lined and actively forgotten. Many inner city neighbourhoods were simply allowed to disintegrate, and its people with it. The local authorities unconcerned about the crime levels within these areas only started worrying when the disease began to spread beyond its confines. For all its futuristic landscape and its scientific advancements gun crime was at an all time high and these pockets of neglect called Zones were the major breeding grounds.

Scotland Yard's Met-1 surveillance cameras didn't help boost confidence amongst the residents either. A police presence would have been more appreciated but that was reserved for the neighbourhoods that had a future.

Yasmeen shrugged at the unfairness of it all and watched as an electronic eye kept a keen interest in her steady progress, moving along its network of wires like an industrious spider, its task of providing a deterrent on these London streets an impossible one.

She may have seemed casual but she was acutely aware of the dangers and far more concerned with being prepared. High above street level, PLI's -Perpetrator Level Indicators, were flashing amber as she penetrated deeper into Zone C154 - an area of high felony occurrence covering the notorious Kings Cross and a thin strip of Camden Town. She was reasonably safe for now as long as the colour remained neutral and the Klaxons didn't begin to scream. Such was the unpredictability of criminal activity in these parts, anything could happen.

Heartbeat thudding dully in her chest, her mouth parched, she struggled to keep her apprehension locked away.

As always it was best not to draw attention to yourself. She was just a lone Rasta woman, going about her business and engrossed in her own world.

Nervously she shifted her focus from the stark terrain in front of her. Leering eyes peered out from open all hour shops, ogling her, the sensualness of her easy sway, long supple legs and small sandalled feet, drawing unwelcome stares.

Some things never change.

She remembered how she used to pray to be ordinary looking, wanting to be less attractive, to be accepted. Maturity and time healed those self-destructive wishes, developing into a confident woman able to give thanks for the gifts she inherited from her Jamaican father and Ethiopian mother. Being a Rasta 'dawta' and with the respect the Nation of Ras Tafari carried, that alone put most people at ease in her company. The rest she did not care about. Yasmeen would not apologise to anyone for who she was.

Wolf whistles came from an open window above her. She didn't break her stride, her hand remained in her shoulder bag, caressing her only protection.

The Close Quarter Stunner customer satisfaction guarantee promised the ultimate in personal protection. Somehow it didn't make her feel any better.

The white rectangles of the zebra crossing illuminated weakly indicating it was safe to walk and she stepped out on the road, passing a group of youths idling on the other side. They had their backs to her, too engrossed in counting credits or stolen goods to be interested. She pushed the large wrought iron gates, walking briskly through, she hurried onto the forecourt of the Tabernacle and breathed uneasily.

An hour or so later, the meeting was at an end and Yasmeen sat talking to her mother's oldest and dearest friend. Although she had not seen her in person for more than a year, she was the closest thing to a mother that remained in her life.

"I'm glad you could come daughter," Sister Ijah beamed, wiping sweat from her brow. "Please, don't let it take so long before I see you again, yuh hear."

Yasmeen hugged her warmly.

"It won't sister, I promise."

She remembered fondly when Miriam was alive how they would sit and swap stories about their homelands. Miriam would talk of Shashemane while Sister Ijah joked about her village in Jamaica. The little woman's vibrancy and humour as she recounted her life, had brightened many a depressing evening. What she didn't realise, was how she painted a picture of the Island so vividly in Yasmeen's head, with descriptions like detailed brush strokes.

She had welcomed them into England after they fled Ethiopia, making sure their acceptance into the Rasta community was as painless as could be expected and when Yasmeen became an adolescent, Sister Ijah's was always a shoulder that would support her.

"You would make your mother proud, yuh si child." Sister Ijah stroked the insides of Yasmeen's palm, her eyes bright. "The whole community talking about how yuh moving forward in life. Is yuh mother an her blessings following yuh."

Yasmeen nodded respectfully.

"There was nobody like her." She said.

"Jah bless her memory and dat's why I'm worried sometimes."

"Don't be, Mom," Yasmeen smiled. "I'm fine, honest."

"Yuh make it difficult feh me to keep my promise to her." Sister Ijah sighed. "We need to see each other more often child not just talk over some cell phone."

"I'm sorry for that, Sister. I've been burying myself in work trying to prove I can fight with the best. I suppose I gave a bit too much but I'll do better, we won't be such strangers this time around."

"Good." Her plump cheeks puffed up as she smiled. Then she looked her up and down with an appraising eye. "By the way, when was deh last time you go out an socialise?"

Yasmeen shrugged.

Sister Ijah shook her head as her finger wagged.

"Don't turn out like me, with not a chick nor child. I want you to introduce me to yuh King man."

Yasmeen laughed at the outdated term for a man in her life.

"I haven't got a King man, Sister. No one will have me." She joked.

Sister Ijah kissed her teeth long and hard, then said, "What you telling me!" She shook her head disbelieving. "All dem fool, fool bwoy that come to worship here don't realise what a beautiful and intelligent girl yuh are. My God, them don't know dem bed head, from dem bed foot. But don't you worry, mi dawta." She threatened. "I will have to do some inquiries myself on dat matter."

Yasmeen could only laugh, throw her arms around Sister Ijah's neck and plant a kiss on her plump cheeks.

The prayer meeting had been inspirational and Yasmeen was glad The Tabernacle of Abuna Paulos, the Ethiopian, in Camden Town, had continued to be the focal point on weekends for a dedicated group of Rasta women.

It had ended on a high note as everyone chatted about spending United Africa Day contributing something to the community and not just celebrating. Yasmeen would be doing neither and would be working but she would say a prayer like most who held the continent close to their heart and pray for an end to the conflicts.

The children had been restlessly occupying themselves in the background, excited that they were not in bed but fought against tiredness with their last reserves of energy. Sister Ijah had seen the exhaustion reflected in their eyes and ended the Itations promptly. Soon after discussing their celebration plans they went on to gather their belongings.

Yasmeen had felt a sense that anything was possible after quiet meditation. She had prayed for guidance and, although she still did not have the answers, she now believed somehow the options, would be much clearer.

Heels and soft shoes echoed through the aisles of the vast

building as the group headed for the main door. Their voices remained whispers as if they did not want to disturb the calmness and peace their place of worship required.

The children seemed less concerned about the respect the adults showed, but were convinced quickly with a few stern words. The large motor-assisted doors groaned open. It had suddenly become chilly and quiet outside.

The atmosphere outside seemed to absorb all sound. There was an absence of traffic and even pedestrian chatter as people went about their business.

Yasmeen shivered, suddenly she had a strange feeling that someone was watching them. Her scalp rose into a mound of goose flesh. She hesitated.

She lingered for a while, waiting for the other sisters, so they could accompany each other.

"Yasmeen!"

Silence.

Her name had exploded out from the darkness. She turned expectantly but no one tried to gain her attention. She was not imagining this, someone had called out her name. Someone out there.

The cold hand of fear would have touched her if she had realised the street were darker than usual. If she had realised street lamps had been broken and their fragments strewn across the pavement, or felt a sense of gathering chaos like an upcoming storm.

But she knew nothing of this.

Ezekiel the temperamental son of one of the youngest in the group was already impatiently sitting at the bottom of the stairs. He was still huffing from a slap he had received earlier and peered into the darkness beyond the wall.

Even he found it peculiar. And even more so as a man appeared from the shadows. A mass of locks fell untidily around his shoulders, his piercing eyes searching and a flaming spliff jutting out of his mouth.

The dreadlocks winked at him.

Casually he took the big head from his lips and used the red-hot end to ignite what to Ezekiel's eyes was a flaming fire ball.

The man smiled at him, again.

Drawing his arm back as far as it could go, he lobbed the fire ball skyward. The small boy just sat there, watching in detached awe as the missile arced over his head, spinning and blazing in slow motion and then violently exploding on the steps above him. Ezekiel turned frantically in every direction as more of the fire balls rained down from the darkness beyond, exploding on impact. His desperate gaze held only by the assailants as they came into view.

The abnormality of dreadlocks and skinhead together, raced through an immature mind that was unable to evaluate the unlikeliness of what he had seen. In the distance, the man stood impassively observing the damage for a moment, and then he was gone, disappearing into the midst of a savage-looking group of tattooed and white baalheads spewing racist abuse.

To the boy, they were the bogeymen of his nightmares. His voice returned as a terrified shriek and with it his presence of mind. Desperate to find his mother.

Flames were everywhere.

Yasmeen's scream locked in her throat. The situation unravelling before her eyes was unreal. Coughing, the propellant fumes stinging her eyes and the heat overwhelming, the reality of it became all too evident. Their only escape lay behind them, back into the Tabernacle.

Yasmeen scanned the confusion for Sister Ijah. The instant that Yasmeen's eyes met the elder's, her confused senses met with a tortuous scream of her name. Then Sister Ijah erupted into a howling furnace of flames. The human torch rolled down the stairs, thrashing and screaming.

Yasmeen stood back, shrieking at the horror in front of her, tears streamed down her cheeks, her mind wiped clean. She could do nothing to save Sister Ijah.

A wave of guilt welled up in her as the realisation that she had seen this horror re-enacted before. It had been in her dreams.

And like many times before it had lurked in the shadows of her consciousness and allowed destiny's hand to play itself before revealing itself.

What use was a gift that was unable to protect you before the fact?

******

HACKNEY TOWN HALL, LONDON.

One week later. United Africa Day.

"Soon dun!" Yasmeen repeated the man's words with shock, her eyes blazing while she shook her head trying to extract some sense from what he had just said. "What does that mean exactly, Elder?"

Elder Jeremiah took in a deep breath.

The proceedings had taken on a decidedly chilly atmosphere.

One he had expected but could do nothing to prepare for. Now the situation was beyond calming. He looked around at the members of the Rasta Forum, confidently expecting some support.

They met the elder with silent stares. His eyes focused on Yasmeen again and recognised the cold glint of determination.

He had been warned about her in his briefing before coming to London from Jamaica to preside over the congregation. In his many years of diplomatic service for the Nation, he hadn't met any woman quite so determined.

Somehow the Rasta hierarchy respected or feared this sistah. Jeremiah felt none of those emotions, he just did not care much for her tone.

"The elders know about the escalating situation here, sister," he said calmly. "We are not blind and deaf. It is at the top of the Council's agenda."

Yasmeen's brows twitched, her eyes were glistening reservoirs of tears, as fragmented images danced behind her eyes. Sister Ijah's screams, the stench, the heat...

"I think I speak for everyone here, Elder," she spoke softly leaning forward on the chair in front of her. "This violence has plagued us for nearly three years and, of this time, the elders have literally ignored the problem. Sending a few observers, who saw nothing and did nothing is not enough. They are attacking our tabernacles. We want to know from the Council exactly what is being done. You are the council's representative here. Don't insult our intelligence by dancing around the real issue. We want to know what is being done?"

The elder's head tilted backwards from the onslaught, his fingers touching his cheek as if he was checking for blood. The diplomat in him resisted confrontation while the old traditional Rasta man wanted to discipline her on the spot. His fist clenched and his eyes narrowed as he took control.

"You're new to the running of this Forum, aren't you, sista..." He paused. There was something vaguely familiar about her. He brought up her personal file on the VDU before him. "Sista Beyene. Here, things follow a particular process. Being in a position of prominence yourself, you must understand." He grinned slyly. "We deal in due process here. There's no place for individual opinions guiding our decisions."

Yasmeen shook her head solemnly.

"People are dying and with all due respect you still want to play games of protocol with us." Their eyes locked and for interminable seconds Yasmeen matched him, glare for glare, the only messages communicated were hostile ones. "You can try and side-step the reality as much as you want, Elder, it won't go away. We demand to know."

"You 'demand'." Elder Jeremiah's voice was edged with annoyance, still wondering what it was about her that made her feel so familiar.

Yasmeen was ready with an acidic reply but a young man behind her stood up, pushing his glasses up the ridge of his nose.

"The sister is right, man. It's about time we had some hard facts, not speculation."

"Yes, iyah, it due." Another voice in the meeting agreed.

"If the Nation has some solutions to this craziness," an older woman in colourful headgear added, "why can't we hear it?"

Voices rose as feelings mounted.

The elder stepped back from the podium with a look of frustration and defeat. His fingers massaged his chin while his eyes focused into the distance. The muscles of his jaw tensed as he made a decision that was an unsavoury one. With renewed vigour he cleared his throat and returned to the podium. Staring at the forum members with quiet intensity, he used the time they took to calm down to decide on how he would approach their ultimatum. His aide, a man with a ram rod straight posture, thin faced and humourless was standing vigilantly at the end of the raised platform. The elder summoned him and they exchanged words, briefly. The man then briskly walked away and approached the secretary recording the proceedings. With no care for the secretary's protests, he reached over and switched off the recording equipment.

Silence.

The Elder's cue.

"First I would like to say Sister Ijah's vicious murder has horrified us. Our prayers are with her families and friends."

"Dat nuh good enough." Someone kissed their teeth. He ignored the outburst, adjusting the sleeves of his gown.

"But I bring you good tidings my bredrin and sistren. The Council of Rasta Patriarchs are going to announce to the Rasta flock around the world, the date for the celebration of the Ascension."

Gasps of surprise rose from the audience. They had talked about the occasion for some years now, strong opposition in some quarters had delayed the final decision - the Nation of Ras Tafari would have an ordained leader.

Negusa Negas.

"Rasta has been a faith of resistance against all the odds," he sermonised. "And this blight on our name in London is just another string of tests we've had to endure and conquer from time."

Calmly the elder placed both palms flat on the podium and leaned forward.

"In seven months time, we will have made history and we want it to be made with this blight resolved. The Council has already taken the initiative to actively find solutions to this disgrace happening in your midst. Without it being resolved our way of life cannot turn a new chapter. I can say positively, that as I'm standing here, secret plans are under way to deal with these false lions killing in the name of the most high."

"Secret?" Someone cried out. "We need specifics."

Jeremiah calmed the man's apprehensions with a reassuring to and fro motion of his hands.

"This is a delicate situation, brethren, understand. The Spear of the Nation is fighting a religious and racial war, which the Nation has no part of. When the public sees their lion's mane and what they are doing, they think they are Rasta. They are heathen!" He shouted. "Innocents are suffering in the process. Murder is a government issue, a police matter. We will only reveal the plans we have made with the authorities to particular members of our community who can contribute within the law. It has to be that way."

"And the Pure Blood?" Someone asked.

"The Pure Blood will be dealt with within the framework of the law of course."

"Dat nuh bomboclaat good enough, Elder." Brazenly, a young man stood up amidst a group of youths. "If you want to be at the mercy of them murdering baalheads that's your choice." He spat. "The Rasta yout will not be at anyone's mercy."

The group and its spokesman stormed out.

Yasmeen shook her head regretfully and turned back to the elder who had just experienced yet another taste of the people's depth of feeling.

"I suppose you expect us to take your word for all this, seeing as we have no formal record of what you've just said."

Jeremiah nodded his head to her as a sign of distaste or

respect, she was not sure which and did not care.

"My word as an elder is exactly what I'm giving you, sista. My word is what I'm giving all of you. We will resolve this situation at all cost."

THE TABERNACLE OF RAS, KINGSTON, JAMAICA. LATER THAT SAME DAY.

"Praises to the most high, from whom all good tings come. Amen and Amen!"

Figures dressed in traditional African robes sat around the huge slab of polished wood silently absorbed by the blessing. Shrouded in smoke from all sides, the remains of the burning ganja forming wispy shelves like ethereal staircases to the cracked ceiling of the meeting chamber. The 'Healing of the Nation' had blessed the ceremony and while the essence rose from the Kutchie symbolising their supplication to the Father on high, they reflected. Today was the anniversary of the fulfilment of a life long dream that had been lamented in song and literature by Rasta for decades.

A prophecy the Nation of Ras Tafari held close to its heart.

From an area in the centre of the lacquered slab an iris portal noiselessly opened. The shiny chrome head of a Holographic Projector came into view, the metallic frame locking into position with a sharp snap and Lite Globes floating above their heads dimmed, throwing the chamber into darkness. With a piercing whine beams of light burst from the projector head to fuse into a sharp three dimensional image. The elders relived the hour long ceremony which culminated with the elegant figure of Denise Mbeki, the president of New South Africa, graciously addressing a group of African leaders. Smiling, and with an air of relief some might say, she leaned forward and placed the first signature on the African Concorde Agreement.

The World Service anchor man Richard Hall began his commentary as the events of the past unfolded in the background.

"Today millions of viewers witnessed history in the making.

It was the dawning of a new era. The pragmatists amongst us, says it will end in more turmoil and bloodletting, while others shed tears of relief as the president of New South Africa, Denise Mbeki, great, great granddaughter of Nelson Mandela, put her signature at the head of the list of nations participating in this new chapter in African history. The African Concorde Agreement has become a reality and with it a semblance of hope burns. While the world doubted and debated, from the ashes of the ongoing conflicts came the Commonwealth of Democratic African States. And with it the possibility of a common market, the development of a single currency and an established and centralised parliament working only for the member states. The West has never witnessed such a concerted political force emerging from the continent.

The darkness skittered away just so far and then slowly it formed a figure that seemed to dislodge itself from the diminishing shadow.

Both silhouette and man stood as one.

The light had caught Patriarch Yamu just as he had eased back his chair and stood up gently shaking the hood away from his head.

An impressive figure.

Grey locks hung long, shrouding his face as he bowed.

Someone cleared their throat as if to speak, the sound hollow in the great hall.

His reaction was immediate as it was surprising.

The patriarch's head snapped upright, much like a man preparing to defend himself. His ears cocked, he listened for the expected remark, the derogatory comment that would indirectly question his worthiness for the honorary position he held.

None came.

Reigning in his defences, he relaxed the taut muscles of his face.

Honorary position, my raas!

Instead of it being a sign of respect for his achievements and his unceasing efforts in developing the Nation, it became a constant homage to his dead brother's memory.

Reminders of the man who joined the way of life of Ras Tafari with the ancient faith of the Ethiopian Orthodox Church, the man who had literally swayed African States into accepting unity, a man whose compassion for the wretchedness of the human condition was a well-documented fact, a man whose very presence assured millions of avid viewers for his speeches.

A self-righteous dead brother, whose visions every Rasta man, woman and child swore had guided them into the future. A brother who the Nation chose stubbornly to remember at every conceivable moment for his supposed contributions.

The 'Dread' as the flock called him - with misplaced affection -had taken enough of what was his.

Only his twin's untimely death had given Yamu an opportunity to show his true worth.

Jah damn every one of dem!

The flock was besotted with his brothers 'Ism's an schism's'.

Yamu just had to look around at the men and women seated with their insipid looks of devotion to remind him why he hated these festivals and why he held them all in contempt for giving his brother's life works so much significance.

Everywhere he looked, everywhere he went, constant reminders of the Dread and the legacy he left behind. Old fashioned and weak ideas which in today's world would put the black man under the whip for another two hundred years. Unity between the races, instead of African supremacy and Rasta world order.

And they had listened to him. That was why the Nation was lost in the wilderness and only he could guide them back to the promised land. Just as they were patiently sitting now, waiting for him to speak, they were waiting for him to give them a new focus, to guide them.

The Commonwealth of Democratic African States was much more than a spiritual event. To Yamu it was a solid platform for all out war with the European downpressors and their offspring.

War inna babylon!

Under his spiritual guidance he would make them pay for hundreds of years of injustices meted out against the African people. Like the Jews, WE must never forget.

His dream was to make sure they never would and as Negusa Negas he could make it all possible. For Negusa Negas was recognized worldwide as king of a nation.

Whoever seh, 'Widout war there cannot be peace and that one cannot exist without the other' is trying to lead us astray!

Yamu shook his head, trying to block by force of will his brother's sickening words of non-violence from echoing in his head, but couldn't.

It had him worried. The frequency of these occurrences was becoming more and more regular and startlingly vivid. Fragmented images - through his brother's eyes.

The Dread was alive.

It was that simple. He didn't know how, he only knew it was the truth. He could feel him. That's why he couldn't sleep. The Dread - the one person who could stand in the way of his ordination. He would destroy him and everything related to him and this time nothing would remain. His brother was not the one spoke of in the Prophecy.

Negusa Negas was his destiny and no one else's.

For now his concern lay with the outspoken patriarchs who felt they could sense the dangerous undercurrents to his plans but not knowing for sure if they were right.

He was watching them, while his plan hatched. A cunning plan. He smiled.

A smile from the face like some ancient African ritual mask used to evoke evil spirits and armed with a small protruding mouth which you feared hid needle sharp teeth. It struck you more as a weapon of destruction than a means to deliver words.

The patriarch walked faway from the table, his hands clasped tightly behind his back then gracefully he turned, masking a hunger behind features that seemed to glow with passion.

"Jah!" He chanted, his voice powerful. The word reverberated around the chamber.

They echoed his praise, uncertainly at first, as he took the ceremony away from its usual format. Only Yamu had the power to do that and he abused it at his pleasure.

"We have lived to see the final struggle for peace in Africa in our lifetime, my brothers and sisters. Now, as the father has promised, one of our numbers will lead our people and become the first in the line of Negusa Negas, Shepherd of the flock of Jah-Jah."

"Raaastafari! Ever living, ever sure." They chanted.

"Yuh must open your hearts an pray dat when the time comes for you to choose, yuh will have read the signs an have no doubts who should lead the flock."

"Yes I." A majority chorused.

A self-assured snicker came from the other end of the table.

"Of course we will know, brother." The calm tone from the Trinidadian patriarch carried a severe intensity. "As you know, the final decision is ours." He motioned to the seated leaders with a savage sweep of his hands. "If I didn't know better I man would think you were trying to tell us where our votes should be placed."

Yamu smiled grimly, his eyes narrowing. They were, smouldering light brown, piercing and alert.

"No need for dat, breddah Samuel." Yamu raised both palms to the ceiling with insincere submission. "Jah will guide our hands an heart. I'm confident we will make the right choice and Rasta will finally have its Shepherd."

"Just so that you don't believe YOUR will, is the will of Jah, almighty."

"Father forbid, mi breddah."

Yamu bowed humbly, concealing a hatred he did well to keep concealed. Brother Samuel returned the gesture and took his seat.

Yamu did so too, his eyes skewering the elder across the table from him.

A savage, cruel gaze.

Ras Tafari History will praise only one name as deh First, he swore to himself, and believe I and I it will be mine alone.

COCKPIT COUNTRY, JAMAICA.

His scream was short lived.

The Dread filled his lungs with short sharp breaths, his austere gown soaked in sweat and his head pounding to the beat of his panicked heart. In desperation his gnarled fingers searched for the cool bed linen. He buried his face into the folds of the material in relief.

The intensity of this vision could not be ignored any longer. He stared into the darkness, trying to forget for a moment.

After twenty-five years hidden here and never once even a dream, he reasoned his gift was dormant or dead.

But the Babylonians were at the city gates baying for his blood, again and it had reawakened.

They wanted to break him, destroy his seed - his true legacy on earth. He smiled grimly.

Man a plan but Jah a wipe out.

They won't tek my only family from me!

A pea dove chirped in the distance making his threat sound hollow.

He shivered in the warmth. Gingerly, he rubbed his palms over the protruding veins at the back of his hands and wherever he felt beads of perspiration he massaged them into his dark skin.

Closing his eyes, he breathed in, his body odour blending with the smell of decaying wood.

His vision blurred and a vista that belonged in his nightmares opened. The screams of pain, the blood. Her mutilated body. His baby.

As his waking nightmare subsided, he found himself huddled into the wall like a cornered animal, tears streaming down his cheeks.

He took a moment to gain control and swung his legs off his bed. He supported himself on trembling hands, the white ropes of his thick hair fell over his face, obscuring his already dimmed vision. He could still hear her calling.

Shaking his head, his eyes clenched shut, he tried to will the real or imaginary sensations away.

With care he brought a dried cashew nut slung around his neck to his lips and kissed it.

His confidence building, he grabbed his walking stick. Now with more purpose, he shuffled over to the cast lamp hewn out of a smooth stone, its centre hollowed out with a cotton wick imbedded in a reservoir of hardened coconut oil.

He brought a match to it.

It flared and crackled to a constant flame.

The darkness was sucked away suddenly, revealing the rough cut thatch walls and spartan decor.

He made his way to his study hurriedly.

Old volumes - that had gone out of print circulation and advancing technology decades ago - lined the walls of the space he used when he was engrossed in his more academic work. Dusty scrolls from far-fetched institutions lay untidily about, official accolades from governments and organisations were thinly layered with dust and sat alongside faded photographs of a proud past.

His eyes focused on the pristine computer terminal outshining everything else in the room. He switched the solar energy generator on and waited for it to reach its optimum output, powering the very few electronic commodities he possessed in his basic home perfumed with the faint whiff of prime ganja and moist soil.

"Yuh will not harm my family." He mumbled.

A gold chalice lay in the corner - the only real extravagance he had in his life - with a bundle of his home grown cannabis beside it. His Maccabees Bible took a centre stage on a metal podium, and the skylight above directed shafts of sunbeams onto the Word at midday.

It was like the Almighty was blessing it and that image buoyed up his spirits.

He stared absently through his plexiglass window at the far end of the room. His thatched kitchen outside was surrounded by the greenest, most lush vegetables you would ever hope to see, blending inconspicuously with its covering of bush and making his home invisible to only the closest scrutiny.

He absorbed the world outside.

A hummingbird hovered nearby. Its long beak and probing tongue tasting the dewy nectar from a hibiscus flower. The Dread watched the frantic movement and was transported for a moment.

He recaptured his thoughts as the mild throbbing from the generator, rose up from the floorboards. The fluorescent light in his study flickered on and the old man seated himself and recited his message to the awaiting terminal.

Minutes later a bird burst from the foliage. A grey and white messenger pigeon left its masters home banking sharply on the upward currents of heat breaking from the valley below and headed for the village in Trelawny.

Thank Jah he was not totally alone in the world.

Solemnly he followed the bird's path, contemplating.

He knew his family's life hinged on the steps he had devised over these last three days. And whether those same plans were at all possible would depend on the answer to the message, strapped to the bird's leg.

If the answer was yes, he was trusting the lives of his baby with a yout. A yout, he himself had entrusted his life with.

If the answer was no, it did not bear thinking about. He couldn't be sure how long his daughter had left.

He cursed his frailties for he could do no more but remain within the confines of Thro-Weh district and that was virtually nowhere at all.

He knew he could change nothing only follow the path fate had set. What will be, will be.

But he had to try.

He wiped tears from his eyes and watched the image of the pigeon blur as it stroked its way to the horizon.

"Guide an protect," he murmured. "Guide an protect."

TRELAWNEY, JAMAICA. THREE DAYS LATER.

The ganja fields stretched as far as the eye could see.

A green bed of chlorophyll shimmering under the midday sun, flowing in graceful waves from the gentle breezes like the currents in the sea. The lone Rasta man imagined that the Father himself had dropped it from heaven.

All rambling hills and rivers.

My Zion dis.

Trevor's wiry locks flashed from left to right as he swung his machete to the roots of the sensi plants, grunting with the effort. His powerful right arm swinging from left to right like a human combine harvester. His string vest clung to his chest, dust and humus changing his complexion to earth black. Cannabis leaves settled to the ground on both sides of where he worked, in flurries of green and dark brown.

He didn't have to be doing this. His team of ten men and women tended to all twenty-five acres of Rebel Vineyards with a wide array of agricultural machinery. There was no need for this kind of back breaking work but it helped him to think and kept him in shape.

And he did have a lot to think about.

The beams of sunlight able to penetrate the canopy of tall ganja trees above his head, reflected off his glistening back like obsidian. Engrossed with his efforts he swung the cutlass effortlessly through five or six plants at a time and then threw them behind him. Trevor had been cutting away steadily at the weed plants on this plot for at least an half hour.

The old man told me that they would come.

His muscles ached and his stomach complained but he had to be patient.

He glanced around quickly.

Behind him a magnificent mango tree. Its leaves stroked the soil as it was weighed down with green fruit. A wood-fire burned away below it a charcoal black breadfruit perched on top and steam issuing from its stem. Two big-eyed red snappers lay beside the staple food, stuffed with seasonings and herbs and roasting evenly for a lunch he was looking forward to.

Just till the messengers arrived, he thought. Just till he could give his performance an done.

Trevor's eyes burned red as the fumes from the herb plants permeated the air. Midday especially he had to wear breathing apparatus. It was necessary if he wanted to work at his peak and not be slowed down by the intoxicating gases thrown off from the extended buds.

He was prepared but the birds fluttering on the ground, drunk from the smells were not. Insects hummed giddily as the heat rose in shimmering curtains. Trevor stopped for a moment and wiped his face with a dirty rag limply hanging from his back pocket. In the same motion as returning the rag he quickly took a file and began to keen the edge of his blade to a silver finish.

Dem deh yah.

He gave a satisfied flash of his mane and commenced chopping again as if he had heard nothing, his senses acutely aware of movement.

The bushes to his right parted suddenly and sandalled feet stepped through.

He kept chopping away.

The men edged closer to him, their steps absorbed by the moist fertiliser.

One, two, three...

Trevor spun unexpectedly on the balls of his feet. He drew the razor-sharp machete low and with lightening speed lunged forward. He hesitated just in time, freezing in a stance resembling some savage Samurai warrior, in feudal Japan.

"Dreadlocks!" The words exploded from his mouth.

His hands tensed for a moment as he twisted the blade upwards, relaxing as a smile brightened his face.

"Be careful how yuh creep up behind me, natty, dem last day yah, you can't be too careful. What a guh dung?"

Ruben was straight-faced, an intense man in his late twenties, a small goatee beard stuck oddly on his chin with spectacles covering intelligent eyes. His hair was only shoulder length and he preferred to wear the yabesha lebsse traditional garment popular in Ethiopia.

The younger dread respected him for his fairness and his vast knowledge of the crops but was uncomfortable with Trevor's laid back leadership style.

The bwoy needed to mellow.

Beside him was the Nation of Ras crop supervisor, standing with his hands behind his back, sour-faced as usual. The older man, they called Papa - a baalhead, who travelled to plantations around the island making sure the Nation received its fair quota of the best sensi - stood there with a worried frown on his face.

Ruben wet his lips self consciously.

"We just got a message from town." Trevor nodded at Ruben's words urging him on. "The elders need to see you urgently. They expect you to come and meet with them in Kingston in two days time."

"Why?"

Ruben shrugged.

"Yuh must be bloodclaat crazy." Trevor snapped. "Dem think they can just snap dem fingers an mi just come running? Dem nuh know me, boss." Trevor's eyes blazed. "I have responsibilities yah suh. In one week my crop must get reap an sell. Nuthin else is my priority."

"They are insisting." Reuben added somewhat cagily.

Trevor kissed his teeth.

"Mek dem insist." He turned away to look at his roasting fishes.

Ruben looked down uncertainly and used his sandals to dislodge some loose dirt in front of him, still unable to understand Trevor's outright hostility to the elders. But knowing also he had a track record of deviously getting his own way.

Ruben tried to make him see sense, not that it mattered.

"The only Bloodclaat man mi answerable to is Jah-Jah himself," Trevor assured him.

"Well today that is about to change."

Trevor grunted.

"Change?"

"Unfortunately, they have made sure your passion for creating your own choices has been curtailed."

Trevor swore and his hand snapped upwards releasing the machete with a defiant flick of his wrist. It flew into a twirling arc, its spin a blur of motion as the flying guillotine ended with the blade buried deep in the bark of the lone mango tree in the distance.

"Fuck dem." Trevor's voice was low and menacing.

Papa spoke.

"Calm down, young lion." His voice rose gruffly above the breeze, like granite stones falling down a hillside. Still his uneasiness was obvious, as his eyes shied away from Trevor's intense stare.

"Ruben right, Trevor. Look at this."

Papa handed Trevor a sheet of paper. The official Rasta seal was at the far right-hand corner. He read the communiqué and chuckled at the audacity of their request.

The powers that thought they governed his life, were threatening to revoke his licence to sell his 3000 metric tonnes of reaped sensimilla. They knew as well as he did that without a licence he would be unable to sell his harvest and rot would eventually set in. It was no idle threat for the whole economy of the village depended on that harvest.

They had summoned him before, just as they did today, three years ago. The transgression he had to answer for - even after the court of the land had found him not guilty - involved seriously wounding a six-man raiding party who had tried to relieve him of a truckload of his finest genetically modified sensi. The old men at the Tabernacle in Warricka Hills had all sympathised with his actions, except for one.

Dem want mi, badly.

Trevor crumpled the paper with disdain and flung it aside glaring for a silent moment at Papa.

The paper rapidly decomposed.

"Dem choose to fuck wid deh wrong man."

"Maybe so." Ruben said.

Papa looked skyward, losing his balance slightly, the white rum still coursing through his veins. Then he said in his alcohol assisted voice.

"Don't worry about a ting, Trevor." He gestured expansively. "Yuh thirty acres is safe in my hands, boss." The merest of smiles smeared his face. "Providing you meet up to your obligations."

Bare face raas, Trevor thought. But I will play deh game.

"It's all been arranged," added Ruben. "You leave in two days time. You'll receive your itinerary when you get to Town." He pushed his glasses back up the ridge of his nose and his lips pouted apologetically. "I'm sorry my friend but it's out of my hands."

A brief gesture by Ruben, a few words spoken to Papa and the two men disappeared, leaving Trevor standing in silence, unable to shake the ominous feeling gripping his vitals.

His elaborate charade of surprise at their presence was convincing enough but his disbelief at the lengths the elders were willing to go to summon him was no amateur dramatics.

A mosquito bit his arm.

He slapped it and rubbed the remains between his fingers.

Four of his best men would accompany him to Town just in case the elders had any bright ideas to kill him on the way. Whatever else lay ahead for him in Kingston wasn't clear but the sham the old men in the hills would present to him was somehow linked to the more important mission he was dedicated to carrying out.

The old man had seen it.

And who was he to argue with the higher powers.

Trevor sat where he had stood, taking the small cylindrical shaped paper - that had earlier been attached to a carrier pigeon - from his pocket and unfurled it.

He read the Dread's request again.

Now Thro-Weh district had the first opportunity to repay the old man for everything he had done for Rasta worldwide and for them.

A debt of gratitude he would willingly risk his own safety for.

His mood darkened as he thought of meeting Yamu's henchmen.

Instead of dwelling on that unsavoury confrontation, he prepared to build himself a spliff before he ate.

He had a lot of planning to do.

******

The United States of Europe Airways cruiser bucked as it descended. High winds from all sides buffeted the huge Airbus as it flew through the harsh weather for landing.

Asim peered out of his window, moodily watching the slow progress of the black clouds and the rumbling thunder. Forked lightening in the distance illuminated their rolling underbelly. He fixedly watched the bubbling cauldron outside and imagined the pelting London was receiving down below.

The rains had followed him from Africa and like an omen, the dark skies opened up and welcomed a long lost friend.

Glad to be back, Asim said the BA Cruiser zoning for its last circuit before landing at Terminal 6.

A wonder what yuh have in store for me? His question was directed at the Hounslow suburbs looming through his monitors. He sighed heavily, the seat straightening from its reclining position and seat belts snaked out of concealed compartments to secure him. His sudden movements aggravated the wounds in his back. Not even the luxuries of a first class private cabin could help that. Another addition to his catalogue of scars. If they could be read, he told himself, flicking through the pages, would give accounts of his survival from sniper fire in Pretoria to a broken bottle gash to his chest in a bar brawl while undercover in Angola.

A book of blood and scars, whose words were fading but never totally forgotten.

Today could have been suh easily my memorial ceremony.

The doctors had still been taking minute pieces of shrapnel from his back and legs after his final operation in Jo'burg.

Providence or luck.

What deh fuck, he smiled. He was alive and that meant a second chance.

He was seeing things much more clearly, today. Taking the opportunity to look forward to the future and bury the memories.

An hour later he was standing in the Arrival's Hall, his heart sunk as he listened to the message over the tannoy. His family would not be meeting him after all. The information desk had not been able to fill in the gaps on whether it was an emergency call or not but he was requested to go home immediately. The first thing he did was call no response. His paranoid instinct took over. How could he ever have imagined that coming back would be trouble free? An hour in the country and already he felt something wasn't right.

Welcome home, boss.

London hadn't changed much. The black cab took the quickest - and the most expensive - route from the airport to Harlesden. Few people could afford to pay the astronomical amounts of credits needed to drive their cars through the most direct roadways in the capital. If that wasn't to your liking - and it wasn't for most people - you had to make do with the least financially demanding and most congested routes.

Asim peered through the window and reacquainted himself with the familiar sights. The traffic ran smoothly until they were out of central and into the heart of north west London. The Compu-Cab was crawling along but it was flashing lights ahead that made him realise something was up.

A black van emblazoned with an eagle, forensic officers in pristine white jump suits and Met-1 officers weilding the latest weaponry. As they passed the crime scene, three skinheads - Bloods they called themselves -lay spread eagled, wrists bound behind them and guns pointing at their heads.

London never stood still and neither did its problems.

The night-workers were hustling amid the flurry, well covered from the rain, hurrying back to their desks after their midnight lunchbreaks.The arial lanes were busy tonight, too. The stars in the sky were already obscured by light radiation from the streets and with hundreds of hoverjeeps scooting along the predetermined grids of space hundreds of feet above his head, the likelihood of ever seeing a twinkling star was remote.

His anxiety mounted as he drew closer to home. Undeveloped mental pictures of Akilla formed in his head.

I just hope everyting criss.

He had a funny feeling.

Maybe that was because in ten minutes time he would be facing a challenge he had not trained for and one that should come naturally but didn't. He shook his head at the irony of it.

The test of his life in the form of his five-year-old daughter.

Everyting safe, he kept repeating.

Life couldn't be such a 'bitch' to finally bring him home and then...

He shook his head as if to clear it of those thoughts and switched on the taxi's Digital TV.

Just relax, boss.

The Compu-Cab pulled up smoothly to the kerb of 112 Fontaine Street, the magnetic suspensions eased down gently while Asim peered out across the road to see the darkened house.

The cab doors hissed open. And in that moment he relived the many nights he'd legged it from cabs without paying. This generation of fair dodgers wasn't so lucky. The thought crossed his mind that maybe he and his ruffneck mates were the reason behind these drastic measures.

Stepping out, he casually looked around. The wet pavement shone from the reflected light, like a river of black ice on an alien world. He turned and palmed the driver a money.

The cab pulled off, leaving Asim standing with his hands in his pockets absorbing the sights of his old turf.

A quiet residential street. Nothing out of the ordinary.

Dads, Moms, one point teight youts, a dog, a cat, goldfish and a fifty year mortgage. Everything in its proper place, dull and boring and that's how he liked it.

This part of Harlesden hadn't always been like that. It had the distinction of being, only the second area in Britain to have its Zone designation revoked by Met-1. The residents had fought against gang violence, drugs and one of the highest crime rating across the capital. With communal solidarity and not to forget the combined clout of the Nations of Islam and Ras Tafari they had battled the beast and won. The result was a peaceful neighbourhood, where you could grow your kids and not worry for their safety.

It was good to be home.

His parent's home was as he had left it. Memories crowded in on him. The large terraced house stood as refined as it always did, its sharp lines and inspiring paintwork, was like a Pavlovian trigger making him relive in a split second his childhood. He peered across from where he stood, to the small front yard bordered with short hedges and enclosing a rectangle of manicured grass. No fancy embellishments just plain and simple. His father's philosophy in a nutshell.

He smiled knowing exactly where he gained his fondness for things from the past.

All the mod-cons the average families couldn't do without were absent from the Marshall household.

But there was always that buzz about the place.

Tonight it lacked the vibrancy he remembered.

The muscles of his jaw tensed.

The nerves in his injured back tingling, he dragged his bulky duffel bag behind him, opening his all-weather coat and rubbing his finger tips lightly across his holster. He peered down both sides of the street, just as a cyclist spluttered by.

Strange - no cars.

He pushed the gate open and walked up to the front door. The brass numbers on the lo-tech front door - a slab of wood attached to hinges - shone under the street lights, as Asim lifted the ancient door knocker - the one his mother wouldn't change for the world - and slammed it down twice. He tried the door knob. It gave way as he twisted. He eased open the door and stepped in, his ears straining and his eyes trying to focus in the darkness.

Something was not right.

He was not alone, his instincts needed no prompting of that.

The Equaliser slid away from where it was attached to his ribs and fell effortlessly into his hand. A special gift from his superiors as he ended his tour of duty, it rarely left his side. Let's say, we're giving you a fighting chance on Civvie Street, they had told him. Yours to use until you become a bona fide civilian in three years. London is a dangerous place.

He kept the weapon concealed under his coat and listened carefully.

Nothing.

The house was comfortably warm, the way he remembered his father loved it, and the furniture was neatly in place. His mother's touch.

No signs of a struggle.

What puzzled him were the conflicting aromas. Delicious food smells and perfumes. An explanation formed in his head. Relaxing he smiled. Jut as quickly, the smile disappeared. He had to make certain.

He gripped the gun tightly under his coat, his finger a hair's breath away from the...

...Trigger?

He blinked rapidly some sanity returning to him.

This is Harlesden, he reminded himself.

Get a mother fucking grip, turf bwoy.

He breathed uneasily and let his hands fall to his side.

******

Surprise!

The lights in the entire house came on all at once, reggae music blasted from speakers and a wave of familiar faces appeared from up the stairs, through the kitchen and in the dinning room.

A sigh of relief burst from his lips.

Luckily for him his weapon remained concealed. A fuck-up of huge proportions had been averted.

What began as apprehension evaporated with every hug and kiss. There were faces he remembered, their names forgotten in his past and then there were 'faces', he knew intimately.

All friends and all making him welcome again.

His mother was crying as she ran to hug him.

"I've missed you, son!"

Asim held her tightly lifting her off the floor as he spun her around and whispered, 'I love you' in her ear.

His stubbornness he learned from her. The best teacher he ever had. And still as beautiful as ever.

The Field Marshal wasn't one to complain. He loved the idea of his 'spars' looking enviously with no possibility of ever touching.

Asim smiled inwardly.

Mr. Marshall saw him from a distance and walked over with outstretched arms. They hugged long and hard.

"It's good to have you back, bwoy." He grinned, the dome of his head showing sparse grey in his low-cut hair style and reflected nearly exactly the shape of his son's own.

And the keen mind in it.

His blue silk suit was just a bit too forceful a statement for a man of that age, Asim thought, but Mr. Marshall had been rewriting the rules all his life, he was not about to stop now.

"She may be your mother," he continued, laughing after their embrace lasted too long for his liking. "But she still is my wife."

He broke up the tearful reunion and kissed his wife on the lips. And it wasn't a familiar peck you would expect but the kind of embrace and kiss he would give to a girlfriend - not a wife of thirty years.

The Field Marshal had not changed.

"Won't you learn to behave yourself round people, Rupert?" Anne said.

Thirty years had not dampened their love.

"Listen, you have deh boy to yourself for God knows how long, let him mingle a bit, man."

The Field Marshal winked at him.

"Come."

Anne weakly resisted as her husband gently put his arms around her waist and led her into the kitchen.

Asim stood there, still being showered with kisses, pats on the back and handshakes from friends, whose faces had dimmed but never faded from his memory.

He was glad to see them all, but throughout the excitement his eyes were searching.

Where was his daughter and, come to think of it, Fatima?

Passively, Asim absorbed the atmosphere, trying his best to trap all the sense impressions of this evening to memory.

He was actually back.

It was funny how he dreamt of coming home to a quiet family gathering. His parents still not forgiving him for leaving them with the responsibility of a baby he was never certain he had fathered. They would sit for a family meal the tension palpable and then, in an explosion of anger and resentment, their true feelings would emerge. The mental scenario he had constructed in his head was far removed from the reality of the moment.

His thoughts were fuelled by paranoia and in his haste he had forgotten to add love to his equation of disaster.

Shame decided to show itself in all its uncomfortable glory.

"Still looking as beautiful as when a left you, Mama." Asim tried to dismiss his discomfort as he stepped into the kitchen." The old man is still doing a good job after all these years."

Anne laughed out, her voice light and vibrant. Tears of joy streamed down her face as she rested her head on her son's shoulders savouring a long over due feeling of relief.

Fatima was so like her.

But where was she?

Anne was never the one to keep her problems locked away. The longing in her eyes, her lips parting in hesitation as if she wanted to speak, but deciding against it and the way she subtly redirected any conversation relating to the family.

If it wasn't Akilla, it had to be his sister.

Growing up together, Fatima had been the highly strung one.

There were a few run-ins with school officials and the Field Marshal himself but as time went on she found an outlet and some direction - much to everybody's relief. He loved his sister dearly but she had a wild streak which surfaced from time to time.

Her absence could mean this was one of those times.

He would soon know.

Shrugging, Asim conversed with the guests as they shovelled coconut rice in their mouths and tore into fried chicken. He caught up with the word on the street and the fascinating ghetto stories that were never made available to the average man. It was good to immerse himself into the London runnings again, if a little uncomfortable with the respect he was afforded.

They were calling him a hero, but they didn't know the half of the, raas story.

A hero didn't run out on his family and then feel ashamed to ask about a daughter he had abandoned in the process.

A hero.

To whom?

Everyone thought that his return from the 'Peace Corps' in Africa was something to celebrate. The world knew about the selfless work being done by the Corps in the fight against terrorism on the continent. For one cf their own to be a part of the process of homeland security in Africa made them proud.

The facts of what he did would not be accepted that readily.

They were congratulating a man who had killed time and time again. And not even he could justify each one of those assassinations.

Democracy had a high price and so did a family.

Asim had had a bellyfull of other people's patriotism and idealism. He was done with the politricks. Being with his family now meant much more to him than any cause could.

His eyes continued to search.

Anne's smile seemed permanent, more pleased than any mother could be. She looked adoringly at her baby, drew his cheek to hers and kissed him.

Little else mattered. Her son was back with her - those many tearful prayers had not gone unanswered.

She watched him looking around eagerly at the small children playing in the hall way. Trying to see an image of himself in any of the bundles of energy threatening to wreck her prized possessions. She saw the disappointed in his eyes and watched him look away confused and anxious.

"We have to talk Asim." Her eyes glistened with tears making them seem mischievous and maudlin all at once. "There's so much we have to catch up on, son, but come, first tings first. Let me introduce you to someone before you start tearing your hair out."

She rubbed his bald head teasingly and laughed, leading him into the familiar sitting room. A multicoloured banner was stretched from wall to wall with the words 'Welcome Home Son' printed in large letters. Helium filled balloons bobbed up and down in dancing hands.

The tiny micro-sound was being handled by none other than his 'spar' Pato. He was grinning from ear to ear, the single blue streak in his neat hair glistened as he held up his fist to his passing 'bredrin'.

"Respect, rude bwoy." His voice booming through the surrounding speakers. "We'll talk later, man."

Asim nodded, showing his clenched fist and chuckled to himself as the selector moved to the music.

He hadn't changed one bit.

The mad professor was in his element and Asim new his guests were in for some serious Reggae Revival.

It was so hard to believe he had left all this behind.

In a corner with no dancers just a few chairs and a sofa, a woman and a child sat playing and giggling.

He stood transfixed for a moment but felt that it was much longer. An overpowering sense of deja vu struck him and left him reeling. Time folded, his past and present, places he had been to and people he had seen and suddenly he became uncertain whether he had dreamt this.

The young woman was a Rasta, her hair hung down to her shoulders, like dark vines. The silk African gown was long but still left her sandalled feet exposed. Awash with peculiar emotions, he felt strangely confident they knew each other. Not a passing fancy either, he KNEW her. But it seemed it was so deeply buried it would not or could not emerge completely.

Jesas...!

He guessed, she was of East African extraction. Stunning. He found it difficult to tear his gaze away from those smouldering brown eyes. Her face was cloaked with skin that was a rich earth black that seemed to throw off a brilliance of its own. Her beauty obscured everything and the electricity she extended made him hold his breath.

His focus narrowed.

She was playfully tickling the little girl on her lap, her smile showing teeth that glistened white. The little girl laughed out.

Asim was slow to spot the signals but it became clear to him as the child's eyes lit up on seeing Anne beside him. She jumped from the Rasta woman's lap, laughing loudly with her arms outstretched.

"Grandma, where's my juice?"

Anne lifted her up, a more serious look on her face.

"Shush, about that. I've got somebody I want you to meet - more important than that stomach of yours."

The little girl had already locked her eyes with his, tilting her head to one side, her childish mind evaluating this stranger.

"Say 'hi'. This is your daddy," Anne said. "He's here especially to see you."

Asim was speechless.

His mouth was open and although his reasoning mind told him it was for only seconds before closed it, his tongue felt like a strip of desert.

Trying to swallow proved difficult too and so did stringing two or three words together to make a comprehendible sentence.

Asim stood there nonplussed.

What the fuck had he done.

A sorry arsed victim of too many rash decisions made in the past and now haunted by painful emotions he was struggling to put under control.

A proper father, a good father could draw on happy memories of his daughter growing up.

He had nothing, sweet FA.

Instead of the healthy emotions a father should feel for his daughter, an uncomfortable sense of guilt pricked him.

The knot remained in his throat.

Akilla stared back as if she were reading the turmoil on his face.

Another set of hard facts outside of the world he was used t was just being forcefully rammed down his throat. As hard to swallow as it was, he would handle it.

Akilla had grown beyond anything he had expected. She was so mature for five years. Jesas, he couldn't even remember her birthday. In his mind's eye he had pictured a tiny baby, gurgling and giving that toothless smile like a little cherub. Now he was staring at a mini reproduction of his late wife. Long frizzy red hair, plaited with ribbons and crystal bubbles. Her small lips pinched at the sides - another trait of her Irish mother - with those determined slit eyes and her straight nose, flared at the tip.

An unmistakable Marshall trait.

His daughter. Man, he didn't deserve her.

"You wouldn't remember me, would you?" he asked the question awkwardly and then wished he had phrased it better.

The little girl shook her head, a pout forming on her lips.

"You know I've come a long way to see you, because I want us to be friends." Asim stretched out his hand unable to make his first physical contact seem as if he was about to close a business deal. The little girl recoiled, hugging her grandmother desperately around her neck.

"It's your daddy, darling, don't you want to shake his hand?"

She shook her head in the negative. Sternly. Her father's heart sank.

Anne squeezed her son's shoulder, reassuringly.

"Give it time, son," she said softly. "She needs to adjust to the idea of actually having a father again. It's not the easiest thing to accept - especially for someone her age."

Asim nodded.

"I know that, mama, she needs time."

Even in agreement, his disappointment was impossible to hide.

But what the hell did he expect. He was the one who had ran out on her and not the other way around.

"In the meantime," Anne went on quickly, not wanting him dwelling on Akilla's behaviour. "I want you to meet the young lady who your daughter has taken a liking to. Yasmeen, my son Asim."

The Rastafarian beauty stood up, bowed slightly and offered her hand.

He took it and felt how soft it was. Her fingers seemed to be subtly stroking the grooves of his palm as they shook hands. Asim found himself tilting his head back slightly, the perfume she was wearing reminded him of the Jamaican countryside. For a second he was there, giggling rivers, the smell of grass, the hum of gal-a-wasp.

He drank in her poise and elegant movement some more without being blatantly obvious. She shifted position and the directional lights hit her full on. He saw the outline of her stout breasts as her nipples nudged the silken material. The gown was translucent and the shadow of her enclosed figure made him swallow hard.

Moments later he was still holding her hand.

Shit!

She gently pulled it away.

"I'm sure Anne told you it's bad manners to stare." She laughed. "I could be some jealous Rasta man's queen."

Asim snapped to attention, blushing slightly as his less than subtle ogling was discovered and exposed.

"I didn't mean to embarrass you or anyting... beautiful women have that effect on me."

It was Yasmeen's time to blush.

Asim switched the subject quickly.

"Akilla really loves your company. Smart girl."

"She's my little sister." Yasmeen said. "We weren't so close at first though. The more we talked I realised we had so much in common." Her voice lowered. "She loves ancient history - which is my speciality - pizza and computer games. She's a very perceptive little girl, you should be proud."

Asim's eyebrows twitched upwards.

She continued.

"Don't be too worried about her reaction, though. Even with an above average IQ, she's still a little girl. You've been away from her for so long and it's only natural there'll be some trepidation on her part. Just go slow, give her time and she'll begin wondering how she survived without her dad."

Yasmeen made it sound so easy.

Anne broke into the conversation discreetly. "I'll leave you two to talk while I put this young lady to her bed. Now, say good night."

Akilla shuffled out of her grandmother's arms and ran over to Yasmeen.

"Good night, Auntie Yasmeen," she said, kissing her on the cheek and turned to face her father. She stared intently at him her chubby features, expressionless.

"Good night..."

Akilla didn't finish the sentence and ran to hold on to Anne's hand.

Asim grimaced.

"Bed time." Anne announced and they were away.

Funny how Yasmeen had not only sparked these strange and totally unexplainable flashes of recognition but had brought to the surface a buried memory he had thought forgotten.

He was nine years old, an asthmatic, his grandmother was at her wit's end and had rushed him to Compound - a Ras Tafari community at Nine Miles in Bull Bay, Jamaica. His cousin, Jah Thomas, the herbalist was his grandmother's final option after a severe attack. If it hadn't been for the bushes Jah Thomas had picked, crushed and boiled to make an infusion, Asim would have surely died. He never was able to properly thank his cousin but he developed a deep respect for the faith.

In his eyes it was a sign of strength to wear the crown of locks. And Yasmeen was obviously a woman with plenty to spare.

"So you and Fatima went to school together," Asim asked after sipping his vodka and orange juice. Grinning, he shook his head like he was confused and then swallowed the liquid in his mouth. "It's just hard to imagine what yuh an my sister could have in common."

Yasmeen smiled, showing those sparkling white teeth.

"Adversity can bring people together, you know. We met in college. I had a project that needed me to reproduce the garments worn by the people of Benin in the 12th Century. Fatima was a drama and fashion design student, I was majoring in Ancient History. I had lost my mother at the time and she was going through some personal problems herself and we gave each other strength. Opposites attract they say."

"Suh dem seh." Asim said. "I bet you at least left with a degree. When Fatima graduated, it was with a 'better luck next time' pat on the shoulder."

Yasmeen picked up her glass of sparkling water. "She just needed time to grow up and find her way."

Asim smoothed down none existent hairs on his slick bald head and nodded.

"I suppose you're right. Where is she anyway? I was expecting her to be here."

The flow of their conversation had been quite spontaneous and relaxed up to that point. Asim's innocent question made Yasmeen hesitate.

"I expected her here too, especially after being as excited as she was about your arrival. Under the circumstances..." She changed emphasis quickly. "I'm sure she'll call to explain why she's couldn't make it."

"What do you mean?" Asim's brows were knitting, prying open his half-closed eyes.

"I'm sorry. I've said too much already."

"What's going on, Yasmeen?"

But she refused to say anything more.

The curse that had formed in his head, surprised him by braking out of the confines of his thoughts.

"Fuck!"

Something was up. His happy homecoming was about to be dealt its second blow for the night. He could feel it.

He came to his senses quickly and saw Yasmeen calmly sipping her last drop of water, fine tendrils of her locks obscuring one eye.

"I'm sorry I swore, it wasn't directed at you," he said.

She laughed.

"Don't apologise, I'm a woman of the world." Her soft voice trailed away with the music.

For a man who had been trained to adapt to the most adverse of terrains, learned to make life and death decisions quickly, judging characters and personalities and leading from the front, Asim had a lot to learn about everyday life.

He felt like an inexperienced teenager given the task to chat up a girl for the first time

Next time, keep your expectations within reason.

Instinctively he held on to Yasmeen's hand again, his eyes were fixed on hers.

He wondered if she could hear his heart pounding.

He excused himself with difficulty after a few more minutes of conversation. He had hoped to talk with her later but Yasmeen had mentioned an urgent appointment.

Appointments in the early hours of the morning? Very cloak and dagger.

He looked forward to unravelling her secrets.

That pleasant thought brought him back to the situation at hand.

What was going on with his sister, this time? The questions brimming in his head, just couldn't wait.

The welcome home party had wound itself down.

The reaminder of Asim's guests sat drinking and in conversation. A large wafer screen in the lounge drew a small group of eager men as they relived the historical match of the legendary fighters Muhammad Ali and Geroge Foreman. The unforgettable 'Rumble In The Jungle'.

Asim finally managed to confront his mother in the empty kitchen.

"You've been trying to avoid talking to me about Fatima all night, why?"

She frowned, her defences slotting into place.

"You've had enough on your mind as it is. I just thought tomorrow after a good rest would be a better time to talk about her."

She dried her eyes and sat upright preparing herself.

"BrainTech!" She said softly. "I found it in her room."

Shit!

"They'd featured it many times on TView Crime Hour so I recognised it. I was so shocked and confused. I told your father and we both tried to talk to her later that evening. We argued. Your sister stormed out with your father threatening to box her."

"An she would deserve it too!"

Mr. Marshall joined them with his comment, seating himself on a kitchen stool.

"Can yuh believe that we were worried out of our heads for this gal and she have the gall to stand up in front of us and cuss, her parents in the most disgraceful of fashions." Mr. Marshall's gaze rose to the ceiling as he remembered the incident, the anger in his voice returning. "By the time I cooled down, I found out Fatima pack her tings an gaan."

Asim gave that passive impression that he was not overly concerned, but internally he was scared. Raas scared.

BrainTech! He kept repeating in his head.

The new trend on the streets was for the ultimate high. Why inject or sniff when you could wire your rush directly to the brain for a high like no other. The technology behind its development had been outlawed the world over. The crippling addictiveness was unacceptable to any medical council. But as was expected, BrainTech hardware was available on any front line. All you needed apart from that was a broadband line and a credit card.

BrainTech was designed so the punters kept coming back for more.

This shit belonged on the streets - "Not in my yard."

Even here, in so-called respectable society it was clear to him that the basic instincts of human nature, couldn't be held at arm's length.

******

It was like the rainy season 'back-a-yard'.

Undulating sheets of water whipped by high winds, relentlessly battering everything unlucky enough to be exposed.

Unlucky, that's how he felt.

Trevor was huddled under the canopied bus stop in the driving rain, a thick leather jacket draped over his shoulders and his face a mask of frustration.

Suh dis was the part of London, yuh wouldn't find in the brochures.

He was stunned.

He'd read and listened to reports about the crime and the economic difficulties certain parts of the U.S.E. were facing but seeing the effect of it with his own two eyes was a chilling reminder that nothing remained the same. His rudimentary history lessons had taught him about the colonial super power, one of the bastions of capitalism and the land of opportunity. The stark landscape before him contradicted all that.

Police patrolmen suited up for war, beggars intimidating passers-by into crediting their accounts, garbage mountains so huge he guessed refuse hadn't been collected in months, while vermin were breeding out of control.

With the negatives aside, what was regarded as London for the visitor, held no appeal for him either. It was much too densely populated, unnaturally clean like some sterile operating room, and claustrophobic. He could understand why people were so uptight and angry. The city, the steel, the concrete, seemed to create a formula for frustration. And these 'natural areas' were a joke. They were as much good as pissing on an out of control bush fire.

What had persistently bothered him was why generations of Rasta had made this there home. The Nation owned Black Star Liner was still busily repatriating families to the motherland from all parts of the world. But for some, nowhere nuh bettah than yard. Even if your yard was as inhospitable as this.

His only consolation was, at the end of his assignment, if all went well, he'd be back on the Rock.

All of this forgotten and done with.

His journey to England started when,he had arrived at the Tabernacle of Ras on a rainy Friday, two days after the ultimatum was issued to him. The Air Jamaica floater had taken only ten minutes to get to Kingston from Mandeville before flying on to the Ras compound itself. Tappa, Ras Badu, Piper and Son-son had shadowed his every movement since he left Thro-Weh. Escorts led the group into the vast grounds and then through the complex of buildings which made up the religious headquarters. After entering what could have been a drab-looking storage facility, they were led through a maze of interconnecting corridors. They stopped at an imposing mahogany door manned by a pair of stone figures kneeling. The escorts walked forward and knocked curtly on the doors and without any hesitation ushered only Trevor through.

Ras Tobias sat in front of a wraparound plasma screen. The elder was known to Trevor from newsreels. One of Patriarch Yamu's aides who, before growing his locks, was a technical advisor to the Prime Minister of Jamaica. He was smiling. Obviously enjoying his work in cyberspace.

"Ah! Trevor. Glad you could make it." The voice of Ras Tobias sounded excited. "Was your trip a good one, I hope suh?"

Trevor frowned and wondered why the elder dread's lisp annoyed him so much and then became concerned about how he knew he was waiting there.

The elder closed down his system, his fingers touching unseen controls clear to him in his cyberspace environment but in the real world making him seem like a mad pianist overcome by the brilliance of his own composition. Bowing his head, he kept his eyes closed for a moment as his senses adjusted to Real World.

"You're the man for the job whether you know it or not." Ras Tobias came away from the equipment and sat at his multilevel work station a grin appearing on lips that resembled a snout. "I can tell these things." His eyes widened. "You may have needed some convincing but that is just because you don't know how important a job this is."

Ras Tobias had a haughty air about him, a man who understood his importance and could have had years of formal training that told him so. But his lisp, the protruding lips and how his eyes darted everywhere impatiently, made him an open target for humorous comparisons. There was no denying. He had the look, the manner and the speech of a mongoose - if a mongoose could talk.

And Trevor didn't trust mongooses.

"Why did you drag me all the way up here, Iyah, an yuh know we can't see eye to eye. It is no secret the elders don't trust me, and I man don't trust dem. You say I'm deh best man for the job but me know there must be thousands a man more capable than I." He paused for effect. "What is deh real reason yuh want me involved in dis?"

The elder shook his head.

"You are too paranoid and just want to be confrontational as always. For once, use this..." Ras Tobias touched his forehead with a slender finger. "Why we chose you is because the elders have a history with you. They know what you are capable of Trevor, therefore you are a more predictable factor. The old men tend to like certainty and to guarantee that they have promised to reap your priced crop while you are away and to re-consider your licence...?" He let his threat trail away and with a cunning smile began to explain to Trevor what he wanted him to do and why he would do it.

Trevor shivered from the wind and reached into his shoulder bag fumbling through the contents. A small Maccabees Bible, a battered Palm Pilot, a spliff he had built earlier in his hotel room and a few other miscellaneous bits and pieces. He reached in and took out the spliff and fired it up with his cheap lighter.

He sucked hard and shivered, again.

His inspired choice of location was the product of spontaneity. The hotel Ras Tobias had arranged from Jamaica, in downtown London, he had no intention of staying in. H ecouldn't be sure that it wasn't bugged and that there was no one on his tail. So tonight he had slipped out of the Cumberland unseen and left a message for his contact to meet him at a spot he had randomly chosen. He wasn't to know he had ended up in one of the few defunct Zones in the city. Once a thriving neighbourhood, its fortunes turned sour as the manufacturing facility that provided the most jobs became ninety percent automated. Months later it had been assigned a Zone status and began to slowly deteriorate until it self-destructed. Graffiti bigging up both Bloods and Spears was sprayed everywhere - remnants of a hotly contested turf war. What was left behind was an empty husk, a ghost town, abandoned by its original inhabitants and unable to be redeveloped because of its history.

An ideal place to meet if you trusted no one.

Trevor watched his surroundings warily.

The message he left his contact was to come alone. If he so much as saw another living soul he would disappear.

The Nation may have misguidedly thought it would be easier to murder him here than yard but he would prove them wrong.

A hundred metres up the road, a streamlined Eco Bus screeched to a standstill at the edge of the no-go Zone. It blasted air from both sides, lowering itself to the sidewalk. Its traditional luminescent red winked under the street light. Trevor observed it in the distance, his stiletto's spring mounted under his sleeves. He pulled his leather hood down over his face.

The driver u-turned quickly and pulled away.

The sound trailed into the distance and left Parchment Street quiet again.

"Tribal war inna Babylon." Ras Tobias had quoted melodramatically.

The memory of his voice was as irritating as the real thing.

"For three years Rasta in London have had to hold their heads in shame because of this conflict between man and woman with the locks but not the heart of Rasta. Spilling blood of another human because of the colour of his skin. Racism and religious intolerance has been the reason for the death of both black and white, and it must stop. All our best efforts in trying to end it have been wasted and we intend to approach the problem from a different angle. We want peace, breddah, but we may have to make war. You have the required skills we need to find the information that is so important to ending this bloodshed. You are a survivor with a vicious streak that will match the wantonness of these people. The time for dipplomacy has ended and we have to match them, fire fi fire. We need to know who is leading these men killing in Jah-Jah name. Report back to me with your findings. Only you and your contact in London will know your true purpose. Use whatever means at your disposal. Leave no stone unturned, yuh hear mi. No stone."

No stone?

"Bullshit!"

Trevor cursed silently to himself.

The wind howled through the disused buildings.

He lowered his head and brought up his collar around his cold ears.

The only good point about this location. Nothing or no one could approach him without him seeing them. Total isolation. No houses or estates, no casual strollers just gloom.

A window slammed shut from a gust of wind. The dilapidated bingo hall on the other side of the road, a grotesque reminder of better days.

He squeezed the damp material of his jacket, the time flashed on his coat sleeve.

Twenty raasclaat minutes late.

Suddenly the wind changed direction again, splattering his face with icy rain. He was on the verge of engaging his portable TView, calling a taxi an teking his raas back to the hotel.

Throwing down the remainder of his spliff and grinding it with his heavy duty Cats, he hunched his shoulders and turned to go.

He looked up the road concentrating his eyes against the swirling flurry of water and then down the other way.

A luminous haze approached from the distance. He stood watching with interest.

The car slowed to a stop beside him purring like a contented cat.

"Yow!" he said, knocking his knuckles on the darkened window. "Wha time yuh call this, boss? You know how long mi deh inna this rain an wind waiting for you to turn up?"

The gull wings pivoted upwards, the interior expelling warmth and the smell of perfume.

"It was either being late or not coming at all, brother." The silky voice said with just a hint of sarcasm. "You should be glad I wasn't held up further. And, by the way, 'boss' sounds too formal. My name's Yasmeen, Yasmeen Beyene. I'm your contact."

"T-T-Trevor," he stammered, taking her hand and bowing his head, all signs of violent intent evaporating.

Standing there dripping wet, with a sports bag slung around his shoulder, she would be forgiven for thinking his stammering was due to the wind and rain. But Trevor was more than cold, he was in shock.

So this was Yasmeen Beyene, the old man's daughter.

The woman he was sent here to protect.

******

Peace.

It was quiet at last.

Asim sat in the kitchen with all the lights out, slouched over the wooden counter, beside him a glass of coke and a near empty bottle of J. Wray and Nephew rum.

He looked deep into the depths of his glass, nursing the remainder of his drink contemplatively and wincing as the strong rum scorched his insides on its way down.

When you can't remember what your fighting for, it's time to pack it in. It seemed like sound advice, a week ago. But tonight he was not sure. He felt as if he was more comfortable with the threat of death in the field than to face the battles rising on the home front.

There was no pretence in counter terrorism, there were rules, procedures. You could depend on the danger and risk to always be there. You could prepare. Here he was a fumbling novice who wanted a rule book to guide him and then realising to his horror there was none. This is what it's all about, turf bwoy - reality outside of a barracks.

Asim stretched on the stool and froze suddenly. A blanket of pain shot through his back. For an instant he found breathing difficult. Swallowing uneasily he tried to ignore the discomfort, but mind over matter did no good. He gritted his teeth, feeling every fragment of shrapnel lodged in his back and with slow rotation of his shoulder blades felt the pain subside.

Many raas rivers to cross.

He swore again and flung the remainder of his drink down his throat. The lights shining through the louvered windows draped him in stripy shadows. Asim looked like some hybrid creature incapable of camouflaging itself. Stuck out in the open and trying to mimic its environment to survive but failing.

"Yuh all right, bwoy?"

Asim turned to see his father, dressed in a paisley night gown, his eyes droopy with sleep.

The lights came on and remained soft.

Asim smiled calmly at him as his father sat in the chair opposite.

"It looks like you've got a lot on your mind, son, yuh want to talk?"

Asim reached over the table and patted his hand.

"I think I've just had my hopes up a bit too high. Clouded

judgement, pops."

Mr. Marshall nodded.

"Five years away from home makes a man start thinking and hoping tings will be right."

"Hoping." Asim repeated the word as if he was analysing the resonance of its sound.

"The truth is different though." Mr. Marshall folded his arms and leaned on the counter. "We all can wish an hope as much as we please but family, like anything in life, takes effort. Five years ago, your mother and I wished too, but the fact still remained that you had disappeared and left us with your daughter. We had to face that, just as we have to face this. Now, imagine that same feeling of fear, you feel for Fatima. We felt that for you." He laughed, punctuating the steady drone of his voice. "For Anne and me, this is nuthin new. This is what parenting and family is all about."

Asim took a deep, frustrated breath.

"A lesson I'm yet to learn."

Mr. Marshall smiled.

"Don't be too hard on yourself. Just promise me, Akilla will get the same sorta patience and selfless dedication from her father, that we gave to him."

"That is a promise."

Mr. Marshall stood up and poured himself a cup of Camomile tea from the instant tea pot.

"Yuh want one, son?"

Asim declined but watched his old man stir in his secret additives. The Field Marshal had always been a brilliant cook, even in his days as a printer. He was slow to discover his real calling but once that was clear in his mind he retired early, dedicating his life to his family and his passion for cooking. He established The Pepper Pot Restaurant and his hobby became his livelihood. His father's Saturday soups and Sunday dinners, his mom's punctilious attention to the upkeep of her home, Fatima's nagging. Unforgettable parts of his childhood. Memories he drew on at the most challenging points in his life, memories that helped to mould him. He wanted them back again.

"Am I really cut out for this, Pops?"

Mr. Marshall smiled, a stray light beam making his eyes twinkle.

"I know yuh are son. But don't convince me. You need to convince yourself. And then your daughter. And that, believe you me," he chuckled, "will be a challenge in itself."

This time Asim had no illusions about the truth of that statement.

******

Asim refused to try and sleep again.

He sat on his bed watching the morning unfold through his window and waited patiently for the sun to peep over the obstructing buildings. Ask him and he would say jet-lag and too much alcohol had thrown his normal sleep cycle out of sync.

That wouldn't be quite correct.

He didn't want to go back to sleep even if he could. Not with the nightmares.

There was never a night he was free of them. Sometimes brief snatches, at others he was forced to experience a lengthy opera of anguish. And it was always the same, always horrific. He was held captive and forced to watch in painful detail his wife being gang raped , while a child he knew intuitively was Akilla - kept screaming in his face, accusing him of being a coward, over and over again.

His nightmare fading, he headed for the bathroom.

His morning ritual done, he stared back at a face refreshed, and controlled a rising tingle of excitement.

His first day back pan deh street was going to be a good one. He could feel it.

He stepped out of his room clothed in a comfortable Irish linen suit and matching light loafers. He clenched his fist, the luminescent figures showing boldly through his skin and silently edged his way to his daughter's room. The floorboards creaked under his weight. A smile came to his lips. The Field Marshal's 'early warning system' had caught him out many times in his more rebellious days, but it had never - as yet - caught a thief. Being caught so many times by something as stupid and lo-tech as that was embarrassing and then trying to explain to his spars why he hadn't turned up for a clandestine night on the town was even worse. The days.

Passing his parent's room, he stopped and listened to their rumbling snores.

Free from his adolescent stunts for many years now, they had let their guard down and wouldn't have known if he blew the hinges off the door with a claymore.

Akilla's room was beside theirs, and conspicuous by the colourful three-dimensional sticker of a Gummy Bear adorning it.

He pushed the door open.

His eyes adjusted to the darkness.

For someone so young the room was disturbingly ordered and clean. The cupboard on his left was packed full of cuddly toys and a library of educational software. Atop the little desk-cum-dressing table was a 10mm thick slimline laptop, a well-worn drawing pad and crayons. And to his right another closed off wardrobe where her clothes hung. Completed magnetic puzzles sat like prizes on a glass shelf directly over her bed next to models of complicated molecules, architecture and planets with their surface detail lovingly assembled by her hands.

Shaking his head, he moved over to her bedside and saw her contented face as she clung unto a fluffy space Yogi Bear. Her mother's face - the resemblance was uncanny.

For a brief moment he lifted his eyes to the ceiling.

If God listened to men like him, he wanted to say a 'thank you' and ask for a special blessing for his 'old people'. They had made the sacrifices, bared his responsibility and showed him even more love.

If the shoe was on the other foot...

He kissed his daughter lightly on the forehead and closed the door behind him.

******

It was nearing noon when Asim stepped out of the Angel metro station. He had visited his wife's grave and asked for her forgiveness. He somehow felt she had understood.

A dirty green duffel bag was slung obliquely across his muscular shoulders as he strolled out with confident ease, his mirrored Ray Ban shades flipped up. He squinted at the sun encroaching over the billowy white clouds and turned right down the high street.

His mood had improved with the weather, though a shroud of despondency still clung to him, remaining just beyond conscious reach, as it did whenever his mind settled on Eva. And that was often.

Asim sighed wearily. Up ahead a crowd gathered around an Info Point, their tiny network cards locked into play as they downloaded the day's news. He caught a glimpse of an advertising page on one of the screens - a micro bikini-clad...

That reminded him. Of how long it had been.

Mentally, he ticked off another item on his Things-to-do list.

Organisation was the foundation on which the army was built. It had become second nature to him.

He made a note of his progress.

The list had been whittled down to a handful of items, one of which he was about to take care of.

All in all it had been a busy day, and he was gaining a feel for the big orange again.

It was a manic Saturday in Islington, no different from a manic saturday afternoon in many of the towns he had visited in Africa. This was definitely the London he remembered and loved. Summers had become somewhat longer than they used to be (a legacy from the don't-give-a-fuck-about-the-environment generation of the twentieth century) and everybody agreed that it made Britain a much more pleasant place to live.

He turned into Liverpool Road and kept on walking until he came to a serious-looking security gate. The look on Asim's face said he was pleasantly surprised. Beyond the barrier was a spatial configuration parking area that spiralled into the ground, a pristine looking drive way snaked up to the once shabby building now reconverted and expanded into a gleaming corporate headquarters. The new home of Zulu Security Systems Inc. shone under the sunlight.

Fuck me, Ricardo! You've been busy, boss.

His partner had managed to keep all his expansion plans secret. So this was the slick bastard's surprise.

If anything could make you believe in destiny his involvement with Ricardo would do just that.

They had been spars in the paratroop regiment but had lost contact for a while as he had gained stripes and moved on. Ricardo's army career was short-lived and he had ventured into civvie street with a great idea and some family money. The enterprise - technological security solutions - had been a success and when their paths crossed again the Ghanian was looking to take his business to the next level. Asim remembered how contagious his enthusiasm had been and how they drank and chatted into the early hours exchanging ideas.

For Asim, the outsider looking in, the solution was quite clear but he waited for an invitation before he made his recommendations.

He had been on leave from Aldershot when Ricardo asked him to view an optical surveillance system he had acquired for sale. It had been the first time he had been to his friend's office and what he saw impressed him. Ricardo had tried to lure him away from the army by throwing large sums of money his way. Maybe it was his growing sense of disillusionment with the financial benefits of the military that made him start to reconsider the offer. The next time they met he had come armed with a business plan that was designed to spread the company's emphasis from importation to consultation and development. Asim wanted to provide the expertise needed to use the equipment, suggest security arrangements, keeping ahead of the competition and even going into development himself.

Ricardo wasted no time working the plan into the overall

operation of Zulu Securities Inc, giving Asim the opportunity to spearhead some of his own initiatives. It grew from strength to strength with the aid of brilliant young technologists recruited into Zulu's fold and who were responsible for fifty new patents in five years. Ricardo was able to float the company on the stock market and hold controlling interest in a very short space of time. Asim shook his head at the irony of it all.

He walked up to the console and waited for the robot to detect him. His features mapped and his voice print confirmed the barrier swung open and he made his way in.

"Easy nuh!"

Kehinde jumped into his arms. Hanging unto his neck as he twirled her around, she kissed him on the lips. His partner's PA, couldn't quite believe it was really him.

Asim grinned shaking his head. What was the bwoy waiting for? Ricardo should have jumped the broom and made a honest woman of the poor girl, if he had any sense. She was the same slender and elegant young woman with the most calming eyes.

They hugged again.

"Why didn't you tell us that you were coming back to England?" Her voice held just the right balance between love and reproach.

Asim laughed. "An miss that look on your face? No way." He paused and squinted in her direction. "Looks like your putting on some weight as well girl and all in the right places, I might add."

The secretary's dark cheeks flushed as she pouted her lips and acted as if Asim's statement had cut deeply.

"The boss has been treating me to too many three course lunches." She complained unconvincingly.

"Wha!" Asim shouted. "Preferential treatment to certain members of staff. It's disgraceful."

Asim held her hand and turned full circle, peering through the office's glass walls to an area down below.

"Jesas! How much staff have you got working here now?"

"Thirty-five. Technical staff, management, sales and transport. Four years of hard work and invaluable inside information from you, sir."

"Me!" He jerked his thumb to his chest. "Obtaining data for you guys was the easy part. This is where all the hard work took place. Believe." Asim walked back over to Kehinde's desk, standing by it, arms folded.

"So how is deh old dog baring up, anyway?"

"Working too hard. He believes no one can do his job, except for you that is.

He's under a lot of pressure. I'm doing my best but..." She sat down and leaned back into her chair. "You are back for good, aren't you?"

"Try getting rid ah me."

Kehinde smiled uneasily.

******

Ricardo Opoku, stood looking intensely at the picture of himself with a few of his compatriots from the 47th Paratroop regiment that always sat on his book case. The regiment's motto, All for one, made him reflect on those days. They had been the reason for his success, despite twelve months in military prison in Colchester and a dishonourable discharge. His family in Ghana had never recovered from the shame. Even now many would not speak to him. His present position as CEO of Zulu Security Systems Inc. made no difference to them, and their petty malice meant nothing to him. Today was the tenth anniversary of his father's death and that held more significance to him than anything they could ever say or do.

One of the few men he could sit with and who understood what he stood for. He missed him.

"Yuh know something." A voice behind him made his guts tighten. "In my limited experience only two tings fall from the sky. Bird shit and paras."

Ricardo stiffened and then relaxed. The possessor of that voice should be thousands of miles away in New South Africa.

He turned, an expectant smile formed on his lips.

"We'd have had your cojones for that in the airborne, brother."

Ricardo's bass voice boomed.

"You could have tried." Asim threatened.

Ricardo's chuckle was deep and amiable, belying his immense size.

"Where in hell have you been?"

"If I tell you, I'll have to kill you." Asim grinned.

Ricardo laughed as they hugged and backslapped.

"Gently does it, big man!" He said, wincing at Ricardo's vigourous greetings.

"Active duty hasn't left me totally free from damage, yuh know."

Ricardo chuckled.

"So you're not invulnerable after all?"

"Guess not, boss."

******

"Cheers mi breddah."

The crystals tinkled.

Asim filled his glass again with the highly aromatic brandy and swirled the contents. They dispensed with their laughter and sat in companionable silence for a moment.

"To future success." Ricardo toasted, finishing the last mouthful of his Martini Dry. "We did it brother." He continued, licking his lips. "The competition was immense but Zulu Securities has developed a name for getting the job done."

"You did it." Asim added.

"Modesty will get you everywhere." His partner disagreed.

"Let's jus say I helped Zulu along its way."

Ricardo nodded.

"When you started recommending security systems to the Arabs and Africans, that's where it all began. A simple shift in method moved us away from sales, into the lucrative high profile security and technology consultation. Not to put too fine a point on it, we struck gold." He straightened the seams of his tailored pants. "My only regret is you were not here, to see it develop."

"Well let's see if I can make up for that. This time around I intend to play a more active role in tings." Asim gestured to the company logo on the wall.

"Something I should have done years ago."

Ricardo leaned back in his seat, his size making the sofa seem small. "I didn't realise your tour of duty was over."

"Over an done. And they didn't kick me out, either." Asim grinned. "I left of my own accord."

"That was a long time coming, my friend, and I know your family must be relieved. Get settled before you start thinking of business."

"Cool!" Asim agreed.

"Now for money matters," Ricardo announced. "Check this out."

Asim's eyes fell on the A4 size sheet of info-wafer. The figures seemed to jump off the page at him. He swallowed hard as he saw the size of his bank balance and recalled his initial investment of zero credits. Okay, the dossiers he had provided his partner on the influential men and women in Africa and the east, had not been obtained entirely above board. But if he had known the risks he had taken to give the company the vital edge were that valuable, maybe he would have given the army the elbow much sooner.

An I.D. Logic Card and two old style metal keys dangling from Ricardo's fingers were next to grab his attention.

"Warehouse 401 and my Porsche?" Asim blurted out.

Ricardo gave him the thumbs up.

Asim whistled and laughed.

"Bwoy, if I had any doubts about the nastiness of human nature, don, you would prove me wrong every time."

"We're not just business partners remember, we're brothers."

"So were Cain and Abel." Asim deadpanned.

It was Ricardo's turn to laugh as they locked hands again.

******

They left Zulu Security Systems together near midnight. The otherwise tranquil night was bruised with the sounds of sirens and flashing lights. Armoured vans loaded with armed police on call to another gang related incident sped by.

Their first stop was Ochies Restaurant on Acton Lane, where they filled up on fried dumplings, plantain, ackee and salt fish befor heading into the Bush.

Five years ago, when Asim decided a suicide tour of duty was his best option, Ricardo became the executor of his holdings. That was something else he had to thank his spar for.

Warehouse 401. Akilla needed somewhere to stay, her own bedroom and playing space. The very idea of converting his place for her was an exciting prospect. He had a good feeling about it.

Ricardo taxied into the lighted driveway, the Merc crunching gravel under its tyres. The first thing he noticed was the warehouse's exterior had been cleaned, polished and painted. It looked great.

At first sight as you drove up to it, the lower levels were nearly totally obscured by shrubbery and large sycamore trees. Composed of wood, steel, concrete and glass, what it seemed to lack from a distance it subtly revealed to you up close.

Ricardo said, "I've got a busy schedule in the morning so I can't stop. Just relax and familiarise yourself with the old place."

They touched fists.

Asim held him with his eyes.

"Thanks, man!" He said. "For everything!"

Ricardo shrugged as if he was being overly sentimental and drove off.

Asim flipped the I.D. card in his hand and mounted the stairs disabling the perimeter alarm system from a junction box half way up the flight. He fed his card into the slot and downloaded essential information into the House's main frame. He continued upwards, his soft loafers crushing leaves and small stones underfoot as the warehouse came into view. The place lit up like a beacon on his approach. In a mixture of surprise and pleasure, Asim stepped back and shook his head. He wiped away some weird liquid shit pooling at the corner of his eyes and entered.

The old place had been refurbished inside also and kept in superb condition.

You could see right through the house and it looked as if it had no boundaries, just multiple dimensions of open space. There was some Japanese influence in the sparseness with artistically set Scandinavian furniture of glass, wood, steel and leather.

The Ghanaian pimpernel had struck again.

Ricardo had made sure all of Asim's tastes were catered for, including his love for African pots.

Man! Surrounded by so many good people he did not deserve. His life style had to change.

He entered through one of the sliding glass doors and inhaled the smell of newness. He sat in his single sofa chair facing the urban light show over Shepherd's Bush.

A silken female voice startled him.

"There is a message left for you on your TView, sir, should I replay it for you."

"Raas!"

"Excuse me, sir."

The voice his home's core intelligence unit had used in the past had been dramatically overhauled from an over powering male vocal to very sultry and sexy female tones.

Laughing he said, "It's nothing, just replay it for me baby."

"Baby?"

"Oh!" He grinned. "It's just another term I'll use to address yuh with."

"Entered, sir."

"And House."

"Yes, sir."

"Drop the 'sir' ting. Call me Asim."

"Asim. Entered."

There was a short sizzling sound and then a recording with simultaneous visuals that floated in-front of the glass panel.

Shit!

Fatima's face smiled back.

"Ricardo said you would be here eventually. Sorry I missed your homecoming.

Anyway whenever you get in, ring me. Talk to you later. Bye."

Asim found himself staring at the fading image.

"House." He said distantly. "Trace the number for me, babe, and connect me up, nuh."

"My pleasure, Asim." House answered.

He was beginning to understand why Drill Sergeant 'Maggot' Malone, got the 'hump' when you mentioned family. To him they were a pain in the ass, especially when your focus should be on more important things, like a forced march with full thirty kilo kit through the Brecon Beacons at minus ten degrees.

'Happiness!' He would holler, 'is having a large, loving, caring, close-knit family - in another fucking part of the world!'

Come to think of it, the sergeant did have a way with words.

"Sim, look at you?" Fatima grinned broadly, bouncing forward on her seat. "Five years away and - god! What have they done to your hair?"

Asim stretched in his sofa and tried to create an illusion of calm. As the image of his sister came sharply into focus, he made a rapid appraisal of her. A wave of relief, made his taut muscles sag. Fatima looked healthy, vibrant and composed. Her eyes were focused, she maintained her sense of order - the room she was transmitting from was agonisingly neat, and her dress sense was sharp.

These were not the signs of a developing prog junkie, not a victim of Street Trash software.

He relaxed and met her laughter with a smile.

A smile of relief.

"Well?" Fatima demanded an answer to her question.

"Lack a sex," He said." My hair just decided to fall out."

She laughed some more.

It felt good seeing her, happy.

"Nice place," he said. "Must have cost yuh a bomb."

"It's a friend's pad."

As abrupt as a scene cut.

"Did you like that little touch at the airport?" She said. "The announcement I mean."

Asim grinned, treading carefully.

"It had your signature, stamped all over it, gal. Don't even start thinking you're slicker than me."

"You never did like to think a girl could outsmart you, did you."

"Damn right!"

"By the way, whatdo you think of Yasmeen? Beautiful isn't she?"

"Very."

"She'll be pleased to hear that."

Asim snorted amusingly.

"I've just arrived and I can't believe you're already trying to fit me up."

"Somebody has to. I can't wait to hear about your adventures in the Motherland over a gin and tonic."

"We have plenty a time for that. Right now I've got something on my mind and no answers."

Fatima's eyebrows rose innocently.

Asim dispensed with the subtlety.

"I've seen the BrainTechTM module in your bedroom. Talk to me."

Fatima's face twisted as if she was recovering from a short sharp slap. She flopped down in her seat and flashed her braids out of her face, glancing wickedly across the electronic distance.

"You know, Asim," her voice had raised a notch. "I was looking forward to you being back."

The TView projection suddenly blurred and shrank to a central vertical line. The disappearing point of light caught Asim with his mouth open.

The fucking gal hung up on me.

He jumped out of his sofa and screamed a command at House to redial but an automatic block had already been placed on the line.

This isn't happening, man, tell me this isn't happening.

His fist slammed into the head rest of his comfort chair fiercely.

Nice an easy, remember.

He couldn't have done a better job, if he had planned it.

He held his head in his hands.

Man!

MUSEUM OF ANCIENT AFRICAN HISTORY, CENTRAL LONDON.

"Mind your heads ladies and gentlemen." The words seemed to trickle through the Safety Officer's nose with a note of excitement. For short minutes he was an explorer leading his small party from the bowels of the building, up the rungs of a fixed metal ladder and through a hatch that led back into the immense display area of the Ethiopia Hall. His safety awareness talk out of the way and ahead of schedule, Mr. Hawkins had jumped at the opportunity for some hands-on 'instructing' while he indulged his fantasies of adventure.

Yasmeen's irises painfully adapted to the sudden change in light. It had been her second time down to the World War II bomb shelter. The faces were different but like some crazy style deja vu, she listened to Mr. Hawkins assemble his charges and complete his 'presentation' in the exact fashion he did three months ago, gesticulations and all.

"For you recent additions to our staff, who I understand have a lot to absorb, let me repeat myself for emphasis." He turned up his nose, the voice of pompous authority. "The bomb shelter houses the auxiliary power and safety systems. In case of main system failure, which I might add is highly unlikely but in the event, activation of secondary systems takes place there. The Ethiopia Hall is the oldest portion of the building with the most antiquated emergency network, we need to be extra vigilant there." He pointed to where they had come from and fixedly kept his charges in frame, preparing to gauge their reaction. "I take it we have all been trained on this straightforward procedure. Hmmn?!"

There were over eager nods. He snorted indignantly, ignoring them.

"In this portion of the museum, there are only two ways in. Here and here." He pointed to where they had exited from sometime earlier and then to another manhole hidden by a display in the far corner. "The other entrances will be outlined on your Info-Tablets after Ms Beyene updates them. Any further questions?"

He took their rapid departure to mean no.

The lift swiftly made its way to level one. Most offices were transparent but a few were offered a computer generated vista of their choosing. Yasmeen loved the scenery of an African Savannah with the sun perpetually setting in the horizon.

It was one of the privileges of the executive package. She smiled to herself, her breath fogging the glass. After all this time it was still a joy to work here.

That tingle of excitement in the pit of her stomach still remained and her sense of wonder had not diminished. The museum was her passion, as saccharine as that sounded. Contrary to what her girl friends believed, it wasn't a replacement for a man in her life, either.

The 'museum of compromises', the Tories had dubbed it and quite unfairly so. It was simply a case of sour grapes because it was their Labour counterparts who had successfully achieved something they had only given years of lip service to.

Africa had become more forceful in its reacquisition of its treasures scattered around the world, plundered by the imperialistic powers of the time. The West was unable to dispute the continent's rights to its own property so the United States of Europe held talks to resolve the problem. Having had these treasures in their possession for many centuries, Britain was understandably reluctant to part with them. The powers that be felt they should remain in the United Kingdom, as they were acquired by patriotic Englishmen of past who risked life and limb for a sovereignty that had been abolished.

So they reached a compromise.

Now, Africa could look to its heart's content, but not touch. The historical pieces were never able to leave European shores but effectively they were controlled by the Commonwealth of Democratic African States. The arrangement hadn't pleased them completely but there was nothing they could do, short of declaring war on the U.S. of E.

The expansive complex was built over the foundations of an old World war two art gallery and now housed a department of Ancient African History, archaeology and linguistics as well as the most prized and largest repository of African historical artifacts outside of Zimbabwe. It had more than a hundred million electronic book files, videos, digitised photographs and manuscripts - modern and ancient.

It was a historian's dream.

Tour groups and roving sightseers milled around the Ethiopia Hall, sampling the computer generated worlds of Ancient Abyssinia or viewing the many interactive exhibits.

The dreadlocks man reached out to the exhibit as if the signs saying, Do not touch, did not refer to him. The man inched closer, nothing else existed outside of what he saw in front of him.

Yasmeen's eyes locked onto him from a distance. The locks man had leaped over the roped area and was making his way to the sealed display. Casually she walked over the ropes and into the Rasta man's field of vision.

"Don't do that, brother!" She said. "You're not supposed to touch the exhibits."

Yasmeen pointed to the sign above his head.

The man turned to look at her, withdrawing his hand slowly. A lopsided grin stitched to his face.

It froze her to the spot.

"Do you know why yuh stepmother died Yasmeen? Why she was screaming out your name, to save her an yuh nevah?" The man's voice was a whisper.

Yasmeen stared fixedly at him, the strange man's words had her captivated in a snare of fear.

"She died for you. Died in your place. How dat make you feel?"

Shaking her head in the negative was all Yasmeen could muster.

Inadvertently her fingers stroked the personal alert system

disguised as a lion brooch. It felt rough under her finger tips, its usefulness blatantly apparent for the first time.

"The longer yuh breath Jah-jah air the more people will die in your place. Is you we really want, sista, just you."

His face shone hatred.

"The longer yuh draw breath," the man snarled. "The longer will be the suffering of everyone dear to yuh."

There was a sudden surge of blood to her tensed muscles.

His grin was crazy, his eyes wild.

Yasmeen squeezed the brooch and kept on squeezing.

******

Asim sat comfortably in his parent's lounge his grey Nike track suit patched with sweat and his magnetically cushioned running shoes still laced to his feet. He wrinkled his nose and frowned. An offensive smell oozed from deep inside his trainers.

For a misguided minute life felt uncomplicated.

In a moment of madness years ago he had said this little treasure was someone else's child. A starker illustration of how fucked-up he was in those days, he couldn't think of.

Akilla was his blood, make no mistake. How quickly she had grown. From his first glimpse of her in the maternity ward, screaming her lungs out and now look. Just being around her and the rest of the family was working wonders for him.

Akilla came strolling out of the kitchen, engrossed in her own world, her guard down. Swinging her hands from side to side, she stamped out into the hall her frizzy long brown hair springing uncontrolled from her scalp and her lips pouting in confrontation. An imaginary tiff with an imaginary friend Asim guessed. She was a fiery little sumting.

"I hope that's not me, you're cussing." Asim controlled the timbre of his voice making it as unthreatening as possible.

Akilla stopped in her tracks and turned to look at him as if he was an irritating glob of chewing gum she was about to scrape off the soles of her shoes.

"Well, are you going to talk to me or just stand there with yuh mouth wide open."

Akilla's determined pout transformed into a cherubic smile. Immediately he felt a rush of hope. He was making progress.

"Yuh know, you can't keep running from me, baby. I'm going to be here every day until you're tired of seeing me and then some more."

She took two uncertain steps toward him, her big toes pointed upwards from the carpeted floor like antennae while she bit on her lower lip. Asim was silently wishing her on wanting her to make the decisive step away from hostility to friendship. As she bashfully placed her hands behind her back, the door bell rang.

Jesas!

Yasmeen's voice came across the house's speakers and her image swam into focus on the wafer screen. That was all it took. Akilla spun on the balls of her feet and shot away to the main door squealing excitedly.

Yasmeen two, Asim nil.

His frustration was short-lived. He hadn't stopped thinking about her for the last two weeks. The sexual attraction was powerful and he knew she felt something too. Still it was too much of an effort resolving that question, now. He was just eager to see her step through the door.

And 'eager' felt very good.

******

Yasmeen's perfume proceeded her, the subtle blends of her eau de toilette making Asim's heart race.

Damn, he was acting like a love struck pickney.

She stood at the entrance to the lounge, smartly dressed, her head wrapped with a see-through scarf and those beautiful hazel eyes flashing.

Akilla was already comfortably lodged in her arms, the child's hands around the woman's neck and her head on her breasts. As stupid as it seemed, he felt that he needed to stand up as she came in.

A subconscious sign of respect, was all he could think.

Maaan!

She swayed in and stopped in the middle of the room, her bare feet sinking into the carpet. She nodded, unable to complete the traditional Rasta greeting with her hands occupied.

"Highest regards," she said.

"Highest." Asim answered his words sounding awkward to his ears.

"I missed you... both," she said honestly. "So I tore myself away from work this afternoon and decided to drop by. I'm not interrupting anything important am I?" Her eyes fell on the pile of papers beside the couch.

"Nothin that can't wait." He used his heel to move them out of eyeshot. "Actually I'm glad you came," he admitted, smoothing an eyelash with his fingertip.

Akilla didn't like being left out of any discussion that involved her Rasta sister. She whispered something in Yasmeen's ear and giggled.

"I like that." Yasmeen said turning to Asim. "Your daughter has just come up with a brilliant idea." Yasmeen leaned back and gave Akilla a long appraising look. "I'm not sure what her motives are." Akilla looked on with that innocent stare of hers unmoved by the comment. "But I must admit, going to the park in this weather should be great fun and therapeutic for the stressed out amongst us."

Asim stood back and looked at her with a wicked grin on his face. Both hands in his pockets, he stretched the material absently.

"Does it look dat obvious?" He joked. "Or is this a scheme you girls have planned to root me out of the house."

Yasmeen smiled weakly.

The decision to come here today had been a good one. She needed to get away and try to take her mind off her surrogate mother's murder. The threat in the museum had stuck with her also. Normally she would have discounted it as the ravings of a madman if not for what he had said. Who was he and how did he know her? Why would Rasta want her dead? It made no sense, nothing was making any sense.

She shared in Asim's jibe.

"It just proves how little you know about woman, doesn't it."

She nudged Akilla who nodded, shyly.

"Educate mi nuh!"

"I think we may need to."

******

The Eco-bus silently pulled up to the kerb. Asim, Yasmeen and Akilla disembarked, weighed down with some quickly prepared food, the Geo-dome of Hyde Park in the background. The Dome had been built in the early Twentieth-First century. And with it had come the changes.

Tight security into the facility, all protest marches through its leafy walkways had been banned along with the ancient tradition of speaker's corner. Now the park was a monument to the environment and held the fourth largest artificially controlled climate facility in the world. It was actually a working research laboratory open to the public. It allowed them to experience every weather condition and climate on earth past and present. Set like a shiny multifaceted diamond with the glistening bio-engineered waters of the Serpentine and its attached sports facility, this expanse of land drew stares and tourists.

The trio passed through the electronic turnstile. The consensus was they should find a shady alcove and do what everyone else seemed to be.

Flake out.

Endless lines of bodies lay in various states of discomfort like slowly roasting frankfurters over a medium fire. All the Chief Medical Officer's warning's about ultraviolet light contamination had been ignored.

A hedge plant caught their attention, sprouting wildly near one of the many paths that veered to the northern region of the park. Prime spot.

Yasmeen set up camp while Asim began to realise what he was missing being cooped up inside the house.

A spectacular looking dark-skinned woman loped across the

grass in front of him and then lay down on a towel. Her eyes closed, her face and body toward the sun, knees drawn up and slightly apart. Wispy tendrils of pubic hair escaped the sparse confines of her G-string and her nipples poked the material of her bra to its limit.

Asim's lips curled.

Nice.

They sat comfortably under the shadow of the leaves, the food they had prepared spread beside them. Children's laughter rang out unrestrained, no one caring about anything but the moment. All the problems of the city were left outside the fenced boundaries, where they belonged. Asim felt the urge to just lay back and chill.

Yasmeen sat curling her feet under her like a cat and self consciously pulling her skirt over her knees. He admired the gesture which to him was very sensual but made no reference to it. Instead they both watched Akilla dig into her rucksack for her voice activated doodle-ball for some high impact ramping.

The Rasta woman had been silent for a long time, turning away from her antics only to see Asim relaxed with his head hung back and his eyes closed.

She had an uncomfortable feeling of fear. Yasmeen couldn't say whether it was everything that had been happening to her over the last few weeks or Asim and how attracted to her she was.

These dangerous urges were twisting their way to the surface, cracking through the mantle of her jaded morals like roots breaking ground. Urges she had almost forgotten she had.

Asim's eyes snapped open.

"I can't figure you out. A beautiful woman who isn't caught up in herself. How come?"

"Don't be fooled by what you see," Yasmeen's high cheeks rose. "I'm just as self motivated, result orientated as the next professional woman."

"You had me fooled." He grinned lazily.

"Let's just say you're looking at a woman who has learned what the true priorities of life are."

"Your family," Asim asked. "Where are they?" Yasmeen's body language subtly said 'uncomfortable'. He regretted having asked.

Then her eyes brightened.

"My mother Miriam died four years ago and my father died while I was still a child in Ethiopia."

Yasmeen paused.

"The rest of my family is back home. We lost contact with them as a precaution."

"Family 'ruptions."

"We had to run from Ethiopia because of political problems. All family contacts had to be severed for our safety and theirs."

"You've had some rough times, then."

Pragmatically she said, "They can only get better."

Her entire being was screaming out that he was the one.

Asim kissed her fingertips. A whisper of pleasure escaped her parted lips.

"No!" Yasmeen breathed, the word lacking any real resolve, she just knew it could go no further or the responsibility for her actions would not be hers. Reluctantly she withdrew her hand.

"Do you know what your name means?"

"Guardian or protector - in Arabic, I think." He replied puzzled.

"More to the point it means the protector of the faith. In Africa we believe a name can direct a person's destiny. Who named you?"

"Funny yuh ask that." He nodded the memory amusing him. "My grandmother Miss Mac was given the name in a dream, by some breddah she figured out to be a Muslim spirit guide."

Yasmeen smiled as if what he said meant something to her.

"Are you a believer in destiny?"

He twisted slightly on the grass, making sure he faced her.

"I must admit, that is something I've never really thought deeply about. Never had the need to."

"Maybe it's time," she said. "Did you feel it when we first met?"

"I felt...someting. Yeah."

"Even before that moment, your image made me feel I knew you."

"How come. An we never met..."

She put a finger to his lips, relieved.

"Don't ask me to explain it because I can't. I just know we knew each other intimately in some past life."

His expression was impassive. What in hell was his reaction supposed to be. Surprise, shock, what?

He knew exactly what she was saying and couldn't deny experiencing that powerful sense of deja vu when he saw her for the first time. Goose flesh had crept along the back of his neck. What he was being asked to believe was crazy. Lust at first sight, maybe. Reincarnation? Nah man! A year and a half without sex could fuck up your reasoning. Right.

"Somehow I never figured you'd believe in that spiritualist ting."

"When the proof is sitting beside me, what choices do I have."

Yasmeen's eyes left his and followed Akilla's movements in the distance. She was spinning about in the grass her cries ringing out, the silvery doodle-ball suspended inches from the ground, awaiting her verbal commands before it skimmed along the grass.

The Rasta woman drew her knees up to her chest.

"That's why I'm afraid." She said.

"Of what?" Asim asked curiously swallowing.

"Of you."

"Me?" He laughed. Instead of surprise he felt flattered.

"Questions." Yasmeen said slowly.

"Questions?" He repeated.

"You've made me begin to rethink many things that I had taken for granted for so long."

"I did all that?"

She nodded.

"I never considered the possibility of being attracted to someone outside the flock. I couldn't imagine that my feelings had been mapped out for me already by higher forces."

Asim could say nothing to that.

Her confessions should have felt strange but didn't. If not for that fleeting inner tension that clouded her eyes sometimes he would go as far as to say he even expected it. She had never changed, an inner voice seemed to say.

The bewilderment didn't show in Asim's eyes.

"Makes you wonder who is in control, right."

Yasmeen nodded.

Abruptly, she felt an overpowering need to tell him everything. Tell him she was frightened for him, not of him. Being around her was dangerous. Sister Ijah paid the price, who would be next?

Asim slicked his palm over his smooth head.

"Questions like those demand answers. Do you have any?" He asked.

"I have my own answers but my congregation has its expectations. And I must live up to them."

"Even if that means sacrificing your own happiness... or your destiny?"

"Maybe."

The spider-shaped scar on his right cheek twitched. Why did he get the impression she was building walls. Or was she testing him? Suddenly, he wasn't so sure of her intentions.

"Are you saying a baalhead is not good enough for a Rasta woman?"

"You know that's not what I mean," she said calmly. "The Rasta nation has been through a lot to maintain its values and it's important we protect them."

"Fair enough."

"The locks are the most obvious symbols of who we are," Yasmeen explained. "But not the most important. Deep in our hearts we must believe in Jah, the blessedness of our homeland Africa, the sanctity of human life everywhere, and the family. That is the core of our future and they want nothing interfering with that."

"They don't want baalheads corrupting their beliefs. Are we

that much of a threat?"

She didn't answer instead she stared into his eyes.

He interpreted the silence as a cue to continue.

"It's good to have high ideals but Rasta is flesh and blood, with the best and worst of ideals, like every other way a life." Asim gestured out to the streets. "People are killing one another, Rasta and baalhead alike. Because of the colour of there skin and what they believe in."

Yasmeen solemnly agreed.

He continued.

"Man is man and you'll find we are the same. We may speak differently, have different customs but when it comes down to the meat and grizzle - one."

He lapped his two fingers tightly together.

"I wish it was so simple."

"Well answer me this." He said, his head raised back on his shoulders. "Why are there so many caucasian people around the world embracing Rasta? A long time ago the white man was considered Babylon. Today they are a part of the Nation of Ras Tafari. How come?"

Her pause and intake of breath eloquently showed her frustration.

"Mankind originated in the savannahs of Africa." She recited. "It should have spiritual significance for ALL people. Rasta embraces ALL people."

"All people," Asim repeated. "So if you can give deh Babylon a chance for redemption. Why not me?"

"I want to." She stood up and began walking to join Akilla in the grass. "I'm just not sure I can."

She left him with a vague uneasiness. A sense that something sinister was lurking underneath the barriers she had erected. Something that scampered from view at the slightest hint of discovery.

He wanted to call after her but decided not to.

"I can wait."

COCKPIT COUNTRY, JAMAICA.

Sundown flung a blood red canopy over the valleys of Trelawney. The Dread hobbled out of the bush as if it was his cue. He patiently twisted the handle on his ginep walking stick and pulled out a sharp blade, marking some inscriptions in the dirt. Replacing cold steel carefully into its sheath he sat on a large stone in a clearing, placing his walking stick on his lap, a fire crackled in front of him. Mosquitoes hummed about disorientated by the smoke, fire flies - or peenie-wallies as the locals knew them - periodically lit up the dark recesses beyond the clearing. The cacophony of insect song fell into the background but only to familiar ears, of which his were. Head held down, his gnarled fingers reached back, undoing a bind holding his hair in place. Milk white dreadlocks fell to his shoulders and eyes that moments ago were soft and unfocused became intense as he looked over to the eager faced children seated in shadow.

How he wanted his thoughts to be free from any fear or bitterness. The children deserved no distractions. But he couldn't give of himself wholly, not yet. Solving the meaning of his premonitions demanded his full attention.

He came to know that the inner certainty he sensed when discerning visions involving others, did not apply when he himself was the focus of his own gifts. The symbolism that used to be so clear in meaning, had become obscure and less reliable. They had a significance he needed to fathom, completely. And their urgency was making him frantic. They wouldn't let him rest.

Distantly he looked into the fire blazing and warming the soles of his feet. The air was filled with glowing embers, swirling and spiralling into the night sky buoyed up by the thermal currents.

Fame and international recognition would have been best served if it was heaped on another man's shoulders. His popularity eclipsed the reputations of leaders within the flock. Amongst Twelve Tribes, Nyabinghi Theocracy, House of David and Orthodox, he sensed strife. Jealousy became aggravation and aggravation turned into threats to his family. So he stepped back, arranged his own death. The elders in Thro-Weh district promised him safe haven, and to the rest of the world he became history.

Now, twenty years later they were trying to kill his only child. Why?

The Ascension, it could be nothing more.

Wolf an leopard are trying to kill the sheep and deh shepherd.

The time for hiding, done!

His own life was unimportant. What mattered was the future. Peace, the Rasta children.

And his girl child.

He had set his plans in motion and could only pray his assumptions were correct.

"Yuh a guh tell wi story, Elder." The shrill voice of impatience abruptly snapped off his remaining thoughts.

The old man smiled warmly.

"Of course mi young lion, this is your time. What do yuh want to hear?"

He taught the children of the district the traditions of the islands, the stories of Africa and its legends.

Excited shouts rang out as every small voice demanded to be heard. He calmed them with his walking stick outstretched.

"Calm dung, I will decide for yuh." He thought for a moment, licking his lips. "Tonight yuh will hear of breddah Anansi, the spider man."

They huddled closer.

Shanna, the youngest of the group of twenty, brazenly left ranks and with her thumb plugged firmly into her mouth, sat comfortably on the Dread's lap.

He stroked her hair.

"Once upon a time," He began. "Breddah Anansi knocked on breddah Tiger door an wake him..."

HARLESDEN, LONDON.

Asim stood in the cluttered kitchen with his hands in his pockets. What should he do now? Maybe bringing out the sandwiches was a good idea, or start on pouring the drinks into the cluster of paper cups. Then again, keeping them occupied should be his main priority, so definitely start handing out streamers and whistles.

Better yet, ru'bwoy, just stay out of their way and hope for the best.

Anne smiled.

His indecision was amusing and dangerous at the same time as his frantic preparations was reducing her usually neat work area to a bomb site. After calming him down she said, "Are you sure you want to go ahead with this, son? It's not too late for me to take over."

The offer was a tempting one. The fiasco at the zoo two weeks ago was still vivid in Asim's mind and he considered his mother's offer very carefully, indeed.

Again he had masterminded the festivities, but learning from the experience of recent past, he made sure Akilla's friends were situated in the small confines of home and constantly monitored. So disaster was less likely. Today would be free of search and rescue operations in abandoned nature reserves.

"Take it easy." Anne warned, but he was just a father with a lot of catching up to do, and an overwhelming need to cram into his daughter's life as many of the things as he had not been able to give her, in the shortest period of time. He wished she would communicate with him but beggars can't be choosers. He was content to arrange the entertainment, the food, music and send out the thirty or so invitations. As saccharin as it sounded, it gave him a sense of purpose and made him feel he was contributing to her development.

A contribution that was long overdue.

High ideals aside, what he never counted on were the children and how he'd control them.

They started drifting in early and he started to panic - the showbiz dictum, never work with children or animals came to mind for some strange reason. Flashbacks from the results of his last brainstorm and all that had gone wrong made him freeze up.

Awful premonitions of disaster lensed through his mind burning away any confidence he felt in pulling this gig off. Damn, he was going to be host, for thirty screaming pickney.

Anne could see the shuttering of his eyes while the scenario played on the screen of his mind.

"Just help me serve the food, Mum," He managed. "I'll handle the rest." His voice sounded hollow in his head. And the words 'famous' and 'last' just seemed to hold odd significance to him at that point.

A decision was made on the spot that it would be better for all concerned if he stayed away from handing out pointy hats and cheesy grins of welcome. They both agreed to confine him to the kitchen for the time being.

Good idea, he thought. Damn good idea.

Three quarters of the way through the party he was getting into the swing of things.

Asim watched the ambulance leave before he returned to the merriment.

The casualties were actually lower than he had imagined. One dislocated arm, what seemed like either food poisoning or appendicitis and a few cuts and bruises, was a real result. Akilla was enjoying herself, her friends, infant party crashers and all, seemed to think he was tops. For an adult anyway.

Even the Techno Wizard who had been booed at first, gained their respect by threatening to make someone's robot bear disappear. This he promptly did in anger and couldn't - or wouldn't - conjure it back again.

Besides the tears and the apologies, it had been a success.

It had actually worked out.

The only thing left to do was to inform the parents of the fallen heroes being sped off to the hospital. That was done on his way back to the music and mayhem.

His thoughts were occupied with how the mob would react when he told them party time was swiftly drawing to a close.

He was too tired and relieved to care.

Where was she?

Asim stepped out of the kitchen into the back yard and looked around. Akilla was still avoiding him but it had become habit to keep her in his sights and receiving few smiles when their eyes met. Being the great hostess that she was, Akilla was never in one spot for too long. She mingled as you do and engaged in small talk.

Five years old, to backside!

He shook his head and walked through the kitchen, passing the Field Marshal wiping the mouth of one terrorist dressed in full camouflage gear. The garden was an erratic mess of pubescent colour and sound. Asim rounded the corner, just catching sight of Akilla's blue and white track suit.

He hesitated.

Something told him to step back and he did.

Peeping through the crack in the door, he saw his daughter holding hands with another boy about her age.

Boyfriend?

He blinked and shook his head. Nuh way!

Fatherly concern was telling him he should go and break that 'shit' up but shameless inquisitiveness won out. He cocked his ear to the panel and listened.

- You've got a great dad, Keela. Where woz he all this time?

- Away.

- Away, where?

- Africa.

- Wow! Did he see any dinosaurs?

- Dinosaurs are extinct, Moran.

- Monster Watch says they're not.

- He carried a gun.

- Your dad did?

- Yep!

- Cool!

- That's not cool.

- Was it one a them EM cannons that burns you up and there's nothing left and...

- I don't know, Moran.

- So he didn't shoot things then.

- I don't know.

- Come on, Keela, tell me what he said.

- Nothing.

(Pause)

- You don't like your dad do you?

- I dooo like my dad! It's just...

(Laughter)

- My dad never did nothing like this for me. He must love you a lot, to come back here, when he could be shooting stuff in Africa.

- Guess so.

- You're lucky. When my dad left, he never bothered coming back.

He had heard enough. Silently, with his head lowered, Asim turned and walked out of the kitchen.

******

Fatima could scarcely believe she was in here. The reality was even wilder than the stories she had heard. Every vice was catered for and every outlandish request possible for a price.

The Pleasure Arena was draped in wispy layers of mist. Pulsing spears of red and green laser light from the ceiling mounted rigging, punctured the CO_2 clouds. Shadowy dancers on the crystal floor swayed to the digital sounds of reggae fusion. Some were flesh and blood, others VR images invisible to the naked eyes but seen only through filters that rose from the floor to cover them in a transparent dome.

The insincere smiles were broad, the laughter unnecessarily boisterous. Liberated women paraded topless, nipples taut and glistening in the light. While the men who were equally expressive paraded their manhoods like coiled snakes in see-through briefs. Men dressed as women, women dressed as men. This was hedonism at its extreme and with no consequences. That's what made the Arena world famous.

Even before you fell victim to its reputation you were struck by its architecture. The design was a scaled down reproduction of the Colosseum of Rome. The designers demanded authenticity to such a degree that portions of the interior included the famous wedge seating from the original. Their obsessive attention to detail created a feeling that prehistory had been flung forward in time and imbued with the sophistication of the 21st century.

It was in this atmosphere that movie stars, pop stars and some of the younger members of traditional moneyed households mingled with the connected commoners, downing traditional alcohol or more exotic drinks spiked with stimulants. Fatima had been swept away with the hype, harbouring no hopes of even walking up the red carpeted entrance. The requirements were high-powered business contacts, privileged family connections and money.

Her luck was changing.

The man who sat beside Fatima was known in hustler circles as Baldwin. A cigarette hitched to the corner of his small mouth, seemingly unable to fall out even when he spoke.

He was so in his element.

And knew without a shadow of a doubt he was the king of cool and the epitome of fashion as he struck a pose of rugged sophistication for all to see. His dreadlocks tied back and exploded in all directions from a platinum clasp that held it in place. A few strands of his hair were adorned with platinum tubes encrusted with diamonds, and his right eyebrow pierced with a ring made from some other precious metal. He wore a pair of self-adjusting Gucci shades on his brow and strutted with an elegant lion's head walking stick. His back-to-the-past Armani zoot suit hung loosely but elegantly on him. Baldwin leaned against the cane, his eyes pinpricks of nervous tension.

Just for a moment he was caught in a freeze frame of contemplation as the music buffeted the interiors of the nightclub. Just at that instant you could evaluate succinctly the type of man he was.

A hustler, an opportunist, a womaniser and a well-dressed cocksman with a physical presence that made him unhealthily desirable.

How could any woman resist that combination?

After all, Fatima was only human.

Baldwin turned away from the dancefloor and smiled at her, a nervous twitch of a smile that held no real warmth. Sparking confidence in no one except for the lovestruck.

He was fond of her. She was beautiful, determined but much too trusting for her own good. He was very rarely wrong about women.

What did the Big Boy want with her?

He was given no reason, just a name. They had paid him well for a job he had thoroughly enjoyed.

The pace of the music had slowed, signalling a break from the frenzied activities on the dancefloor. An old fashioned smoocher slid through the flat speakers. Lovers came closer, their warm breath caressing necks and earlobes, raising pulse rates and expectations. Baldwin was unaffected by the change in tempo, his thoughts remained troubled.

He sat beside her again.

Fatima picked up her glass and took a grateful sip of vodka and passion juice. She let her hand roam along his crotch, her nails lightly running along the length of his bulging organ. He held it there for a moment under the crystal table allowing her the pleasure of his rapid erection, but he kept his eyes glued to the dancefloor, deep in thought.

"Come on, Wyn, I want to dance to this one. Just me and you." She grabbed his hand and tried to pull him up but he simply kissed her neck and patted her backside.

"You go, suga. I'll watch that sexy body whining from here." He pointed his cane to the gathering dancers.

Fatima shrugged and spun onto the floor.

Baldwin had other things on his mind.

He let his shoulders droop and let out a stream of nervous breath. They had wanted this over and done with a week ago. That queasy sensation in his gut was not calmed by him swallowing large doses of brandy. As his eyes darted right he was just in time to see the broad-shouldered white man in a shiny suit lope around the periphery of the dance area.

Bobby Beeton scowled.

As he approached, Baldwin restrained a grin at the pale faced orang-utan. His head was cemented to his body with no intervening neck and his jaw line was broad and powerful. The ring through his nose glinted. It was obvious he was not pleased to see the funky dread. Mr. Beeton - as he preferred to be called - stood their glaring at him, his broken nose twitching as he spoke. He was now an albino bull in Baldwin's minds eye,.

"Where's the girl?"

His voice was all cockney and as gruff as grade one sandpaper.

"Over there somewhere." Baldwin snapped, pointing without looking away from him.

"Tone it down ya black cunt or do you want us to take a walk outside then. Teach you how to talk to your superiors." Mr. Beeton grabbed at Wyn's collar but he recoiled slapping away his hairy paw with his cane.

"Don't soil deh shirt, man, what deh fuck's wrong with you?" Baldwin eyed him up and down and kissed his teeth.

Beeton clenched and unclenched his fist, slowly.

"Don't get cocky with me, sunshine."

"Just take her, man. Take her."

Baldwin closed his eyes and turned away, a burden of shame clung to him, weighing him down like a ball and chain.

"You've come to ya senses, sunshine. You're not as stupid as you look. Now don't talk just listen." He reached into his jacket pocket and pulled out a hermetically sealed, glass ampule. He handed it to him.

"Pour this in er drink an when she gets tipsy, take her out to the motor. We'll take it from there. Awright!"

Baldwin nodded feeling nauseous.

"Now get a fucking move on."

Mr. Beeton walked away, adjusting his collar.

"Who was that you were talking to?" Fatima came over, encircled him with her arms.

"Just a business associate." Baldwin flinched, rubbing his palms together and wiping the perspiration on a handkerchief out of his breast pocket.

He changed the subject quickly.

"What do you think?" He opened his arms in a grand gesture, his eyes on an opened bottle of champagne and two filled glasses.

Her response was to kiss him full on the lips, her tongue flickering in his mouth.

"Thanks darling, for everything."

He swallowed hard.

"A toast then," she said.

Baldwin raised his glass uncertainly.

"To us."

His voice broke as he echoed, "To us."

******

Reginald Thorndike never thought he would see the day. Yet throughout his fifty odd years of ducking and diving, he had seen changes. Changes even he had to accept with stoic resignation, making him shake his head in disbelief but that was the world he lived in.

He looked absently at his empty glass, the waiter was clearing the table with more caution than was usual because his boss hated to wait for anything. Quickly the soon-to-be-out-of- work employee replenished his supply of liqueur and made his escape.

"Take your time." Reggie chided observing his haste.

The waiter nodded, crisply trying not to meet his employer's gaze.

Freddy Tubbs chuckled from a seat beside him, showing his artificial choppers, never once taking his eyes off the show in the foreground.

Reggie Thorndike smiled to himself. Freddy was not as reserved as his other associates, not as refined.

So fucking what. The others wouldn't take a bullet for him if the need arose, Freddy wouldn't hesitate.

Through narrowed eyes Reggie regarded his old school mate

for a moment, enjoying the show on stage like an eager child would their favourite cartoon program. Slightly slumped in his seat, his grey pinstripe suit shimmering under the roof lights with his understated mauve shirt nearly hidden by a broad metallic grey tie. His calling in life was to break people both physically and mentally through what he would describe as expert application of pain, and in Mr. Thorndike's business the ideal man to be beside him in dodgy situations. After all, large portions of his business were established on pain.

He stitched an insincere grin on his face that didn't last long.

Reggie was one of the lucky few who could say -hand on heart - that he was happy how everything had turned out for him.

The Blue Note was the premiere Erotic Entertainment Centre of the United States of Europe. Situated on Broadbent Street in the heart of Soho. The women were the most beautiful in the U.S.E, and the accompanying stallions muscular and well-hung. Their sexual antics on stage were drawing excited reviews and pulling the punters from all over the place. Entertaining them in plush elegance, where nothing was left unexplored and no one left unsatisfied.

The Brotherhood had a substantial stake in the business and, like so many people, Reggie owed them a favour that they could call upon at anytime.

The gang warfare that was gripping London had become a point of contention to the Brotherhood. They never imagined the niggers, jews and pakis would start to fight back with such fury and single-mindedness.

"So what do you think, Reg? Doesn't this show just get better and better every week."

Freddy Tubbs grinned amiably his eyes flicking up and down in time with a well-endowed woman, bobbing her gigantic breasts in beat with the music.

The audience applauded and laughed.

"You should know by now, that whatever I put my head to (no pun intended), produces results, Freddy. It's a gift I've got." He adjusted his thick diamond encrusted chaps mindfully, leaning back a bit more into his chair and folded his arms. "You've stuck with me through all the aggro'. It's been a rough ride in places but now it's done and I'm grateful." He shrugged. "Being grateful isn't enough, though. Later we'll talk about you and your misses taking an all-expenses paid luxury break in the sun."

"Majorca?" Freddy asked eagerly.

Reggie shook his head.

"Think big. Concorde, Five star hotel, limos all the way. Take your pick, mate."

Reggie took another sip from his glass of champagne, allowing the cool sparkling liquid to trickle down his throat and handed his friend a travel brochure.

A red light flashed on the chair's arm rest. From inside the chunky arm of Reggie's seat a small screen folded out of its housing and sparked to life with a view of the main foyer.

He peered at the screen and barked down the miniature microphone.

"Oy! Mick! What's going on?"

The voice and a face came back to him on his screen amidst the confusion in the background.

"We have it under control Mr. Thorndike, it's just some skinhead wankers who think they can gatecrash. Don't worry, they're going nowhere."

Reggie's ears seemed to prick up at the comment. Pure Blood. Tattooed faces and bald heads except for long pony tails. Grimacing, he peered down at the screen and spoke softly, his voice carrying impatient force.

"Those geezers you're trying to eject, take their money, search them for concealed weapons and let them in with a personal apology. And Mick.."

"Yeah guv."

"I don't want a repeat of this incident in the future. Is that clear?"

Mick's eyes widened, unbelieving at the order.

Freddy Tubbs scratched his head apishly at what he had just seen, his mouth forming an incredulous 'O'.

Reggie leaned back, adjusted the sleeves of his jacket and ignored Freddy's expectant glances.

There were some things about him not even his best mate should know.

******

Asim stepped through the turnstiles and immediately felt the tension in the air.

Security around the vast perimeter of Finsbury Park was tight and areas that were not manned by intense looking guards were being cybernetically monitored. He shook his head, a feeling of disappointment at the state the capital was in.

Whether he liked it or not, London had become a very dangerous place to live.

Thousands of people were congregated around a stage set in a natural depression across the landscape. Sounds from the band warming up in the distance floated into the dark blue mantle of sky, joined by the fumes from thousands of assorted fires in mouths and hands.

The park seemed to be alight.

As well as not being here on time, he wasn't able to observe the two minutes silence - a commemoration of the seventy million descendants who had perished in the slave trade.

He looked back at the crowd again.

People patterned the grass in every direction like a cheap maze. Kissing his teeth, he focused on the highly visible mast flying the royal seal of Ethiopia and moved towards it.

Stepping diagonally through the bulk of bodies, Asim carefully picked his way forward, drifting through pockets of earthy ganja smells and food aromas.

His apprehension of being around crowds wasn't evident as he trod on toes and stumbled through groups of people. The mostly warm apologies he was receiving for his own clumsiness were putting him at ease.

Many of those gathered had come to hear the official announcement of the ordination of the Symbolical Negusa Negas in two months time - Yasmeen had explained about the Prophecy of Redemption to him. And told him about one of the founding fathers of Rasta who had seen the coming of a man who would lead them, the peacemaker. But most he felt had come to show their concerns - and their fears - for a city buckling under the burden of racial intolerance and crime. The 'race wars' as the electronic media chose to call them, had served one good purpose tonight at least. It had brought all the different peoples of London together in peace. And what could be more fitting for the cause than for the ambassador from the Commonwealth of Democratic African States to make a keynote speech. Legendary cultural artist I Jah Man Mystic had shared that view and with his Consciousness band had given their services to the cause, swelling the numbers even further. Represented was the racial diversity which gave London it's strength and weakness and amidst that was the Rasta flock, proudly adorned in their African finery.

Asim let out a sigh of relief. He passed a group of young men beating drums. If matters religious were brought up he could hold his own.

Yasmeen's knowledge of the faith was astonishingly detailed. History, fact and what he considered could only be fiction was distilled into an evenings talk.

The Dread, Joshua was what had interested him the most in her historical accounts. A man who if he was alive would be the Negusa Negas no question. A giant whose very involvement in an event blurred the boundaries of fact and myth. The Great Riots of Kingston were a typical example.

Early Millennium and Kingston erupted into riots starting from Rema and Jones Town. The people's angst was directed at a political system that had just raised the taxes on communities struggling to survive. Soon downtown's commercial centre was burning, and the affluent became the focus of ghetto people's anger. The violence had been going on for two days and the security services were fighting a battle they could not win. The religious leaders called for calm from a safe distance but their pious 'chit-chat' had no effect. Not until the Dread was airlifted into the heart of the inferno, unconcerned about gunshots and fire, finding the community leaders responsible amidst the chaos and pleading for peace, did the madness stop.

Eyewitness accounts say he literally walked through fire. All of what Ras Tafari was today stemmed from his exploits around the world. The peacemaker. Because of his example the election of Negusa Negas in Shashamane was such a major world event. The flock was hoping the glory days could return.

Yasmeen saw him enter the VIP tent and called to him. He smiled as he turned and recognised her.

Yasmeen immediately introduced him to a red headed Rasta man who had followed her over.

"This is Trevor, a colleague from Jamaica."

Both men shook hands, both assessing each other.

"Guidance!" The Rasta man rumbled.

"Respect, boss." Asim said, scrutinising him subtly.

Asim saw a man fluid in his movements with a powerful handshake. His eyes never seemed to leave Yasmeen's presence for too long. Trevor was not the cheeriest of individuals but Asim sensed an honourable man and a fighter.

Who he was exactly became a point of interest.

Yasmeen did not stop there. Music execs to lawyers made Asim's acquaintance in such a short time his head was spinning.

"What do you think?" Yasmeen asked as she diplomatically extracted him from another deep and meaningful conversation.

"I'm impressed, but where do you know all these people from?"

She laughed.

"All well wishers and associates."

"Now I can see why, you were concerned about a baalhead in your life." He patted his chest. "You're risking a lot being seen with me?"

"A week ago maybe I'd agree with you."

"What has changed?"

"I've learned life is too short," Yasmeen said. "Experience it all, leave your mark and wonder about the morrow when it comes."

"Yours is not to wonder?" A Rasta with blonde coarse locks and blue eyes interrupted. The headphones parted from his ears with a weak whine and his voice lowered to normal volume. "Because in two minutes the show starts, so your opening speech is now."

Yasmeen looked at him distastefully. He shrugged.

"Sorry!" He tapped his watch.

"Opening speech?" Asim asked surprised.

"Remember, leave your mark." She placed her hand on her heart and bowed slightly.

"Come!" She took Asim's hands. "Give me some moral support backstage."

******

"Wicked job, boys," Asim shouted over to the men. "We'll wrap this up later."

The demonstration had gone well.

Asim turned to face a group of Japanese business heads and tried to gauge the level of interest. A mild hum of subdued discussion - which he interpreted as being excitement - emanated from amongst them.

What more could he ask for as an introduction into his position as projects chief for Zulu Security Systems Inc.

His first project - his first victory.

Impressing the Asian market was no easy task.

"Zulu Security Systems Inc. would like to apologise for not being able to allow you to use recording equipment." Asim said to them sincerely. "This evening's presentation and all the information contained within the Personal Digital Assistants we gave to you is copyrighted and patented material and is regarded as classified by Zulu Security Systems Inc."

Polite nods and smiles of acknowledgement.

Asim proceeded.

"I know there must be many more questions you want to ask

but first I'd like to direct you to our reception area for some light refreshments and our company's CEO Mr. Ricardo Ogun will answer any further queries. This way, gentlemen."

Asim led them from the courtyard into the main building and up the lift to the third floor. They followed in orderly fashion still speaking in their native tongue as the door to the reception automatically opened and Asim ushered them inside. He glimpsed Ricardo smiling at him from the distance, impressed not just with the results but by how the Japanese catering firm had converted their functional reception into an elegant sushi bar.

Everything was falling perfectly into place.

"Asim!" A hand forcefully grabbed him by the shoulders. Surprised, he turned to see Kehinde out of breath and distressed.

"Your mobile was off." The words came out like a busted spigot. "God, I've been looking all over for you." She stopped suddenly unable to say anything more.

"What is it?" Asim demanded.

Kehinde led him out into the corridor and stood him up near a utility room, her eyes pools of tears.

"Tell me it's not Akilla." Asim held her desperately about the arms, his voice raising alarmingly. "Tell me."

Kehinde shook her head.

"Fatima." She bit on her lips, choosing her words with care. There was a sharp indrawn breath. "She's in the IC unit at King's, she was fishe dout of the river, near Battersea Bridge. She's alive."

She swallowed hard as Asim's cold expressionless eyes studied her, searching for more. She couldn't keep it from him.

"She's been raped!"

Asim's eyes locked shut.

******

Yasmeen and Asim left the nurse at the reception desk and headed for the recovery area.

She offered no words of encouragement. She could not speak.

Jah almighty forgive me, this is my doing.

Asim had to know. She had to tell him.

Asim was frightened. History was repeating itself, boss. Life was either fucking with him or giving him another chance. A chance to make the type of scum who preyed on others and seemed to have a preference for him and his family, pay dearly. An ice cold fury welled up in him. The reassuring softness of Yasmeen's hand squeezed his own.

He held it tightly.

Coming down the main corridor, he recognised the huddle of people standing just ahead of him. In front of a set of battered swinging doors was his distraught family. Low wails and sniffling caught his ear as he approached. He came among them, almost unnoticed, their voices respectfully low except for the Field Marshal. Aunt Mazy and Glenda stood sobbing, his uncle John-John was sucking on a nicotine free cigarette with such force it was like he wanted to pull the artificial tobacco through the filter. Anne on the other hand was seated quietly being consoled by Asim's twin cousins. Sensing her son's approach, she looked up.

An unrecognisable mask, stared back at him.

Her eyes were swollen from tears, her face sagging and her hair clumped together on her head, lifelessly.

"Come, son."

She took his arm, her hands trembling and her step unsure and led him to his sister's bedside.

The bruised and battered form of Fatima Marshall seemed buoyant on the white sheets while monitors flashed in time with her steady heartbeat. The young doctor in a long white coat, old fashioned paisley shirt - the collar a size too big - and Levi's consulted his clipboard, its throbbing readout irritating his tired eyes. He checked all the monitoring equipment, programming in all the required dosages of drugs. He then ran a hand-held sensor from her head to her toes, analysing the readout. Then he slowly turned, shaking his head.

"When I said you both had to leave I meant you too, Mr. Marshall."

The only other occupant in the room grunted. Asim stepped out of the shadows in the dimly-lit room to where he was openly visible to the doctor.

His eyes were red and still moist.

"I know." He said flatly. "But you've conveniently forgotten to tell us how my sister's going to be. Yuh see I need to know. I'm inquisitive like that." Asim rubbed the back of his hand over his mouth. "So before you start spewing that medical bullshit, confusing the issue. Make it plain to me what her condition is so I won't leave here with the wrong impression."

The doctor sighed, his head hanging on his chest.

"The prognosis hasn't changed since I last spoke to Mrs Marshall five minutes ago. Your sister was either lucky or she's a bloody good fighter." He said. "Her physical condition is still stable but she's not out of the woods yet. What condition her mind is in, I just can't say. There could possibly be a trauma reaction to her ordeal but we won't know until she regains consciousness. The rest is out of our hands."

Asim stood as stiff as a ramrod, listening. His arms folded across his chest, turmoil raging inside. He had to grit his teeth and clench his fist for control.

Whoever was responsible for this shit would pay. Dearly.

Yasmeen felt helpless, hesitantly placing her arms around his waist, her head resting on his back.

Asim's body tensed for a moment and he turned around to embrace her.

"Tell me what you're thinking."

"The past." He said. "I was married before, yuh know that."

"I know." She said.

"Her name was Eva."

They had met on one of his leave periods from the army. She had been the nurse who bandaged a badly gashed hand that had inadvertently smashed through a pane of glass while he held onto someone's head. Their courtship was brief and they married in Ireland and at the receptio the Jamaican and Irish portions of the family blended seamlessly. Eva had decided to leave her job and raise a family, an old fashioned girl at heart.

They were very much in love.

"My unit had just returned from military exercises in Germany. I can never forget how eager I was to get back to Warwick barracks after not seeing my wife for three long weeks. We crossed lines at twenty-one hundred hours and instead of going straight to my quarters, I made a detour with the boys and had a drink. I should have gone straight to her." He shook his head, his voice fading. "But I didn't. No more than a half hour later, I left the pub and went home. It was a moonlit night - I'll never forget. Clear and cold. I walked up the driveway and saw the door kicked off its hinges. I found her in the kitchen, battered, the motherfuckers had escaped through the back door only moments before I turned up. No one was ever charged, as far as I knew no one was even questioned. If I'd only gone home. Our life was fucked from that night."

Asim stopped and gently pulled her to him. As he looked into her eyes and saw the depth of her emotion he couldn't help but to kiss her. And then kissed her again.

******

Another night with too much shit on his mind.

"Just admit it, ru'bwoy." Asim muttered under his breath. "You're scared."

He stood rooted to the spot, looking up at the twin steeples unable to move forward or backwards.

Hypocrite.

What the raas were you doing here, anyway.

In his time he had torn many lives violently from existence without a misplaced thought - most had deserved it in his opinion - and he made no apologies for it.

A job had to be done and he did it.

Fear wasn't the right word to describe how he felt, a deep-seated respect was more to the point. He just couldn't bring himself to taint any place of worship with his blood splattered past.

Yuh hands an heart mus clean, his grandmother would say.

He looked on with his hand buried in his pockets. He knew

this was not a place for him. Not with murder on his mind.

The church rose up like an immense spike of grey stone. Pigeons circled overhead, fluffy white clouds slowly proceeding in a backdrop of brilliant azure sky. What a location for a place of worship. Right in the middle of a Zone.

Swallowing, he looked around as if seeking reassurance. Even the architecture had a raw power that was dizzying.

Yasmeen was a few steps behind him, her eyes had been plotting his hesitant steps. He reminded her of a little boy intimidated by the awesomeness of their first trip to worship. The structure, the ceremony, the atmosphere, all alien.

As different as it was from any church - Tabernacle, Yasmeen would correct him - he was used to, the sights and smells vividly reminded him of his adolescence.

Every Sunday morning, tired or running a fever of a hundred plus Miss Mac - his grandmother - frog marched him to the temple to share in the community spirit and hear the word of God until it was forged into habit.

He was still a youth then. Innocent, compared with what he had become.

"Come on, then." The voice beside him was Yasmeen's, her arms snaking around his waist.

"If you're expecting an invitation from above, we could be here all day."

"Yeah!" He grunted absently, keeping pace with her, his eyes roaming over the cavernous interior of the old Anglican building. Inside was dimly-lit and that all pervasive feeling of reverence lingered in the air with the smell of cannabis. Walking down the aisle together, the old fashioned pews that would have greeted you a few years ago, had been replaced by mats and stools. The walls were adorned with paintings of African saints and clay figurines. The altar took centre stage an exquisite piece of Rasta sculptor work, hewn from a single tree, stained and polished to a brilliant finish. The Niyabinghi drums seemed to be beating from all corners, lightly resonating in his head as his lungs filled with the aroma of sensi and he relaxed.

"Jah! Excellent is thy name."

The voice of praise had come suddenly from behind them just as they were about to sit and was responded to by other voices spread all around.

"Where two or three are gathered together in my name, there am I in the midst of them." A distant voice announced.

They both sat without making a sound, Asim squirmed uncomfortably, wanting to get up and leave but slowly succumbing to the tranquillity the tabernacle emanated. He felt his anger standing more pronounced in the silence like a beacon and he was unable to conceal it.

Wha guh round bound to come back round.

And what he had been given here was an opportunity for a second chance. A chance to make amends for his lack of resolve in a situation so much like this one. Now was not the time for him to step back, like a good little soldier bwoy so the authorities could tell him they had no suspects. He was going to take responsibility.

Even the Itations being whispered in prayer or voiced so all could hear, were challenging him, preaching a truth he did not want to hear.

There is no sense in hate; it comes back to you. Therefore make your history so laudable, magnificent and untarnished, that another generation will not seek to repay your seed for the sins inflicted upon their fathers. The bones of injustice have a peculiar way of rising from the tombs to plague and mock the iniquitous.

It makes no difference, Asim thought, he would communicate in the only language Fatima's rapists knew.

Violence.

Unfortunately for them it was a lingo he was more than fluent in.

Asim refocused on his surroundings, a few eyes turned to stare, his thoughts felt like loud hailers, announcing to the world that he should not be here.

Yasmeen was on her knees praying as a middle-aged dread came forward from an area near the altar, a smouldering chalice in his hand. He raised it in the air before the sparsely populated seats, chanting a blessing in Ethiopian and lowering it again.

"Deh healing of deh Nation." He pronounced, sitting cross legged on a mat at the foot of the altar, his presence drawing the few men and women within the temple forward. Yasmeen sat back up and turned to Asim.

"How do you feel?" Her voice a whisper.

"I'm not sure," Asim said. "I'm not concerned either way. My feelings don't come into this. Fatima's do."

His face was a dark and complicated study. Yasmeen saw regret, determination and fear all at work there.

"I know, I know." She consoled him. "Still she needs us strong more than anything else." Yasmeen sighed keeping her eyes on the deacon while he handed the Kutchie - the communal pipe - to the circle of people around him, the dense cannabis fumes leaving ethereal impressions in the dark backdrop, like white paint strokes on a black canvas. "Thinking about what happened to Fatima can be the worst thing. It's best to try and place our energies somewhere else. For me it's here. This is where I gain my strength. That's why I brought you here, I thought..." she moistened her lips "...maybe, you would feel better, less angry."

"Shows that much?"

She nodded.

Asim smiled insincerely.

Yuh have me sussed, baby.

"You're worried I'm going to do something stupid, yeah," he chuckled half-heartedly. "I can't blame you for thinking that. Under the circumstances that would be the natural reaction but I'm over that. I just want my sister to pull through."

She didn't respond, just kept looking at him, searching behind his eyes.

"Listen, I've seen enough and done enough to take the knocks life dishes out in my stride." He continued." I'm okay, trust mi."

"Then why do I feel otherwise?"

Fuck it! He thought.

"You tell me, Yasmeen." His voice edged with frustration had risen a notch and then modulated when he realised, half the temple could hear him.

"Sorry." He put his hand on her lap, his expression earnest. "You're looking for something that just isn't there. I'm fine, man. It's just that I'm struggling to get these pictures of my sister out of my head. Images of those cock... those bastards abusing her, just won't go away and so many questions." Asim kept his eyes at the foot of the altar watching the wispy curtains of ganja smoke rising. He said finally. "I'm not saying it doesn't hurt, I'm not even saying dat it's not tearing me up inside but I've got a handle on it. I appreciate everything you've done to help me and the family but if anybody needs yuh prayers and concerns, it's going to be Fatima."

Yasmeen looked at him long and hard her mouth opening slightly as if she wanted to say something then she smiled and approached the altar.

I'm too far gone for prayers, baby, they're wasted on me, Asim thought.

Yasmeen looked back moments later, hoping he would still be there but in the dimness of the temple, he had gone.

As she drove home later, Yasmeen kept thinking about Asim. She switched to manual, isolating the cars onboard computer. A sigh slipped from her lips, more of relief than anything for an uneventful day as she joined the bright lights of Central London.

From the speakers, I Jah Man Mystic preached peace and redemption in mesmeric tones. Yasmeen was picturing herself with Asim in a warm bath with a chilled glass of carrot juice. She swung left down a small one way street that cut out a large chunk of traffic on her way home. Strangely, the street lights weren't working and the company car compensated with a bright beam of light that cut through the darkness like a laser beam, her momentum uninterrupted.

These roads were second nature and her speed was borne of confidence and familiarity. Hesitation wasn't her usual reaction but she did as she waited at a traffic light.

Suddenly, with a crack, her rear window spiderwebbed. Then

the front windscreen exploded in a million shards. Then there was silnce. That was all the warning she needed. Head down, and foot on the gas she accelerated at breakneck speak.

******

Asim's car was snugly parked in its garage. He took the elevator from the basement to the first level and was welcomed by House's sultry tones.

"Welcome home, Asim. Your biorthymic readings are erratic. I have taken the liberty of preparing a cup of your favourite herbal tea and I'm in the process of running a bath at your optimal temperature of 55 degrees Celsius."

"Thanks, babe."

"My pleasure, will there be anything else?"

"A massage maybe?" Asim teased.

"I can't comply with that request, without a robotic extension of myself."

"Yuh disappoint me!" Asim grinned. "Just relax and do something else for mi while you're brewing dat tea. Search for a conversation, I had with my sister a while ago. The I.D. tag is Fatima Marshall and her voice pattern is stored in personal file #45639T. Bring it up in the lounge and put it on a continuous loop."

"Searching."

As Asim mounted the spiral stairs to his low ceiling bedroom, he saw that House had already brought up the visuals. He quickly undressed and replaced his Armani suit with standard issue army PT wear. Comfortable and functional.

In moments he was downstairs again, in the kitchen, and not long after that he had a steaming mug in one hand and the recording his sister being re-enacted in front of him in the lounge. The frame of light that acted as a screen floated inches from the wall. Asim wasn't sure what he was looking for but he just felt that there must be some clues in the footage. This was the only real lead he had available. He had to lick the trail while it was still hot.

He had already come to some solid conclusions from the police report and his own observations. This was no random act of violence. He reacquainted himself with the finer details of the report that the Techheads at Zulu had hacked into. He picked up the laser pointer beside him and sent a pulse of light on the closed icon. It instantly expanded to fill the entire floating screen, flashing the number of pages it contained, security level and help option. Asim read the report.

Fatima's body was thrown into the river from a white Peugeot van. The vehicle had no distinguishing marks. The licence plate had an illegal visual scrambler attached to it, so it was untraceable. In Asim's experience that hardware was difficult to come by without the right contacts and plenty of credits.

Met-1's Police National Computer Network sent out requests to a hundred thousand citizens who owned a van of that make and colour for details of their whereabouts on the night.

They were wasting their time on that score.

The suspect van had probably been atomised long time.

The forensic robot they deployed on the scene had discovered nothing worthwhile noting, either. The most promising development - if you could call anything in this sick situation promising - had been the bite mark on Fatima's body. From the file, the Met-1's pathologists had created a 3-D impression of her attacker's dentition and proceeded to cross reference the London data banks but, as yet, they had come up empty.

So why did they leave her alive?

Someone was sending a raas message.

Time would tell him who and why?

As the report closed and the icon disappeared with a bleep, it left Asim sightlessly peering at the recording of his sister. How alive she seemed, so beautiful and content.

Fast forward. The recording looped once more, Asim peered under his sister's arm through the window and a blurred image. He squinted, leaning forward. The vague structure in the background suddenly started to make sense to him.

It was a clock tower.

Shit, that was it!

He took up the laser pointer from beside a cushion, pointed, and lit up the vague image of the tower.

There was no mistaking now that it was a clock tower of the type found in the centre of some of London's many districts. The inscriptions running around the neck were still blurry.

"Enhance clarity by factor of five." He told House, and his first solid lead boldly came into focus.

'A gift to commemorate the kinship between our two great towns from Kingston, Jamaica to Brixton - Out of many one people.'

THE TABERNACLE OF RAS, KINGSTON.

Yamu walked through the garden in buoyant mood. He had rested and eaten after his meeting and an all over glow of satisfaction continued to warm him.

He sighed. The flowers in the garden struck him with a force of vivid colour that was almost overpowering. He closed his eyes preferring to take in as much of the sweet-smelling air into his lungs as he could and let his thoughts drift.

The Spear of the Nation and Pure Blood had agreed on territorial exclusion zones. Another major triumph for the true prophet. And his involvement in all this never suspected. Securing his position as the most powerful black leader in the world. When the war in Africa ended - and it would when he was good and ready -Negusa Negas would be the spiritual conscience of the continent. A dream he would bring into reality.

His Rasta bredrins who held him in awe. His main crtic Brother Samuel from Trinidad died tragically in a hoverjeep crash in Kingston. A few, believed his outburst at the ceremony on United Africa Day was the cause. Jah, Jah vex, they reasoned. Confirming further their belief in Yamu's worthiness.

But the patriarch's death had a more worldly explanation.

Such a pity. A humble leader who had a listening ear for all.

He would inscribe that personal accolade on Patriarch

Samuel's tombstone in Port-a-Spain. Snickering, he remembered the article written by a CNN correspondent a year or so ago, describing 'Yamu the peacemaker' in glowing terms.

Even they were captivated by him.

It wasn't all fabricated either. A part of him was humble and patient but a very small and insignificant part. The greater part of him wasn't.

It was almost dusk and the sun with only two hours of brilliance left, stained the Ras landscape blood red. Yamu had started his walk from his private quarters on the east sector of the compound and was leisurely making his way through the gardens - of which he had stopped for a moment - and across the artificial streams. In the distance the antagonistic hum of irate mosquitos gave ample warning of their arrival before nightfall.

He shuddered at the thought. His aversion for the 'bloodsucka dem', made him pick up his pace to the auditorium.

From there the Ras World Network would be told the news from the only man whose very involvement in a situation seemed to assure positive results. And in a speech lasting thirty minutes and accessed by millions of Rasta faithful, he would explain in grandiloquent terms what he had achieved with the help of a special few.

The prophet will come as a peace maker.

He contemplated the words.

The report had been filed to the terminal in his private chambers from London, midday. All the players involved had served their purpose and in time would disappear. There was only one loose end to deal with and that was an unexpected development. One of the warrior faithful in London who had suddenly developed a conscience for his ordained role in life and had decided to cleanse his soul by speaking to Trevor Farruka - the dead man walking.

He should have been performing his pious look much earlier that morning. Unfortunately his attention had to be diverted to this matter. His accomplishments as a travelling peace envoy had given him credibility many diplomats would envy. Making the 'miracle', he was about to claim in London just that more believable. Peace would come only under Yamu's direction.

Jah will be done.

And his will was the will of Jah.

Mek nuh mistake.

He set off up a cobbled path towards the auditorium, head bowed slightly forward and hands folded behind his back. A headwrap of white linen covered his locks and a beige gown ended above his knees. A troop of ants scurried away from his sandalled feet.

He stopped and crushed them underfoot, like his enemies would be trampled too. How did they expect to trouble him?

Jah send mi come.

And by the end of the night, the world would share the truth he already knew.

******

Trevor ate while Yasmeen stared in amazement.

The most tolerant of diners would have been irritated by the Rastaman's enthusiasm for his meal. He slurped and snorted wading through a mountain of food in an unbelievably short period of time.

Yasmeen could only shake her head and be thankful their table was set snugly away from the main body of the restaurant.

It was for the best.

"Are you enjoying that?" She asked sarcastically.

"Not three bad, yuh know," he hesitated then flashed a grin. "Not three bad, at all."

A rumbling belch seemed to take him by surprise as he looked down at his stomach.

"Manners!" He pronounced, his copper coloured hair bouncing as he wiped sweat from his forehead.

Yasmeen had never seen him so happy.

"You know, it's nearly as good as deh gungo peas soup my queen Marsha makes for me." He stopped abruptly and peered at her unsmiling face.

"Everyting cool?"

"Not really. A few personal problems, you know."

"Don't worry, sista, I man news should put a smile back on your face, feh real."

He chuckled, whipped out a terry cloth and blew his nose.

"Is one ting with soup, yuh know." He wagged his finger as if he was making a major culinary point. "Wid deh right touch a pepper it can clear up wind, an cut fresh cold or flu."

"Hmm!" She said to that gem of information and watched while he downed two steaming bowls of soup, assorted banana fritters, fry dumplings and fried fish. In his own way he had paid her little hideaway the greatest of compliments.

Nyam was her favourite vegetarian eatery. Nestled in between the Maglev station and a news emporium, the spartan exterior hid a cozy setting of wicker furniture, hanging plants and a glass roof which could be retracted on those humid summer nights. Roots music formed such an inconspicuous background that it sat cozily on the edge of your awareness, mixing with the elaborate murals of the African savannahs on every wall. Sometimes when she sat by herself, the chants of some musical prophet would gently transfer her into the paintings. It was like she could feel the dry dirt between her toes, the sun on her back. It had that magic aura of relaxation about it and, as Trevor found out, its cuisine was unrivalled. Cooking was done the old fashioned way over coal fires. There were no microwave units to be seen anywhere.

All natural preparation and ingredients.

Trevor scooped out the last cluster of peas and liquid on his spoon and chewed on it thoughtfully.

"Sista!" He called out, crooking his finger in the direction of the waitress who hurried over to him wondering if all was well.

He smiled at her.

"A want to try dis fruit salad with mango liqueur. It nice?" The young lady had a penchant for colourful description and as Yasmeen impatiently watched, she convinced him life wouldn't be worth living without tasting the delights of the dessert. He ordered two bowls.

Yasmeen sighed and wondered how he kept so trim.

We live in dangerous times, sista, a Jah-Jah sen mi come, was all he had told her about his mission.

"Have you forgotten why were here?" Yasmeen asked calmly.

"Shame on you, sista Yasmeen. I man can't forget that but a hard working man like me have to eat. Can't reason on a hungry belly." He leaned back into the chair and stretched as if he were making room for the dessert.

Yasmeen cleared her throat testily.

"Still..." He said, watching her eyes raise to the ceiling.

"... Watching I man feed my face is not helping a busy woman like yuh, right?"

She slowly nodded in agreement.

"So mek we reason, nuh."

He sat up straighter, leaned forward on the table and detached the red, green and gold band from his hair and let it fall to his shoulders.

"Is like this," he began. "I meet one man dung Dalston Market. Him details were E-tagged to me by somebody who choose to remain a shadow. The breddah sell bush tonic, an incense. We chat for a while an him show I the London runnings. And by an by, him explain to me his business was in desperate financial problems. I made him taste some a my crop from last reaping. Deh natty never sample any herb like dat before, an two-twos him want to do business. So we strike a deal. I man will supply him with the raw material, him need to make him business work, in exchange him can give me certain information. That's when him tell mi bout the man dem who responsible for the war with the baalheads."

"He knows them?"

Trevor smiled at her obvious surprise, throwing back his head, his locks falling back into place.

"What him really mean is, him know a man, who knows another a man, who know a breddah who knows dem. But when certain man a chirps, it seem like they know it directly. You have to look beyond dat. This breddah here, is not the type to mix with them Black Heart Man. I can tell dat. He is no murderer."

"Doesn't all this seem a little too convenient though?"

"Sista, a nearly four weeks, mi a walk street, seen. And this is the first light mi experience. Remember, is nearly two weeks before him even tell mi anyting worthwhile. To I, this is straight up."

Without making her presence too obvious, the waitress who had been hovering near their seats had skilfully deposited the desserts on the table and without making it necessary for them to break their discussion, scurried away. Trevor looked down at his mound of glistening fresh fruit, smothered in whipped coconut cream and floating on a sea of mango liqueur and picked up his spoon tentatively.

He thought very carefully about his next move and decided to enlighten his impatient sistren some more before he started to tuck into his dessert. His lapse of concentration dealt with, he uncertainly put his spoon down and evaded Yasmeen's penetrating stare.

"Umkhonto we Sizwe - The Spear of the Nation. My man in Dalston, seems to think this man he will recommend me to will have the answers to my questions. He is a man who left the Spear... an live to tell the tale. He is a desperate man. A meeting set up already sista, an all the information we need will come straight from the horse's mouth." He smiled inwardly. "The way me see it, after that I should know enough to please bacrah massa a yard and my job will be done. Then we will see."

By now Trevor was shovelling regular chunks of cream-covered fruit into his mouth, between sentences. He licked his lips and held his spoon vertically in his fist, as if he were about to protest for more.

******

"Ah!" The fielders shouted in chorus.

The umpire wagged his finger distastefully and pointed to the crease. You could see the discernible sag in the barmy army's collective shoulder as the West Indian fans exploded into celebration with steel pan and conch shells. The dejected look on the English batman's face, as he strode angrily to the pavilion, spoke eloquently of their fortunes in this tour of the islands.

"You tink we play cricket," Trevor slurred, "we WAR wid cricket."

His eyelids were drooping and it seemed no effort on his part could keep them open. Rallying his nervous system into action was pointless, he could barely manage a grin and a weak cheer.

"Have to see them bowl out England dis morning." Trevor words staggered out of his mouth but that threat carried weak resolve as he phased in and out of sleep.

A second of rest. Then a brain numbing bleep sounded in the remote distance, drawing him back from wherever he was. A deep-throated snore startled him especially when he realised it was coming from him. Trevor blinked and glared at the wafer screen with contempt. The annoying sound of an incoming message continued to put his nerves on edge. He squinted, a telephone icon in the bottom left-hand corner of the screen flashed, obscuring a fielder in the gully.

Local call.

"Open line." He snorted, sitting up from the sofa and clearing tendrils of hair from his face. "And dis better be bloodclaat, good."

The wafer filled with Yasmeen's weak smile.

"Sister Yasmeen?"

"I'm sorry I woke you," she apologised. "But this is important."

Trevor's uncommitted slouch transformed into what could just pass as attentive posture.

"Yuh all right." He asked.

"No I'm not and I don't think you're going to be either after I show you this."

Trevor tensed, all traces of sleepiness gone and his adrenaline levels building.

"Just hold on a minute while I link this morning's broadcast to your line." Her image shrank back to a small tile at the exact position where the original icon rested. "Watch it carefully and

We'll talk later."

She was gone.

Cricket continued in the glorious sunshine for a moment longer. The screen then turned a solid blue, flickered, and the recording began.

A half hour later, Trevor leaned back on the sofa, more furious than surprised at what he had just seen. He stared sightlessly at some point in the distance, his mouth dry and his pulse pounding in his head. The enthusiasm he had exhibited earlier for the cricket match had evaporated and he just sat there, letting the illumination of the blue screen bath his face

Talks have commenced for possible peace.

Yamu's words.

What a lying, wicked fucker.

For twenty entire minutes, the self-proclaimed leader of all Rasta spewed the most tangled web of lies and with such sincerity that even Trevor would have been taken in by it, if he didn't know better.

Trevor's face - but a different name - was paraded on the patriarch's propaganda broadcast as the man brought in from Jamaica, responsible for organising talks between the Spear and Pure Blood.

The dog was making his move just as he had been told by the old man.

The realisation struck him like a guango stick beating from his grandmother. Sharp and swift.

Everyone now knew Trevor - or as Yamu referred to him on the broadcast, 'Shaka' - was sent here by the Nation Directorate and knew what his mission was.

So much for secrecy. So much for his safety. Now he was a walking target.

Trevor snorted with false amusement.

Him want the title of Negusa Negas so badly, an Yamu was taking no chances of even having mi on the island when him mek him move. That's why he was a part of the patriarch's plans. Or more to the point an annoyance he would have ample opportunity in silencing.

Trevor would have expected nothing less. But what his adversary didn't realise was he had just thrown a very hungry mongoose into the chicken coup.

You think I man have played right into yuh hand, nuh true, but the draught game jus start. You play already boss, now is my move.

******

"Asim!" Jennifer squealed, flying out of her apartment as he was about to press her buzzer again. She leapt into his arms, hugging him tightly and smothering his neck and lips with kisses. Her bath robe hung loosely about her and as she pressed against him, the signals below Asim's belt raged. The surge of blood to an extremity that had been dormant for a year seemed to be constantly reassuring him, he was fully alive.

Still, as sexy as he had remembered her.

He tried to concentrate on his main objective but that would be difficult.

Damn, she smelt good. Fresh water an soap.

"You like the idea of keeping a woman on her toes don't you." She whispered, kissing his earlobe.

Asim grinned sheepishly, trying not to make his lack of self control below, too obvious as they hugged.

He was relieved that he had caught her home - and not for the obvious reasons. This social call, was to be just that a social call. She needn't know Asim had been to see most of Fatima's close friends for information that could help him solve the attack on her. She didn't have to know he had found out nothing that was of use to him and that she was next in line for a subtle bout of questioning.

"Apologies Jenny," He started. "I wanted to call you before I just turned up, believe me. But I was in the area and I thought why not check if she's home. Bad timing?"

She cocked her head to the side and then looked Asim up and down, a wicked smile spread slowly across her face, unravelling like a flower into a full-blown laugh.

"Don't be stupid. We haven't seen each other or talked face to face in years. For you, it's never a bad time. Come in."

Jenny held onto Asim's hand and led him inside. The door slid shut behind them.

"You're looking even more tasty than the last time I saw you Mr. Marshall." Jenny teased. "The old country has obviously cast its spell on you."

The years had not dimmed her smile, sparkling hazel eyes and sense of humour. Jennifer was a very good friend of Fatima, school mates actually and in the past Asim had a hard time trying to convince her and himself he was happily married.

She was that type of woman who believed in the words, 'If you see something you want, go get it'. A free-spirited type of girl who, although living life to the full, had her priorities right.

It would take more than knowing what she wanted from life to tame this girl.

She was just as direct, charming and very appealing as always.

Asim guessed she had chosen the path of remaining single just as her mother before her had. Her mother was part of a generation of single parents who after struggling to raise children on their own questioned the need for a permanent man in their lives.

Those lessons of self reliance were well learnt.

Jenny led him through a maze of free standing geometrical designs and over to the transparent sofa. They sat - Jenny with practised ease and Asim more awkwardly - and the Art Futura material moulded around him to take his shape.

Asim adjusted his backside a few times for comfort and leaned back and for once in days he felt some of the burdens of his thoughts ease. He could feel the strain around his neck and shoulders disappearing and his burning eyes - from two sleepless nights - subsiding. His body seemed to be telling him he was in good company and he didn't resist.

He drifted for a moment and then felt the weight of slender legs on his lap as Jenny made herself comfortable.

"How are you holding up? After what happened, I mean."

Asim's eyes remained closed.

"I'm all right. It's just hard to figure out. I try not to think about it most times. Just be there to help sis if she needs me."

"I can understand how you're feeling but things are getting better." Jenny said "I went to see her today. She's stable and in a way I'm glad she's not awake yet to remember anything. God, I'm not sure I could live with myself!" She shuddered.

"Yeah!" He said uninterestingly. "Be thankful for small mercies."

Jenny's solemn look turned to a smile again, dispelling the morose vibes.

"Look at it this way, with all our help, I'm positive Fatima can pull through this. We've got to be strong for her. That's the very least we can do, right?"

Asim nodded, distantly his eyes locked onto something else.

Jenny's gown had fallen open revealing her legs. He could see her panties - a thin skin-tone lace.

"Ye-ye-yeah you're right," he stammered. "Is just that I've been losing sleep over some things that don't quite add up and trying to figure a way to speed up her recovery."

"What did you have in mind?" Jenny asked, gently rubbing her feet over Asim's crotch.

"How come over the week she's been in hospital, all her friends have come to see her, to show their support except..."

"Except?" She asked eagerly.

"Her boyfriend."

Asim rolled his neck from left to right until it cracked, breathed deeply and stretched some more, his point made.

Jenny continued the rhythmic rubbing of her feet and felt a mound of his hardness rise. Asim tried to ignore it.

"You have a point there. That is weird." She said. "And Baldwin seemed so keen on her."

"Baldwin?" Asim snapped to attention internally, repeating the name with a vicious under current she did not detect. "That's her boyfriend's name, right."

She nodded, that cheeky smile crossing her lips again.

"Fatima didn't tell you, did she."

Asim pouted and shook his head.

"But I've got this feeling, that you're going to."

Jenny shrugged.

"There's not much to it unfortunately. The dirty details I couldn't pry out of her, for love nor money. You know how secretive your sister can be.

Asim sighed, still willing the embarrassment in his pants to go dead but Jenny was intent on keeping it alive. He glimpsed the edges of a large old fashioned bed, draped in black silk sheets and his mind drifted into a tangent.

He sighed.

"Why are you so interested in the boyfriends Fatima keeps anyway?"

Asim's eyebrows arched slightly as she sat back down beside him and uncurled her long legs on his lap again.

Jennifer was as perceptive as she was inquisitive and Asim didn't want to spark her interest in what he was doing, not in the least. Tongues would start wagging and then what. His discreet investigation would be blown.

"You see my theory is, because Fatima wants to keep her private life private, she would have told her boyfriend little or nothing about her family. In other words he couldn't contact us even if he wanted to. He must be going crazy after not seeing or hearing anything from his woman in weeks."

He stroked his smooth chin contemplatively and his eyes twinkled from the ceiling lights.

"Seeing him would cheer her up, more than anything we could do. Between me and you, if I can find him and let him know what has happened, even bring him there myself, it would do her a world of good."

"And she wouldn't be able to thank you enough." Jennifer completed. "That's an excellent touch, Asim."

"I thought so too." Inwardly he relaxed. "She needs as much strength as she can get."

Asim changed the subject as quickly as he could and directed the conversation around to what Jennifer had being doing in her life over the years since he had last seen her. The producer for her own youth show on TView, no steady man, fitness freak, weekend wild child.

She asked him. "Something to take the sand outta your throat?"

"You have ginger beer?"

"I knew it, Asim man!" She cried out. "Don't tell me you're still drinking that Ole Jamaique stuff." Her voice went gruff as she mimicked some seafaring mariner. "You've travelled the world, experienced different cultures..."

"...An there's nothing like a good shot of ginger beer." Asim completed.

Jennifer failed to keep a straight face.

"Nothing?" She asked.

"Well, nearly nothing." His brow arched, suspiciously.

"Relax." She chirped. "I'm only teasing."

That scheming smile appeared on her lips again.

"Somehow I knew you'd want your ginger beer fix. Go check the Re-fridge."

"Cho!" Asim grinned, idling over to the kitchen. "So what can I get you, Jen?"

She answered from the distance but he didn't quite make out what she had said.

"Jenny, what's your poison girl?" He pulled the top off the drink and took a swig.

"Jenny...!" He swallowed some more.

"I'm here."

Asim still had a mouth of full ginger beer when she appeared behind him and was so surprised he almost sprayed it over the floor. His surprise became astonishment as she dropped to her knees, undid his zip and reached inside his trousers.

The movement was so fluid, her fingers were already around his manhood before he could even begin to protest. The minuscule element of male control disappeared with his back against the draining board and the exquisite sensations of Jenny's expert finger strokes.

Mentally he was way ahead of her.

She was stretched over the sink, one leg on the draining board the other barely touching the floor. Her hands held onto the taps as he entered her from behind. With his hands gripping her waist, every stroke making her rise off the tiles on her toes. Inadvertently the cold tap is turned on, shooting water everywhere, soaking them. The cold water adds to the excitement and his thrusts become more urgent. He reaches for her breasts as he rams into her and...

With a 'pop', the fanciful image disappeared and instead of Jenny exciting him it was... Yasmeen.

Yasmeen?

Shit.

His eyes flew open and Jenny was still kneeling in front of him, his member rigid in her hand.

That did not last long as his arousal drained away instantly.

Swearing under his breath he reached down and lifted her from her knees.

"I'm sorry," He sighed. "I want to, believe me. But I can't."

She kissed him and smiled.

"You're just out of practice. Don't worry I'll be gentle with you." She used her fingernail to flip open a stud on his shirt on her way down again.

Asim held her by the elbows bringing her back up.

"It's more than that." He held her hand as she continued to strip him while he redid what she had undone. "And don't get me wrong but I need to sort out a few things in my head first or I'll be no use to anybody." He looked down at himself and grimaced. "Another time."

Jenny sighed seductively, running her finger between her lips.

"I'll take that as a promise, Asim Marshall. Don't think you'll get off that easily, you know I always collect on my promises."

He nodded lamely at the threat, his throat dry and a nervous tick, that tried to be a smile, tugged at the sides of his mouth.

This called for a quick exit.

******

As Trevor looked down his reflection shimmered in the puddle at his feet. The night was warm and the coolness caused from earlier rainfall had gone. Spittle Road in North London was as quiet as it should be, at twelve forty-five at night and reeked with the smell of damp asphalt, cement and sand. Yasmeen was in the car behind. Trevor on the other hand leaned against the warm bonnet, looking up at the stars and remembering his family.

A glimmering ion trail of a hypersonic aircraft cut a gash across the moon's face. Other points of light shot across the sky like rocket propelled fire flies, the usual drone of their engines lost to the ear.

A few lights shone in windows of the recently occupied homes but they soon blinked out. The only remaining sound he heard was a car pulling into the driveway of an adjoining street.

Nice an quiet.

In front of him, mechanical diggers sat frozen in motion, huge cranes overlooked it all. Buildings were being built and torn down standing like the testament to some apocalyptic conflict, surrounded by neat mounds of brick and rock like gutted bunkers from a prolonged skirmish. He took in the entire scene as a whole and just for a fleeting moment the new buildings being erected in the foreground and the old crime ridden estate being torn down gave the impression that some revolutionary cure had been injected into the neighbourhood, spreading across the landscape and destroying the cancerous tumour that had infected the community for decades.

Trevor ran his fingers through his locks and threw his head back in a practised movement, his ropey hair falling back around his shoulders.

Just keep focused, boss.

He cleared his mind for a moment and listened keenly for the approach of anything.

"Take yuh time, boss." He said to himself. "I can wait up to the allotted time."

Trevor was used to waiting, he had been waiting all his life in the bushes of Trelawny. That's what a farmer and bush man did, his calling in life was preparation and then watching as time passed as he reaped the results.

A waiting game.

Waiting for his crop to mature, waiting for that elusive fish on a hook. Skill, preparation and patience.

The arrangements had been made for the meeting at 1.00 a.m. and Trevor would be here until such time. Even though he was confident it would all go smoothly, he was not one to go into any situation blindly. He had turned up an hour early and gave Yasmeen the responsibility of paying attention to the proximity scanners in her car. He was not one for technology, but cars used the scanners to pick up potential intruders while parked and police traps while driving. Similarly he used the equipment to protect his crops from thieves and large pests. They were able to pick up movement at a radius of about three hundred meters and that would give them enough warning to take action.

Trevor spun on the bonnet and peered through the windscreen Yasmeen's eyelids were drooping as she leaned back into the driver's seat on the brink of sleep.

Trevor shook his head and smiled.

And this is the gal, who says she wanted to help.

He had reluctantly agreed that she tag along but with the proviso she stayed hidden but alert.

He watched as her chest rose and fell lightly. Trevor could have easily done without her but she knew the road network better than he did. Making his journey less stressful. It wasn't as if he was totally green about city life but why chose a bucket with a hole in it, if you have a whola bucket. Over the short period he had been here, he was beginning to familiarise himself well with the Metropolis of London. With an A to Z of England on a visual card, and a travel pass, he made sure he visited and talked to as many of the Rasta flock as he could. He thanked Jah-Jah that Yamu's announcement had not destroyed his chances of this meeting. The Nations 'Ole heads may have thought the game was over but he was far from convinced.

Trevor was torn from his thoughts, his attention was suddenly held by a pair of neon arc lights negotiating the corner and stopping some distance away. The lights dimmed and the car crawled a few more meters ahead and then stopped again.

"At least he's punctual."

Yasmeen's voice took Trevor by surprise.

Fucking hard ears pickney.

Trevor kissed his teeth and glared at her.

"Yuh promised me, you would stay in the car. That was deh deal?"

"So I lied." Yasmeen said nonchalantly. "We're supposed to be partners in this. I'm involved as much as you are, so don't expect me to be some shrinking violet because I'm a sista. I'm here to back you up. Or is it that you're not sure a woman is capable?"

"You call nodding off, backing I man up?"

"So I dozed off, sue me. I may be only human and not a superman like you but I'm still going to be here to watch your back whether you like it or not. And next time I won't be asleep."

"Next time?" Trevor said slowly, his eyes never leaving the car in the distance. "I can't force yuh to hear good advice, but if you want to be helpful jus keep yuh eyes on deh scanner and stay out of harm's way."

It was Yasmeen's turn to glare at him but instead of confrontation she disappeared into the car.

Trevor relaxed and stood away from the unit, everything was bathed in the glare of focused bright lights. The Rasta man shielded his eyes and waited for the next move.

Seconds ticked away.

Then the sound of compressed air and the car door slid open. A shadow stepped out of the vehicle and leaned on the open door observing him. Tentatively he looked around, just his head disappearing back into his car for a moment then he came back out in full view.

The temporary I.D. tag grafted to the skin of Trevor's wrist tingled and glowed green. His contact was remotely accessing genetic information about him and cross referencing the data with records held at the World Genome Centre in Geneva, making sure he was who he said he was.

Soon the tingle in his wrist subsided and the tag fell off like a satiated cow tick. He watched the man exit his car and wait for the door to suck shut.

Trevor followed his movement with interest as he came forward making sure he remained at all times in the beam of his headlamps. The silhouette - for that's all he was to Trevor - stopped some thirty meters away. He kept looking around nervously, on the verge of fleeing at the drop of a hat.

A desperate man.

And from his outline he had shaven his crown.

A frightened man.

For a Rasta - even one linked with a fanatical group such as the Spear of the Nation - to cut his mane was tantamount to an act of sacrilege. Trevor's lessons in the faith made what he had done unforgivable. Like the Nazarene Samson in the Bible, Rasta mystics believed that your hair was an extension of your spirit. The source of your strength.

This man disgraced himself before God and man.

Maybe his motives were basic survival.

Trevor shifted his weight more to one leg and felt the encouraging prod of his throwing knives under both arms. He parted his jacket and kept his hands on his waist.

Always come prepared, Iyah.

Trevor was completely still, he didn't want to do or say anything until his contact felt more comfortable with the surroundings. He tried to breathe easy but he could feel the man's fear from a distance and it was disturbing.

Trevor looked behind him as if for reassurance. Yasmeen stared back and then down to the monitor in front of her.

His main concern now was to ask the right questions and listen very carefully to what this man had to say. He was in no hurry.

The man spoke.

"Deh agreement was, I talk to you alone." The voice that had broken the silence sounded sharp against Trevor's ears but there was no disguising his nervousness.

Trevor cursed under his breath.

"Is my baby mudda dat man, she is as safe as they come."

The man inclined his head, not agreeing or disagreeing.

"Right now, I don't give a shit how safe she is. As long as she stays out of sight."

"A nuh problem dat." Trevor replied eagerly and then started to forage in his pockets for a half-finished spliff.

"Careful natty!"

The silhouette's shout was like the report from a shotgun.

And with frightening speed a needle thin laserbeam had formed a scarlet spot on Trevor's chest. He looked down at the hovering point of light, his eyes widened and he could feel the rush of blood through his veins. Trevor's hand froze at his breast pocket.

"Slowly." The silhouette teased while Trevor took the lighter out then the spliff which he bought to his lips with exaggerated caution. He lit the end.

"No sudden moves, natty. As you can see, I get nervous when people mek sudden moves."

"An I get bloodclaat nervous when a bwoy point a gun at my chest." Trevor snapped. "Remember you set deh ground rules. The time, the place. After all that, you still don't trust I?"

The man laughed at Trevor's presumption.

"I trust no one, natty. It's my life on deh line and what's left of it is precious to me."

"So how come yuh here, talking to me?"

"Because you a provide a safe way for me to get some satisfaction."

"Satisfaction?" Trevor repeated.

"Let mi explain to yuh." The red umbilical cord of laser light that had joined both men from the gun to Trevor's chest blinked out. He then lowered the weapon and left it dangling at his side.

Trevor's relief showed in the slump of his shoulders.

"Where else could I get the opportunity to talk directly with a man and know what I say will go back to the right people."

"Dat's why I and I come, king man, to hear what you ha'fe seh and relay it to the relevant people dem." Trevor sucked on his spliff, capturing the fumes between his puffed out cheeks and let it trickle through his nose. The calming effects of his prize winning strain already flooding his bloodstream and relaxing him.

"Imagine the feeling of being able to strike a blow for yuh people," the silhouette started. "Against Babylon. The Spear of the Nation was that to me. A group a Rasta man who nuh give a fuck 'bout the law or the elders. An eye for an eye an a tooth for a tooth. All deh wrongs against our people we could make right. That was what I man dreamed of, from a mixed up yout to a frustrated man. And I did that, live my dream. Take back what was ours and make plenty man pay for dem wicked past."

"So you bruk the first commandment, jus like dat." Trevor shook his mane. "An den you get it into yuh head that you doing the works of the Almighty."

The man in the shadow chuckled humourlessly.

"You think me is a monster, don't it?"

Trevor said nothing.

"This was Jah-Jah mission. I man remember what London was like when Babylon used to detain us, philistine used to bomb us. Nuff breddah died in custody, died at the hands of extremists. I never too young to remember how my father died. Him dead believing the law was right. Those days must never come back and I was making sure of dat. By any means necessary."

"Suh what happen?" Trevor asked.

"What happen?" His tone deepened and his eyes shone feral from the light of a low flying hoverjeep. "We lost direction."

"And what direction was dat?" Trevor asked scornfully.

"Don't you understand, we were being used, boss." The man burst out. "It was no longer a holy war but polytrix."

"Yuh can prove it?"

In his mind's eye, Trevor imagined a sardonic grin forming on the silhouette's face.

"Here is the evidence," he pulled out a Personal Digital Assistant. "I have enough files, stored documents and even video footage. But don't fret bout that, rude bwoy." He said bitterly. "The point is, convince me you can get it to the right people."

It was Trevor's turn to be smug.

"If yuh never believe I could be trusted or even have deh slightest possibility to help yuh, I man wouldn't be here. You've done your homework, I'm the only man who can deliver results."

"I believe you, natty. Just remember that I have killed for reasons I feel was right. I will answer to Jah for that. But the Spear of the Nation are freedom fighters not murderers..."

He paused for breath and in that instant his head exploded like a watermelon.

For a fraction of a second Trevor stood rooted to the spot. In a grotesque and surreal snapshot he watched the spray of blood and brain tissue as the man's body crumpled to the ground like a felled ox. A single laser guided projectile had hit him at the side of the head, tunnelling through the cranium and exploding on exit. His eyes were wide with shock as the crimson tentacles of blood reached out to him from the man's twitching body.

His shock disappeared quickly. Trevor found himself already on the ground scrambling on all fours. He managed to retrieve the falled PDA as bullets whizzed around him.

"Yasmeen!" he screamed but there was no need to rouse her, the car was already reversing wildly. Jumping to his feet he made a desperate dash, shielding his face from flying masonry and dashed towards her. There was no time to stop. He literally jumped in the car as Yasmeen's wheels screeched away, leaving a trail of gunfire in its wake.

******

As beautifully radiant as ever, her hair was wrapped with a beige silk material. Her modest traditional gown did not show anything of her body but her overpowering sensuousness went where she went and that was enough.

Yasmeen came closer, she seemed distant. Her almond coloured eyes met his for a moment and then drifted away nervously. She welcomed him with a kiss on the cheek.

"I need to talk to you Asim." Her hand still in his and her voice unsteady.

Asim paid attention.

"Yuh all right, princess?"

She nodded and gave a fleeting smile.

"I'm fine. But we need to talk..."

"Okay." He said. He sat and put his arm around her. "What's on your mind, princess?"

Sitting there, her posture, perfect, a worried frown on her face and Asim thinking if she were rendered in marble and sent back in time to ancient Africa, she would not be out of place.

"From what you know of me, you'd realise, I've never gone for the easy options in life. But even in my most rebellious of periods, I wouldn't have imagined feeling like this for anybody, especially a... baalhead." Her cheeks rose into an incomplete smile, while she rubbed the palm of her hand gently over his head. "The feelings I've... I'm having, for you are unusual. Maybe telling you all of this is not in my best interest, either. I don't know. But there's something about us which makes it so easy for me to confide in you."

She thought carefully about what she said next.

"Am I doing the right thing, I keep asking myself?" She shrugged. "Right or wrong, I still have this need to tell you my secrets."

Yes!

"It started I suppose when my stepmother was murdered..."

Yasmeen related the circumstances of the murder and attacks made against her and the threats in detail. Times dates and places all from fear heightened memory.

What the raas, was he listening to? Murder? Shootings? Threats on her life? The conclusions his trained mind had already brought to his attention made him uncomfortable.

"Do you know who could be responsible?"

She shook her head too readily.

He tensed. Something about her reaction unnerved him. Maybe it was her sudden show of uneasiness.

His fingers made small circles around his mouth as he sunk into deep thought.

"Easy-target!" Asim's voice was muted and distant.

Yasmeen leaned forward.

"Easy What?"

"Easy-target." He repeated, his brown eyes wider than she had seen them. "I learned tings in Africa. Even when you weren't directly involved with it." He rubbed his palm over the stubble on his head. "We were briefed on contract killings and their MO as it referred to our zone of operation. Sometimes we were even called in to clean up the mess. Our orders were to help keep the peace and that's what we did. As standard procedure we were trained to protect VIPs in potentially volatile situations. The preferred ways for terrorist groups in that part of the world, wasn't direct confrontation with their intended target but the termination of the easy targets - bodyguards, friends, family aides those kinds of people. Creating fear at first, making you believe the attacks are coming from one source when it's not and in the confusion, 'pam'!" He brought the point home with a chopping action of his hands.

"They enjoyed the gamesmanship that it involved." He seemed to shake the memories from his mind. "Anyway, what you said reminded me of that." He tried to dismiss it with an unconvincing grin. "Too many years of army training, ignore me."

That did not satisfy Yasmeen somehow.

She looked at him some of her authority returning.

"You sense that there's a pattern, don't you?" She said. "You think there could be something to what I've been saying."

"I don't know, princess," he stood up from his seat. "Sometimes this shit comes into my head without warning."

And then sometimes it comes into my head and it's telling me something's wrong.

He sat back down and leaned into his seat.

What the fuck could possibly happen next? If anyone should start believing in bad karma, maybe it should be him.

"Tell me again what happened, and make sure you miss nothing out."

It was too late to reverse his suspicions now, the cold hand of reality had already gripped his insides and was squeezing.

Fatima, and now Yasmeen.

Coincidences don't exist, was all he could tell himself.

He hoped for chrissake he was wrong.

******

Asim held onto a cold ginger beer while Ricardo's huge hands caressed a shot of whisky.

His partner got to the point quickly.

"You're hiding something from me my friend I can tell."

Asim's expression became serious.

"Everyting is everyting, Ric, why would I want to hide anything from you, boss."

Ricardo shrugged.

"Kehinde has seen it too and is surprised at how calm you are, after all that has happened to Fatima. She respects your control, but me..." He shook his head slowly. "I know better. Your family has been threatened, the authorities have found no leads and you have been trained by the army for years to be pro-active. Now mix that with your natural impatience." He clasped both hands together resting his case. "To put it simply, my friend, you are calm because you are focused on an objective - finding out who was responsible."

Asim was taken aback for a while but really should have known better. Ricardo knew him well. No need for further pretence, he tried to explain.

"Listen, big man. What I'm doing here is personal. I don't want you especially getting involved because when it starts getting hot, the only man who should be sweating is me. You've got too much to lose, brethren."

"And you haven't?"

"Something like that. I want to find the men who did this to my sister, to my family, to my peace of mind - and I want them hurting, badly."

Ricardo shook his head.

"Have you carefully considered the impact on your family, your freedom and the company if one of its directors is sent to jail for breaking the law?"

"I'm way ahead of you, Ric. I was thinking of doing this next week but we're both here. What better opportunity." He leaned forward pressing on both knees. "Tomorrow I will e-mail my formal letter of resignation." He reached over and put his hand on his shoulder. "The course has been set, Ricardo, beyond even my control. History is repeating itself and this time the story ends on my terms."

Ricardo smiled.

"In Ghana we have a saying,'a friend is life's currency'." He shook his head ruefully. "I know you presumed and wrongly so, that I'm more concerned about the good standing of our company than the need for the right thing to be done, but you misjudged me. I can't accept your resignation and further more I'll be a prime suspect when they realise you had an accomplice."

Asim's expression softened.

"I know what you're trying to do, Ric, but I need to do this alone."

Ricardo smiled cooly and shook his head.

"Having a proper investigation will need operational support, reconnaissance and surveillance equipment. You'll need use of our extensive computer, networking facilities, communication systems and at times another body. Who else do you know, who can provide you with all that and with no questions asked?"

Nobody, Asim thought.

"You know it makes sense."

And he knew Ricardo was right.

Logistically, it would be nigh on impossible to do this alone. He swirled his glass and gulped down the remainder of the ginger beer and stared intensely at him for a long time, then said.

"We need to agree that all the hands-on stuff is left to me, cool?"

Ricardo nodded.

"However you prefer it." He said blandly. "We can talk shop later and iron out a few details when time permits."

He got up to go, his impassive look hiding how much he cared for him. Asim grasped his shoulder and planted a playful right hook on him.

"I owe you nuff, boss."

"We're brothers." He simply said and left the office.

******

It was like coming home again.

Asim stepped out of Brixton underground station into the muggy night air with hundreds of other passengers snapping at his heels.

The sign at the exit said, 'Only the best for the best'. Asim kissed his teeth. He had boarded the crammed underground train and stood for his entire thirty-five minutes journey from Harlesden, pressed against sweaty armpits on one hand and choking on pungent cheap cologne on the other.

At each stop people were being spat out onto platforms heaving with passengers and then as if the carriages were taking a breath another stream of humanity was sucked in again. Air-conditioning units were trying to cool the heat from crammed bodies and scrubbing the noxious cigarette fumes from illegal 'lighters'. MP5 players which were supposed to be personal could be heard by the entire carriage, drunks deposited curries they had eaten previously into aisles while perverts used every opportunity available to fondle their fellow passengers, male, female or animal.

No one seemed to care.

Asim looked on with a degree of amusement and mixed into the subway culture for tonight.

He set his face to dangerous, sending out the clear message, Turf bwoy do not fuck with.

Consequently, he was left alone with only the approving glances from a few sistas in the carriage.

When next he looked around, the main bulk of the passengers had gone.

A baseball cap casting enough shadow over his eyes, extra large quarterback T-shirt, chromo slacks that subtly changed colour with sound, and ultra light Nikes.

The exercise was for him not to draw attention to himself but to blend. Another face in the anonymity of the Brixton bustle.

For a while he stood on the kerb in his new persona soaking in the atmosphere and was relieved that the cultural energy that had made Brixton special had not diminished with time, instead it had become more powerful. The traditional street preacher was there, as he had been for decades, his words of fire and brimstone even today falling on deaf ears. Ridiculed often and seldom listened to. Yet he continued to pace the pavement damping sweat that was popping up on his forehead and quoting the Bible. Fulfilling his part of a bargain, made to a higher purpose.

It was funny how Asim suddenly realised the part the eccentric preacher played in the whole fabric of the community. He served as a reminder to most what it was like to believe in something, no matter what the rest of the world thought.

He pondered the idea. With his head down he headed for the traffic lights.

"Incense!" A Rasta man walked up to him and thrust a stalk of his crudely constructed sticks in his direction, Asim glared at him, the dread smiled, tilting his head. "Calm yuh dung yuh know, boss."

His hesitation made Asim suspicious.

He was much fuller in body and with a considerably larger stall than he had remembered, but it was Benjy all right.

"Later." Asim snapped and moved off.

The certainty in the dread's face faded.

Benjy shook his head and showed his yellowing teeth.

"Peace, mi breddah." He called after him and returned to his business with a shrug. "Incense!"

Asim left the kerbside quickly, unsure if he was recognised and not wanting to hang around to jog Benjy's memory some more. These things had a tendency of coming back to haunt you. The police asking questions, a stall owner remembering a familiar face. Remote but still possible. He had to be more careful.

Threading his way through the night crawlers cluttering Brixton High Street, he headed down Atlantic Road. The familiar smells instantly unearthed buried gems of memory.

The market on his right was close for the night. It had been rebuilt on its original site into a high tensile plastic enclosure. It remained open air with a covering roof. Machine processed foods still played a minor role in the African Caribbean diet and the market, instead of dying, thrived. It was rebelling against the so-called advancements offered and was looking back at its roots, holding on to the standards of the past. A bit like him.

His brisk walk had taken him beyond the old railway bridge. Despite the humidity he resisted the urge to take off his trenchcoat for the express reason that his tool was under his arm. It was subtly camouflaged, but why tempt fate.

Suddenly affluent Brixton disappeared and he stepped into the twilight zone.

Zone B141 to be exact.

In response his stomach tightened and his eyes dilated.

Less than a kilometre square, this no man's land resisted development and revelled in its infamous image.

Asim looked up at the PLI's - Perpetrator Level Indicators - on the building as it flashed red. The demarcation line on the ground, that was welcoming you into the badlands was pulsing the same colour. He grimaced because he knew if he entered the area and the klaxons started blaring he would have to abandon his mission.

The Home Office's plans of closing up to eighty percent of prisons in England and Wales depended on the procedure of biometric tagging of ex-cons. Only serious crimes were now punished with jail sentences - A category offences as they were called - but once a crime was committed and the courts found you guilty, no matter how minor the offence was, you were tagged for life. Category B or C offenders could be prevented from online services, public transport or even shopping areas. Get caught in a Zone on red while the alarms were sounding and you would be immediately immobilised by your implant and Met-1 would be down on you like flies on a turd.

Asim couldn't afford to be caught up in the ensuing chaos if that situation developed. He eyed the indicator warily and decided to take his chances.

A small van hurtled past tooting its horn and the driver leaning out as he blew kisses at a group of women congregated at a corner ahead of him. They hurled abuse, wobbling on stilettos much too tall and showing cellulite on thighs with skirts much too short.

Overhead lights threw shadows as he turned into Cracker Lane and then the environment got dramatically worse.

The lights were dimmer, flickering sometimes.

Burnt out car shells, lay where they had been abandoned like the carcasses of some long dead animals. One or two men leaned on walls, talking or negotiating. Their faces in shadow until they lit up cancer sticks and then their eyes ignited in reflection, hard and cold. The lane opened up into a square, flanked on four sides by residential buildings, shrubbery at the base tried to calm the grey austere look of the place but couldn't. Eyes watched him as he veered left and saw the drab white washed walls of the Emporium looming in the distance. Asim began to understand why this epicentre of crime in south London had never been successfully brought down by the Met-1 and they had tried. It was too well protected and masterminded by a man who knew plenty about dirty wars and strategy. Even when the face of Brixton was changing beyond recognition, this solitary area resisted change, resisted progress.

He squinted up at the PLI's as they continued to flash red.

He would have never found this place if it wasn't for his uncle.

Chips - the Field Marshal's younger brother and black sheep of the family, was a font of knowledge in matters relating to the underworld. He prided himself on it actually.

Chips had gone out on a limb just so he could have words with an old colleague holed up in his personal fortress in South London.

This man was the last word, in his own four blocks of badlands, beyond local government and even the forces of law and order. And that was the man he wanted to see, tonight. It had been seven years but Tyrone Fink owed him and Asim had just arrived on his doorstep to collect.

******

Yasmeen waited.

She stood in the hallway in front of number 34 Carnival House, knowing her presence had already been announced inside. Risto Benji had driven away moments earlier after making sure she entered the flats safely.

The door in front of her hummed and then slid open. She walked in and made herself comfortable on the sofa. The apartment in Ladbroke Grove was silent except for Trevor's harsh curses.

Trevor manipulated one of his throwing knives between his fingers. He didn't acknowledge her. She gave him space and marvelled at how he had transformed the apartment.

All the windows were open and a mild breeze blew inside. One window overlooked a park down below, artificially assisted but still green and lush. Somehow the greenery wasn't simply left down below but magically crossed the building's walls and emerged into Trevor's main room. In the middle of the room was an Ioniser pleasantly charging the air and making it feel fresh. The earthy aroma of sensimilla completed the illusion that they were in the tropics.

A Maccabees Bible was on the bed beside her, opened up to the book of Ecclesiasticus. Her eyes caught his guitar leaning in a corner. It seemed well used.

"Cho!" Trevor spat out, throwing his knife across the room and seeing it impact perfectly into a cork target. Sauntering over to the other end of the room, he gripped the dagger's handle and yanked it out.

He spoke with himself as if Yasmeen was not in the room.

"I man could have got you killed the other night. It was out of order bringing you with me, subjecting yuh to dat type of risk." He walked back over to the end of the hotel room, brushing by Yasmeen's crossed legs. "One good ting, though, I have no more doubts." A touch of humour returned to his voice unexpectedly. "First dem blackmail me den them threaten I livelihood."

Including this development.

The Nation had never seen or heard of a Trevor Farruka before.

She cast her mind back.

After the informant was murdered, Trevor had tried to contact the market vendor. But he had vanished. He then tried to call the Tabernacle of Ras on a hotline they had established for his personal use. The line was dead. He had then contacted the offices of the Nation directly demanding to speak to Deacon Tobias only to discover that the deacon was in Shashemane and was unable to be contacted. The staff at the offices knew nothing about a mission to London except what had been revealed to them from Patriarch Yamu's broadcast.

Yasmeen was scurrying around the fringes of the matter while Trevor in his own terms had got to the meat an grizzle.

Set-up!

A throwing knife flipped through the air and impacted in the target, vibrating violently from the force.

Yasmeen flinched, her thoughts interrupted.

"Do you have to keep doing that?" She asked.

"What dis!" He pointed to the blade in the distance.

She nodded.

"It make you nervous?"

"A bit."

"Sorry, sista Yasmeen," his eyebrow creased, "but it help me to tink."

He walked over, took the dagger out of the target and spun it in his hands.

Trevor had taken the precaution of using this as a safe house just in case he could be tracked back to his hotel. Yasmeen would be safe here too.

If things were red then now they were redder than red. For Trevor this was no conspiracy theory it was all too real.

"This is a set-up, pure an simple. You ever think why dem choose to link you and me together? Dem put two troublemakers together for a reason."

"I don't believe that."

"People are trying to kill wi, do you believe dat?"

Yasmeen nodded.

"Can you see now?" He nodded. "They were responsible for everyting. If not deh Nation itself, somebody inside it."

"No, Trevor."

"Yes, sista. Wake up to the reality a deh world."

"The Nation is a way of life not an organised crime syndicate." Yasmeen murmured, her tone begging for that statement to be the truth.

Trevor chuckled grimly.

"Me is not a reader, but I know dat throughout history mankind a fight war over religion. Nuff man, woman an pickney get wipe out in the name a Jah, Allah or God." He pointed to the Bible. "A nuh mi seh suh, a deh Bible seh suh."

And they both knew that fact couldn't be disputed.

But the Nation of Ras Tafari was different, wasn't it? It had been her life. It wasn't capable of such atrocities.

"Why would they want to kill us, Trevor?" Yasmeen asked standing up from the sofa, her eyes peering through the open window.

Trevor didn't answer, that wasn't his concern. Hidden in the recesses of his mind he knew why and was certain of who. Yasmeen was the one in need of convincing. He walked over to the bedside drawer and took out the bloodstained PDA he had retrieved from the dead man and twisted it triumphantly in his hand.

"Remember this?"

Yasmeen shuddered.

"How can I forget. Have you opened the files yet?"

"A few."

"And?"

"Interestin viewing, sister." He said. "Very interestin."

******

A bulky figure lounged aggressively in the oversize chair, surrounding himself with what could only be referred to as an air of probable threat.

Tyrone Fink loved that pose, nine times out of ten he had wrestled the psychological advantage from the petty villains who felt their bollocks were too big for their shorts.

He looked on with keen interest as the man with the self-assured walk was escorted to him from the other side of the floor. He leaned on one of the huge arm rests and folded his arms, his eyes attracted to the shadow the man was casting on the floor as he approached.

Another potential trader who thought he was topping London's most wanted list. Fink grunted and stroked his face again, his gleaming little pigs eyes watching the controlled chaos of the sellers spread over a thousand square meters of floor space. For all their strutting and parading, the hustlers depended on his protection. This was his little bazaar, selling items the government deemed illegal. He ruled the economic machinery of the underworld in the south, of that no one doubted. It was just that some needed reminding of that fact while others accepted it.

He looked a bit closer at the man converging on him and leaned forward. Fink blinked rapidly and shook his head, the image of someone from his past stood glaring at him, bold as life. Looking remarkably well for a man who had been fucked by the system too many times for comfort.

"Jesus H Christ! Captain Marshall."

"Lieutenant to you dickhead." Asim corrected. "Retired."

Fink shook his head, flung it back and laughed out, his hand coming up to his face, foraging through the hairs as if he had fleas.

Stroke.

Stroke.

Tyrone 'the Wolfman' Fink had not changed much. Except for his hair being longer, greyer and tied back in a ponytail, his face marked a bit more with age and his unhealthy disposition of growing hairs where none should be, remained.

At least he had clipped his ear and nose hairs.

"Will wonders never fucking cease?" Fink bellowed.

His rhetorical question remained rhetorical.

"You know, never in a million years would I have imagined, the straight-up, clean cut, by the book, wipe my ass properly captain, white as the driven snow, would ever step into my little den of disrepute. Which one of these goodies do you want for your personal use then? Laser arms, military, commercial or maybe an old fashioned mind-altering drug. Then again, on your salary I don't think you could afford nish."

"Cut the crap Tyrone I need some information."

Fink cackled sharply, this time he was rubbing the thick hairs on his forearms.

"You always did have the bottle, I have to hand that to you but what makes you think I would tell you, of all people, anything. If my memory serves me right you had me expelled from a glittering career in the army."

It was Asim's turn to laugh long and hard.

"Don't try an bullshit, a bullshitter, turf bwoy. I saved your sorry raas from a court martial years ago, remember?" Asim tipped forward on his toes, one hand in his pocket, the other cutting the air as he made his point. "Peddling contraband in the barracks, if memory serves. And me nearly impeaching myself in a military court because I had some naive fucked-up idea about doing whatever it took to maintain the integrity of my unit. I didn't want to bring this up, Ty, but if it wasn't for me your hairy bloodclaat would be languishing at the government's pleasure right now."

"Bollocks!" Wolfman snapped. "I would have found a way out, I always did."

"Just admit it, man. As your commanding officer I had the power to help you and did, unlike my superiors who wanted your balls. I stuck my neck out for you, remember. Negotiating a dishonourable discharge instead of letting you do hard time. In a round about sort a way, I helped you to build this shit."

Asim made a sweeping gesture.

"Like fuck you did." Wolfman protested but with less venom. The U.S.E. army had given him the edge in his criminal career. The buzz and financial security he always dreamt of came about due in no small part to his desperation after being flung back into civilian life.

Ass-him had a point.

Wolfman's tone softened.

"I heard about your wife a few years ago." He said. "You two didn't deserve that."

Asim grunted and said.

"I still need that information, Wolfman. Like yesterday."

Fink lowered his head, the bristling sound of his hands scraping against his coarse facial hair maintained an irritating rhythm for minutes. When he submerged from his thoughts his frown had changed into a broad grin.

"Okay, lets talk. Right."

They had stationed themselves at a far corner of the trading room. Asim was standing, his back to the wall, feeling more comfortable that way, while the Wolfman sat in a contour chair. Even over this side, the sounds of the grey market bazaar drifted over.

Asim asked the question.

"I need to find dis man. I've got very little intelligence on him but what I do know is from the hard copy." Asim handed him the crystal with the image imbedded in it. "He's a Rasta, hustler, a smooth motherfucker who goes by the name Baldwin."

"Rasta?" The Wolfman interjected, his fingers twining the hairs of his beard.

Asim's eyebrow arched.

He responded to Asim's look of puzzlement before he asked.

"I may be a North London white boy, but I do know a true Rasta wouldn't be involved in my line of business. And Baldwin, the cockroach that he is, is no Rasta."

"I figured this type of thing was your territory."

"How did you find me anyway?"

Asim chuckled humourlessly.

"I'm still connected, boss."

"I bet. And being the proud fucker that you are, you must be gutted coming to moi for help. It must be a major cluster fuck. So why do you need him so badly?"

Asim's impassive features suddenly darkened. Eyes that had seen too many die - a few, dispatched by his own hands. Wolfman knew the look well.

"Let's jus say, he dissed the programme."

A sound like a growl issued from the back of Asim's throat.

Fink remembered his commanding officer to be a passionate man with a degree of self control that made many officers of higher rank envious. Time had taken its toll and he was getting very intense in his old age.

Wolfman twiddled the fingers of his left hand and one of his female aides bounded over. He made another set of finger and hand movements and she disappeared. Asim was impressed by Finks repertoire of hand gestures. Moments later she returned with a computer readout which she placed in his lap. The main man scanned the hard copy with his bushy eyebrows twitching, then held onto his courier's hand and kissed it.

"Excellent, darling."

She smiled and withdrew to a respectable distance.

"Pheromones." He said to Asim's unasked question.

He then shot a satisfied look in the direction of his former commanding officer and flicked the paper with his index finger.

"My records say the wanker you're looking for does actually live in Brixton and that the little cunt owes me money. He's a dodgy customer and even though I know he's making some credits peddling emotion chips, he's running around with some other geezers from the east, some hard nosed bastards I'm told and making more money than is right, for a tosser like that."

The tips of Wolfman's fingers scraped across his face, rapidly.

"Baldwin is a man who thinks with his small head, right." He grabbed his crotch in illustration. "Not his brains. Whoever he's working with will soon find out he's a no hope loser."

"Who is this crowd he's running around with, anyway?" Asim asked.

"That's the funny part. I don't know for sure. My guess is he's become a snitch but their activities are even hidden from my beady little eyes. And that pisses me right off. I like to know what's taking place on another man's patch, the who, whats and whys, right. But this cunt's movements have left me guessing."

He handed Asim the data sheet.

"Still, he's not top priority on my list, just one of those annoying loose ends I hate leaving. His last known address and other relevant bits and bobs are on that paper, memorise it. I don't make it a habit to give out sensitive information like this to any Tom, Dick and Raj, but for old time's sake I'm making an exception. I just want to ask you one thing before you break him in half. Deliver a message for me."

"Break him in half? My days of violence are over, rude bwoy." He said insincerely.

The Wolfman shook his bedraggled head.

"Yeah right." He grinned, his two canines showing over his lower lip. "Just tell the little toe rag from me. If I don't get my money very soon, I'm personally going to climb so high up his arse it's going to take a search and rescue party to dig me out."

Asim grimaced at the thought and said.

"He'll get it."

******

He tried to duck but couldn't.

Even as the space Yogi pillow smashed into the side of his head and he rolled with the blow, he knew it was pointless.

Asim's lesson in reality, had just come to an abrupt end.

The picture he had carried in his head up to this point - and this point being the first time he tucked his daughter in bed - was one of, reading Akilla a bedtime story and watching her blissfully drift off to sleep. A kiss on her cheek and him sneaking away, satisfied.

Wake up, ru'bwoy!

And he did, just as pillow number two sliced his mid-section, quickly followed by a salvo of cuddly toys and smart blocks.

That was when his fantasy bubble burst.

Pop!

Her contagious giggling got louder while she continued to reduce her room to a bombsight. Asim caught himself laughing raucously with her and strangely it had surprised him. It felt out of place, just the act of unrestrained laughter gave him a feeling of being someone else. Like some liberated soul looking in on himself.

God Almighty yout, he thought, you are a sad bastard, psychoanalysing a moment of happiness.

Asim chuckled to himself and sat up from Akilla's bed. He was expecting her grandmother to come in any minute now, annoyed from the noise they were making and only too happy to negotiate peace in the pillow wars that had extended way past her bedtime.

She didn't.

By now it was a certainty that he was really on his own and it was his job to calm her down and tuck her in. He took up the stuffed toys off the floor and placed them on her dresser as she bounced in the centre of the bed like a trampolinist, with her tongue sticking out. Tidying up quickly and ignoring her name calling, the temptation to send a flying pillow at her was strong. But he held back realising their 'ramping' would never end so he tried to look like he meant business and found that difficult to do.

Wrestling the bundle of energy under the sheets, he had to threaten her with calling 'granny' if she didn't settle down. That seemed to have the desired effect as Asim bent over and kissed her. Sighing with relief, he headed quickly for the door.

His little girl was not quite finished with him yet though.

"Daaad!" She drawled.

Asim cringed uncomfortable with the title.

"Yes madam?" He turned slowly with a stern expression on his face which just didn't have the conviction to deter her.

"What was mummy like?"

The innocent question rooted him to the spot. A wall that had shielded his eyes from believing how perceptive Akilla could be, crumbled. She may not have grasped the deeper notion of death but she knew her mother was gone. At that instant he had a brief understanding of the pain she would feel in later life of not knowing her mother and never being able to.

He cleared his throat uneasily and knelt down beside her.

"She was wonderful. The best mommy yuh could ask for." He whispered in her ear. "And just as beautiful as you."

Asim kissed her but Akilla held onto his hand as he rose to leave.

"You have to help me say my praaayers. Didn't Granma tell you?"

Asim's head tilted slightly forward. He smiled.

This he did not prepare for.

"She must have forgotten, baby." He said. "You're a big girl now, do you really need me for dat."

"Don't be silly, of course."

"So what do we do?" He sighed not wanting to disappoint her.

The little woman laughed heartily at that question as she sprang up from under her sheet, eyes alight.

"Dad's never prayed before." She teased in a singsong voice.

"I have but... I'm just a bit rusty, dat's all."

Still smiling with a knowing twinkle in her eyes that belied her age, Akilla took her fibbing father's hands and clasped them together and made him kneel beside the bed. She bounced off and kneeled beside him, closing her eyes tightly. A frown formed on her lips as she suspected a lack of effort on his part. Her left eye flicked open and rolled in the direction of Asim who was feeling like a prize prat as he looked into the middle distance. She nudged him with her shoulder.

"Jah, won't hear you unless. you. close. your eyes. dad."

Surprised, Asim obliged. His first prayer in many years strangely made him realise that it would not be his last.

Now I lay me down to sleep
I pray to Jah my soul to keep
And if I die before I wake
I pray to Jah my soul to take.

******

Asim still smelt of his daughter's baby lotion even as the dark sheen of the glass towers of Brixton loomed ahead. Slowly his Porsche eased its way through the traffic. The night was warm and the commercial centre of south London was awash with neon lighted colour. It was early morning but the streets were filled with automated street cleaners, party goers, blaring noise and swirling colours.

Asim was a stark contrast. He was dressed entirely in black except for a dark-blue wind breaker and perched on his forehead, a fashionable pair of dark specs. From his grim expression and his functional wear, Asim would not be partying tonight.

He had work to do.

The cars ahead slowed to a stop. Drumming his fingers on the steering wheel, humming to some tune he could not remember the words to, he proceeded cautiously.

Soon he drove free along Africa Boulevard, with its banks and office buildings housing multinational companies mainly from the Commonwealth of Democratic African States. Some of the glass towers in the distance rose half-skeletal, half-fleshed, so they looked like an architect's cross-section diagrams. What made the difference was that these diagrams were partially animated. Sparks from laser welders danced off the metal superstructures and robotic workers crawled along the frames like a legion of spiders. Creating the dream while their masters slept.

Asim tore his eyes away from the skyline and manoeuvred his car into Brixton High Road. The onboard computer was already aligning the car in the right lane for the turnoff before he needed to.

The twelve storey NCP car park looked more like a virtual amusement arcade. All bright lights, glass and giant scrolling billboards. He turned into the park and stopped at the barrier.

Time to declare war, he thought.

******

Eyes looked up at Baldwin, gleaming and intense. She drew air through clenched teeth, grunting and groaning. Fleeting smiles from a heightened sexual experience. A BrainTechTM receiver was clipped around her head its central light blinking. All past experiences of an orgasm had been momentarily wiped from her memory by the machine. Her come would feel like her very first but this time under the guidance of a master cocksman.

Both bodies were soaked in sweat, writhing in controlled movements, exploring each other with nothing remotely like loving passion. Baldwin was not the type of man who would make feelings interfere with good sex, especially when this fuck was touching a nine on the Baldwin scale of ten.

Easy.

As his mind lingered, he felt the mounting wave of pleasure, wash down his spine on its way to his swollen member as he sank deeply into her again. He clenched his teeth, arching his back and breathed deeply until it subsided. A euphoric grin lingered on his lips as he slowly lowered himself so only his cock's bulbous head teased its way into her and, with a petulant flick of his locks, he eyed the luminous timer on his night table.

Two hours and thirty minutes. Champion, Baldwin thought.

A new record. He was pleased. And he should be. With Tracy groaning and bucking underneath him it was no wonder he had to use all his willpower not to climax.

The games men play.

He wouldn't have backed away from this opportunity if you paid him. Tracy was a special. He had never experienced a woman with such exquisite control over her vaginal muscles. Combined with her addiction to emotion chips - of which he conveniently sold - she was a beast in bed. One he took great pleasure in taming.

What price a sore penis? That was the price one paid for being a martyr to the cause. With that thought, he felt Tracy grip him inside her and as he moved with the merest gyration of his waist, pubic hairs entwined and the clitoris being stimulated with every movement, she cried out.

With a combination of his probing stabs inside her and the emotion recorder stimulating parts of her brain responsible for sexual gratification, he didn't know how she hadn't exploded already. Then again he knew the answer to that. Tracy was a pro. She had already climaxed twice in the two hours and thirty-five minutes of sex and this would be her third time. It took a special woman to enjoy and take pride in her screwing prowess and his blessing was that these women sensed a kindred spirit in him.

Borderline nymphomaniac.

Baldwin smiled raising himself slightly to increase the friction of his penis against her clitoris and propped her legs back with his arms. For a minute, he had forgotten his Guinness record attempt and wanted only for Tracy to scream out in his sound proofed room with the mirrored ceiling.

And 'bwoy' she didn't disappoint.

******

Wolfman had given Asim a previous address, plus other miscellaneous facts he thought would be useful to source him with. He still hadn't figured out how Baldwin's star sign could help him but he managed to use it nonetheless.

He smiled grimly, reminded of a very apt Jamaican saying that was more than relevant to the present situation. Fling rock stone inna pig pen, whoever bawl out first, get deh lick.

And Baldwin was screaming.

The rock stone he used in this case was his discreet enquires and the pig pen his local haunts. And all coming from a mysterious schoolmate who wanted to contact him urgently. By now he should know, he was never in school with an Egbert

Walters and start worrying. And like a badly plotted comic, he did.

Asim had learned that people reacted two ways to strangers asking about them and that separated them into definite categories of nothing to hide or something to hide. Baldwin fell firmly in the latter. He was not the modest type and definitely did not revel in the idea of a low profile. Driving a custom-built van fully tech loaded drew attention and pussy.

His change from a flamboyant turf boy to the more reserved and cautious type was a dramatic one. He did not like friends enquiring of his whereabouts. The designer dread learned very quickly the benefits of walking and relieving the gridlocked traffic in London by taking public transport. Environmentally conscious he wasn't just deeply suspicious.

The things you could learn from watching.

Human beings acted irrationally on one level but if you looked carefully, they operated on simple rules that seem complex until you know what they are. In Baldwin's case the human frailty of habit let Asim plot his comings and goings and judge with reasonable accuracy the patterns of his day to day activities.

Four different girls in the space of five days slept at his apartment. For Fatima's boyfriend, he wasn't very concerned about the fact he hadn't seen her in the last month. He left his home every day with a back pack bulging full of goodies and came home with it empty. His lunch maybe or he was making his rounds to Oxfam. Somehow he doubted that reasoning. Now peddling, that was more in line with character. All in all Baldwin was a fascinating animal to study in his habitat but there comes a time in every ghetto anthropologist's life where you have to study your subject at close quarters.

Asim couldn't wait.

You were meant to walk down the fire escape of Kuanda Flats in case of emergencies but Asim, always the one to say 'fuck convention', was climbing up it and there wasn't a fire in sight.

No alarms responded to his intrusion and that meant things were going to plan. Asim ran up the zigzag stairs, holding the rails and pulling himself forward and steadily made his way to the Eighth floor.

His first recon of the building a week ago had left him concerned about the security arrangements but he needn't have been. On closer inspection the technology was outdated and typical of local government engineers taking the cheap and cheerful route to the taxpayer's detriment. Asim had attached a little package to the building's main console, giving him uninterrupted access to the winding gantry up the side of the flats' rear face. He had an hour before the system overrode his little toy and started to scream blue murder.

Plenty a time.

For the sake of stealth from his head - he wore a balaclava - to his feet he wore black, everything made from the same light absorbing material. He was a shadow as he mounted the stairs two at a time, his steps lost to the sound of the wind whistling through the metal framework and the distant whooping of rotors.

Nearing the eighth floor, he slowed his pace and silently swung himself up. The windows were spaced evenly along the building's rear face. He stayed in the shadow away from the light shining out of an apartment near him. He had to get by undetected. Silently and with almost casual skill, he tumbled forward on the metal platform avoiding the open window with fluttering curtains. Rolling once and then twice he came up with his back firmly against the wall. The wind whipped at his jacket while he peered across the expanse of Brixton. He was three windows away from the flat he wanted to break into and allowed his nimble fingers to lead his entire body like a fencer across to the point.

A distant sound he had ignored earlier had suddenly started to drown out the whistling of the wind. He froze and cursed under his breath for his lack of foresight. Shaking his head angrily he swore again. A low chopping sound swooped from above, and within seconds it was hovering about a hundred and fifty meters away. The Met-1's metallic black Vampire copter began sweeping the terrain with what seemed like solid beams of light.

Asim's mind went blank and his muscles tensed. If they reverted to heat-seeking mode he was cool, the material of his suit gave off no heat signature, but a full frontal slam by a high intensity light and that would be it.

The beam split and started sweeping the face of the building.

He held his breath.

A thick tube of light came so close, the heat prickled his forehead, Asim tried to melt into the wall.

They took a keen interest in his position, lights dancing around him like they were rehearsing for some cabaret performance. Another moved just below his feet, before shooting down to the foot of the building.

A nervous breath exploded from his mouth.

Swinging away from him they concentrated on two more tower blocks in the distance then, with their noses tilted down, they shot away.

Asim stood there for a moment, breathing heavily, his back against the wall and his head raised to the sky.

He could feel the sweat trickling down his back.

Only four steps more, he thought.

A ghostly reflection of himself from the opaque one-way windows, followed his movements. Stopping, he crouched and came out of his pocket with a small device held between two fingers. He then carefully attached it to the window's frame.

He grinned, just before he depressed the device's housing.

What was this world coming to?

Honest Ed the homeowner was fighting a losing battle against today's high-tech burglars. You were up against thieves who were updating their equipment and techniques every day, leaving the poor bemused model citizen goat fucked.

Better him dan me.

The twin lights on the mechanism flashed red once and then pulsed yellow. There was a muffled 'phut' sound and the window slid open. He detached the small instrument and popped it back in his pocket. Cautiously, he snaked his head through the opening, checking if the coast was clear.

Darkness and silence.

Crouching he entered the apartment, closing the window from inside and found his feet sink into the thick pile carpet, in what seemed to be the main lounge. He stood still while his senses adapted to the darkness and used the time to assess his surroundings.

He was sure this was the apartment his sister had made the call from. The clock tower stood in the distance just as it had in the recording, the furnishings were identical and in the exact same positions from the TView.

There was just one thing. The image he had of the apartment from the tapes had changed dramatically from what he was seeing now. The place had become a tip.

Fatima was an obsessive house mouse and loved where she lived to be orderly and spotless. Asim had been force-fed the lessons of cleanliness from the army but for his sister it came naturally. Her room always looked like something out of the Ideal Crib Show.

Her legacy had not been respected in the least.

Clothes were strewn over the sofa and on the floor. The faint smell of his body odour tainted the air with the smell of cigarettes. Asim carefully stepped over glasses and plates left on the floor and entered the kitchen. It too was in a state of chaos. Greasy tendrils of bacon rind still stuck to plates in the sink and from their state of desiccation were several days old. Asim shook his head. He could only imagine the dutty dread was waiting for the bacon remnants to evolve to a level of intelligence so that they could wash the dishes themselves.

Nasty fucker!

Asim moved stealthily into the hallway opened up some nondescript doors revealing cupboards and storage closets. No surprises anywhere. Moving sideways his back rubbing along the wall, he stopped at a matt black display case situated centrally along the hallway. He glanced at a few expensive looking trinkets inside. Continuing, he headed for the room at the far end. Inching closer and keenly listening for any sounds coming from inside, he stretched out his hand to grab the door knob.

It swung towards him.

Force of will or more sensibly, it was pushed open.

Asim shuffled back using the shadow thrown on the wall by the opening door.

Baldwin stepped out, yawned and stretched his still erect penis - a sign post pointing east, he followed the direction.

Standing perfectly still, Asim watched.

The funky dread headed for the bathroom. Moments later the toilet flushed. Baldwin drearily padded back to his room and Asim whispered his name.

"Big pussy, Baldwin!"

The dread spun, nearly losing his balance in the process. A look of horror and panic on his face lasting only fleeting seconds. Straining, he listened. No sounds.

He relaxed and cursed himself for drinking too much.

"You're not going crazy, boss." Asim's voice was a harsh rasp. "I want you alert an aware."

Baldwin's neck snapped around, like he had been struck with a rock. He shook his head. Cautiously, he moved closer then jumped back.

A ghostly outline, emerged.

"Heyyyy...!"

A furious blow to his Adam's apple cut off all possible conversation and with overwhelming force he was slammed to the wall. Screaming was pointless as he needed air to do that. He clutched his throat, thrashing wildly and, just as he tottered on the brink of unconsciousness, the pressure on his throat relaxed.

He gasped for air, continuing to squirm.

"Lights!" Asim ordered and stepped away from him as the room brightened.

Baldwin slid to a sitting position on the floor, panting.

Asim looked him up and down, squinted at the sight of his erect cock and focused elsewhere. Immediately his attention was drawn to a discolouration on his left arm.

At first it seemed like a large mole but as Baldwin fidgeted, trying to shadow Asim's every movement, he caught the edges of a tattoo with a chilling but unique design. He had to be mistaken, that couldn't be right.

Asim tilted his head and glimpsed the head of what could be a number seven, floating above his dark skin. He stepped back, this time it was Asim's turn for the breath to be caught in his throat. He had hoped to God, he never had to see that ever again. Asim squinted, subconscious sirens were screaming in his head and his pulse raced. He stepped closer and the funky dread cowered, exposing the holographic tattoo. The image may have fooled the eye into believing it was floating above the skin of his forearm but it didn't disguise the fact that it was the so-called sacred circle of seven. The venerated symbol of the Broederbund - the apartheid terrorists of New South Africa.

Asim held Baldwin's terrified gaze with his smouldering eyes and scowled.

"What do yuh want, man?" Baldwin screamed.

"We're school mates, rememba?"

"I don't know you from fucking Adam." He hollered, jumping up and down like a caged monkey.

"I'm Egbert."

"You're a cocksucker, batty bwoy." He pointed at him, making threatening steps in his direction.

"Yuh supposed to say, 'pleased to meet you'," Asim said.

Baldwin looked at the door that led into the passage outside with yearning eyes.

Asim chuckled.

"If you're thinking of running, feget it! I don't miss, turf bwoy." Asim spun the dagger he had dragged from a scabbard strapped to his leg. Flipping it skilfully and wondering if Baldwin's eyesore of an erection would ever go down.

"You're one fucking man. You think I can't take you." Baldwin tested the water and then wished he hadn't said that.

"You're welcome." Asim growled, standing there with unblinking eyes and the shiny knife in his hand.

The funky dread was weak in the knees, pressing against the

wall, his mouth dry and his back moist and sticky.

To die naked, helpless and with a cock stand, no way.

"Fuck you." He bellowed then bolted.

Asim expected that move before Baldwin decided to make it. Scurrying four quick steps to his right, Asim flung his foot up in a roundhouse kick. It caught Baldwin sharply in the hollow of his neck, the force making him stumble, the muscles of his legs going weak. The floor rose up to meet him even too quickly for him to counter. His head struck the hard edge of the door frame, leaving him slumped awkwardly on the passageway wall.

He didn't move.

"Fuck you too," Asim said finally.

Baldwin's erection suddenly went limp.

Eyes partially opened after what could have been minutes or even hours of sleep or even nightmare.

His mind filled with mental fog. He wished that the pain in his head and neck was nothing more sinister than what you would expect from his night's activities. He wished it was the result of slamming it against the wall during sex or because his neck was at an odd angle while he was tantalising her with his tongue. He wished he could open his eyes turn over and Tracey would be beside him exhausted but satisfied.

A vivid nightmare. Pure and simple.

Not so, rude bwoy.

With a shudder of disbelief he closed them tightly again.

This fuckery is not happening to me, man. This can't be happening.

With more caution this time, his eyelids parted and the horror he was desperately trying to tell himself didn't exist, remained.

Baldwin howled, his wasted life flashing before his eyes. Dangling precariously from his ankles, he was attached to a metal rig used by the automated window cleaners to move around the face of the building, Baldwin knew he was dead. He was on the roof of the tower - seventeen stories up - and hanging over the edge, swaying mildly, as the luminous ant colony of cars shifted lazily below. He thrashed like a fish on a hook, his cries dying in the black expanse of the night, powerless. Baldwin cursed in one breath and then pleaded in the next, with a voice that shifted from a hoarse cry to a subdued whimper.

He tried to reach up to his feet but his wrists had been bound and, with gravity and his weak lower body strength, it condemned him to keep swinging as long as his tormenter wanted. The man in black stared at him from his safe position on the roof, waiting or simply lost in his own world.

"What the fuck do you want with me, boss!" Baldwin spat out. "What the fuck, maaaaaan?"

Asim could not get the image of the circle of seven tattoos out of his head. His mind was in overdrive. A multitude of possibilities steamrolling their way through his brain and him trying desperately to extract some rational explanation for it. A black man with the initiation mark of the most notorious extremist groups in New South Africa. A group whose more moderate founders wanted to roll back the tide of time to the 'good old days' of white rule. A well-financed terrorist organisation, who were presently waging bloody war in New South Africa.

As bizarre as it was, the racist Broeders had a trusted network of black informants to provide them with intelligence. But their concerns were a continent away, not here in London.

Not as far as he knew.

In his tour of duty he had personally and with no regret at all terminated some of their leaders and foot soldiers. As he felt the twinge of pain in his back, a reminder of the last close shave he had with them, it reminded him of the score they felt had gone unsettled.

They were linked somehow with Fatima's abduction.

The funky dread was the key and Asim knew he had to keep him under constant surveillance. His job was to 'rinse' him for information and scare him 'shitless'.

If him slip, him slide.

"They say you die of fright before you hit the ground from a fall like this." Asim wondered aloud. "They'd be scraping your sorry raas off the sidewalk for days to come."

There was another stream of abuse from Baldwin as he hung there.

"Just answer the questions and I won't have to test the theory." The dread's defiance was seeping away rapidly.

"What do you want from me, man?" Baldwin sobbed.

"Just some answers."

"I don't know nuthin."

"But yuh do, Baldwin. Plenty."

"You got the wrong man, boss. I'm just trying to survive the system, man. Hustling, ducking an diving, you know how it is broooother."

"Forget that 'brother' crap. I've been employed to get some answers from yuh and personally I don't give a shit how I get it. It seems to me, turf bwoy, you're having the worst day of your life and believe me it can get worse. Providing..."

"Providing what?" Baldwin wailed.

"Providing yuh tell me what I want to know."

"You're making no sense, man."

Asim snorted just managing to control the rage boiling inside. The question was asked calmly.

"What sort of relationship did you have with Fatima Marshall?"

"Fatima who?"

Asim's patience threshold was bordering on zero by now.

He leaned over to the lever mechanism, squeezed on the clasp with the palm of his hand and saw the rope release.

Baldwin plummeted.

His shrieking continued even as his fall ended abruptly, the ropes snapping his ankle bone and spinning him like a bungee jumper. The mechanical winch brought him up from his brief drop until he was level with Asim again.

"Don't fuck with me, dread." He stared into his eyes and could see the near hysterical panic there. "You're not the only source of information on my list, just the easiest to get to. If you were to have a tragic accident, I'd personally sleep better tonight, knowing an asshole like you wouldn't be on the street peddling yuh mind shit. So don't tempt me. Now, back to the question. What sort of relationship did you have with Fatima Marshall?"

"I met her at a club man," he gasped and blubbered, the pain from his broken bone knocking the air out of him.

"Which club?" Asim snapped.

"The Cue Club."

"And..." Asim invited.

"We became good friends. I used to see her from time to time, you know, touch it a few times and that's it. I swear!"

"Bullshit!" He growled. "Ms Marshall was snatched a month ago, raped and you know something bout it."

"Raped!" Baldwin croaked. "She was raped? I had nothing to do with that, man, straight up." He wailed. "Nothing."

"Like fuck yuh didn't!"

Baldwin saw the blade of Asim's bush knife as it was pulled from the scabbard at his ankle. He wriggled comically, trying to twist his body around for a better view at what Asim was up to.

He wished he hadn't tried. The man in black was preparing to cut the ropes. The moisture in his mouth suddenly evaporated.

Baldwin lost control of his bowels and by sheer force of will flexed his vocal chords into a blood curdling wail.

"JESAS CHRIST BOSS! I'm ready! I'm ready!" He screamed. "I'm ready to talk man. Just don't cut the rope, turf man. I'm begging yuh. I'll tell you all I know. Everything boss, EVERYTING!"

Ignoring him, Asim continued hacking into the fibres then he lifted his head like he was sniffing the air.

Baldwin's screams dominated.

Asim slowly sheathed his knife.

"If I ever have to take this out again." He kissed his teeth. "You'll be face down in concrete, so let's get a few things straight." He paused and folded his arms. "I know Ms Marshall was with you the night she disappeared, lover bwoy. I just want to know everything you know."

Baldwin's eyes bulged and his face turned decidedly pale.

Asim smiled under the balaclava.

"Remember, it's you, me and seventeen floors to ground zero, rude bwoy. Take your time, relax and tell me everything you know, in a clear and strong speaking voice."

******

The member of Parliament for Westminster tapped her expensively clad feet to the rhythmic beating of the kente drums.

Her male advisor whispered something in her ear and they both laughed heartily, sharing the joke with the other dignitaries within earshot.

If the atmosphere was anything to go by, the opening of the exhibit, Black Pharaohs in Ancient Egypt, was a success. Five hundred invitations sent out and just about a thousand people turned up.

Yasmeen - who was wearing a slinky, figure-hugging, black and gold sequinned evening gown with matching headwrap, peered over to the assorted gaggle of politicians, academics, journalists, museum staff and the obligatory celebrities who had an interest in African culture and history. A battalion of waiters waded through the crowds with trays of fine wine, disturbing the grazing guests intent on making good use of the free food. Voice of the Skin, the famous seven piece Nyabinghi drumming troupe performed some stirring compositions. The Ethiopian chants especially had the audience mesmerised by their haunting rhythms.

Trevor was right beside her at all times.

"So where do we go from here, what options do we have?"

"Mi a work off deh theory that something a happen, which require that, both a we is out a deh picture. Let's give them what dem want."

"So they lure you here and involve you in this peace process and then try to kill you. But if you suspected why did you come?"

"Because of you, sista."

"Me!"

"Someone told me to come and I man did."

The Rasta man held up his hand before she could ask him

anything else.

"What is important is not why mi come but that mi deh yah to cover your back. And to warn you this is the just the beginning."

"And everything we have been doing here?"

"Chickeeny business." Trevor spat. "Just a small part of a bigger game. A game wi learning deh rules to."

"And you're asking me to believe this was organised by our people."

"Believe dat."

"Why?"

"For now," he lit a spliff, "is better you just trust mi."

She shuffled in her seat.

"That's not the answer I want to hear, Trevor." Her eyes never left his.

"Do you have an open mind sista, can yuh handle the truth?" He asked.

"Try me." It was said with a determined whisper.

The dread leaned back. He looked over to those fiery brown eyes and placed one elbow on the table meeting her stare.

"What is deh biggest event taking place in a deh Rasta calendar?"

"The Ascension of Negusa Negas." She answered.

"An which man, you would put sure money pan to hold the title?"

"Patriarch Yamu." Her answer was immediate.

"What if him never as certain as you? What if him think me and others like me, can stop him from obtain the title becah I know certain things. What steps yuh tink him would tek?"

Her brows rose suspiciously. The patriarch was a man of peace. Then Trevor's warning came back to her.

Can yuh handle what mi have to seh, sista?

She fought to make sense of it.

What could Trevor ever know, that would make the patriarch, a man promoting peace to want to kill him?

If she knew what I knew she would believe.

He licked his lips, wanting to tell her more, but knowing he had promised.

The waitress arrived with the juices and the Rasta man reached for his, then hesitated before he took Yasmeen's.

She was not waitress who had taken their order.

"My sistren asked for a passion fruit juice from your colleague, yuh brought her something different."

The waitress looked at the glass more keenly, the slightly off red contents were making the glass sweat.

"This is pure passion fruit, sir,."

Trevor leaned forward shaking his head, the poor girl oblivious to the fact that she was about to test a man who lived off the land and knew natural juices, a man who also knew the juices had been brought from a Rasta trader who knew Yasmeen well. No concentrate, additives or preservative shit, these were pasteurised fresh from the fruit.

"Look," Trevor said expecting an apology. "Yuh must know fruit. Yuh in deh food business, you taste it."

The woman's face went pale.

She took up the glass and stared at the contents as if she expected it to magically spring from the glass into her mouth.

Yasmeen looked on embarrassed.

"Taste it," the Rasta man growled.

The young woman shook her head and the masquerade she had played out so far fell apart with it.

Trevor lunged at her but she had already left the tray and glass suspended in mid air for a fractured second, backing away from his grasp. Trevor was to his feet quickly, the glass had shattered and the waitress was smashing her way through the guests in a bid to escape, leaving behind a thick head of red hair on the ground.

The Rasta man didn't bother to give chase, he just took out his video two way and informed security who had virtually over run the perimeter like a troupe of excited monkeys.

"What was that about?" Yasmeen asked shocked.

"She was a Blood," Trevor said matter-of-factly. "An if I'm right she was trying to poison you."

Yasmeen's head lowered into her outstretched hands and it was there she asked her question.

"How much longer can you keep on protecting me."

Trevor massaged her shoulders.

"Until yuh have no need for my protection or if mi dead."

******

The day had started well.

It was his daughter's tenth birthday and a little-knees up at home had been planned to celebrate it. Nan was there, his uncle Farlo and his sister Muriel in from Australia. A real family affair and he was forced to leave early.

Unforeseen circumstances, he had told them.

So a sterling good mood - and they didn't come often - was in tatters, while he sat on his tod waiting.

"Where the fuck is that cunt? I want him here!" His finger jabbed down to his feet, at a spot where his shoes sunk into the plush carpets of his Rolls Royce.

The demand and the question were directed to no one in particular but the men beside him felt an overpowering urge to shrug.

Reggie Thorndike blew a wisp of impatient smoke through the window and watched as the tobacco vapour was snatched and devoured by the oppressive darkness outside. He leaned forward. His eyes darted from side to side straining to see anything beyond the glass but couldn't. He leaned back. The men paid to protect him, ignored his impatience and kept scanning the scarred terrain with night scopes. The disused industrial estate in his old Tower Hamlets neighbourhood was ideal. He only wished he didn't have to be here under these poxy circumstances. Tongues were wagging in the wrong mouths.

His favour for the Brotherhood.

Somehow, someone had followed a trail back to him. Now how was that possible? He asked himself.

B a l d w i n.

He recited the name, carefully dissecting the letters from it, one at a time. The bastard had fancied the bitch hadn't he? It was a balls up waiting to happen and he should have seen it coming. Reggie leaned back in the plush leather seat and frowned, extinguishing the cigarette in the ashtray. He lifted his jacket's cuff and consulted his luminescent timepiece.

At that moment a mobile crackled and one of the men spoke into it briefly and nodded. The guards stepped outside looking into the distance as headlamps cut tunnels of light through the darkness. Like choreographed stage lighting the headlamps from other cars parked in a crude semi-circle, lit up the centre of the open area. The industrial ruins became instantly free from the depressing gloom.

Reggie favoured overkill tonight.

The muffled sound of bass proceeded what turned out to be a black 4x4 van. It screeched to a stop as it came near the parked cars stirring up a cloud of dust much to the disapproval of the heavily armed men.

"Shut that racket off." One man bellowed as he swung up on the van's door and peered in. The dancehall\hip-hop track immediately went dead and Baldwin hopped out on crutches, his ankle still in plaster. He didn't look his usual cocky and arrogant self.

Frisked on the spot he was then gruffly led over to the Roller. The door opened and a ringed finger beckoned him in.

Baldwin started to hyperventilate long before he lowered himself into the luxury car. In fact from the moment he received the high frequency data burst confirming he was 'called' he had been in a state. Four days of intensive thinking on how best he could deliver this sensitive news to the man, had kept him awake and worried. The man in black had found out everything he needed to know and if he was smart the trail led to Mr. Thorndike. He couldn't just sit back and wait until Mr. Thorndike put two and two together. And that left him in the unique position of being called a grass, for in their eyes he had broken their code.

The words Death Sentence, sprang to mind.

In his haze of tiredness and confusion nothing made any sense to him, except the vicious reputation these men had. He sat and stared into the frigid blue eyes of Reggie Thorndike. The car door hissed closed behind him.

Suddenly, he felt so alone and shit scared.

******

"Oh man!" Asim spat out remembering his dinner engagement at the worst possible time. He was supposed to meet Yasmeen back at the warehouse in about an hour. He pulled the binoculars from his eyes, scratched his nose and replaced them. He turned up the electro-optical gain to maximum until he could clearly see the framed image of Baldwin shakily slip into the Rolls Royce.

No need to worry, though, she could let herself in and wait. Things would be wrapped up here shortly. Yes, Baldwin my bwoy, exactly what a want yuh to do! What I'd give to be a fly inside dat car.

The building had been an ideal vantage point for his little surveillance operation. The warehouses around here had been originally built to store goods that would eventually be loaded into ships on the Thames back in the day when the east of London was a thriving dock. The banks of the Thames housed various business enterprises whose net worth had skyrocketed in the early part of the century.

While these sites thrived, the industrial estate's fortunes waned as social opinion and economic bases shifted, this part of the east became very undesirable. Hence the dereliction.

Baldwin had reacted just as he had anticipated. With panic.

He hadn't interfered with him for days, allowing Kehinde to monitor his movements from Zulu Security Systems Inc. Most of the time Baldwin had spent at home, forfeiting his partying and his women. Then he started limping out. Asim followed the funky dread on four separate occasions and ended up with nothing. Then ah mind seh stick with him and he did for three consecutive nights.

Then ba-dam!

Result.

His sister, Yasmeen, the South Africans, Baldwin. What the fuck was going on?

He kept the Rolls Royce in his sights and got as comfortable as he could.

******

"You did what?" The question exploded out of Reggie Thorndike's mouth, shattering the cool demeanour he had exhibited throughout their five minutes talk. Baldwin fidgeted, chilled by Reggie's subzero eyes as they impaled him to the seat. He felt like some inconsequential cockroach about to be squashed underfoot.

"H-H-Heee was going to kill me." Baldwin stammered, making space between them on the refined leather.

"He's going to kill you?" Reggie repeated, his voice more modulated. "He won't. Not if I do it fucking first."

"I had to get him off me, off my back, off your back." Baldwin was rattling off his words frantically."

"So you told him about my night club. What else did you fucking talk about?"

"Nuthin else, nuthin."

"So how did he find you?"

He shrugged and said," A just knew if I didn't warn you..."

"Covering your bollocks, then."

"He is a dangerous man, Mr. Thorndike. He's not going to let up."

"And how do you know that?"

"I just know, man. It's how he looked at me. He knows."

Reggie Thorndike stared at Baldwin with sheer contempt. Thinking, evaluating. Why didn't the man in black kill the little cunt? Why had he kept him alive? The black man's words looped through his head. "He isn't going to let it go." Why? "He knows." How? Reggie Thorndike asked himself again.

You could almost see the mental machinery in his skull churning away at the problem, his fingers roughly intertwining in conjunction with the process.

Reggie's face seemed to drain of blood. What replaced it was a gruesome mask of terrible malice and awful intent.

"You grassed us up didn't you?" Reggie whispered. "Why?" He screamed the question, globules of spit exiting his mouth. "You stupid, lying bastard, you grassed us up!"

******

Asim squinted when the Rolls Royce's door flew open, making him grip the binoculars tightly.

Suddenly, there was a bright yellow flash, a tearing sound followed a second later by Baldwin's limp body being violently catapulted from the cars interior as if he had been yanked out by some invisible rope. The dread lay there unmoving, a tendril of smoke curling up from his wound, his back to Asim's prying eyes.

"Raas!"

He left the image of Baldwin and swung back to the Roller just in time to see an Italian styled shoe and silk socks touch down on the ground and then hands gesticulating wildly behind photo-chromatic glass. He tried to will the phantom - with the good taste in footwear - out into the open where he could I.D. him but he was the type of creature who preferred the background, executing his judgements undetected. His performance finished, the door slammed shut and the Rolls Royce sped off.

The gun men scattered kicking up dirt in their haste and took up positions near Baldwin's van. Two entered while one techno type - a man wearing a long black coat, glasses and carrying some sort of detector in his hand - slid underneath the chassis.

Asim was getting edgy.

Then the impossible happened.

The man under the van rolled out holding up some small object pressed between his two fingers.

The fucker had found the transmitter!

A discovery he exhibited no excitement about. Instead the man in the long leather coat, plopped a pair of goggles over his eyes and watched the screen of the instrument he had in his hand. He punched at the key pad stepped forward and made sweeping movements with his arms and then stood very still.

The binoculars still at his eyes, Asim looked on confused and interested at the same time.

He magnified the image and recoiled as an intense pulse of light left the handheld and hurtled skywards. Remaining still throughout, as if he was waiting for some announcement, the merest whisper of a smile on his lips, the man lifted the goggles triumphantly from his eyes.

Turning slowly, moving in a clockwise arc, he hesitates looks down at his instrument then back up again.

Asim couldn't lip read but knew something was wrong as all eyes focused on the building he was holed in. When the cocky son-of-a-bitch waved at him that confirmed Asim's suspicion.

"Shiiiiit...!!!"

Asim dropped the lens, like it was on fire and then looked down at the portable Locator hanging from his neck.

The image on the screen blurred from tired eyes.

"Yuh fucking idiot!"

The red blip on the screen kept flashing, the real betrayer of his position showing no remorse.

Asim backed up, stumbling over the debris behind him, escape being more important now than stealth. The men below, in the mean time, were hustling towards the building, their weapons close to their hips and bloody murder in their eyes.

Asim had no time at all.

This was a fuck-up waiting to happen.

His attempt at escape was not a dignified one.

Reggie Thorndike's men circled the derelict building, the less fit men coming up from behind out of breath. Guns at the ready, they positioned themselves so that every escape route was covered.

Fingers flexed near hair triggers, eagerly. A few of the boys were about to barge in through the main entrance but a middle-aged man, his hair greying at the sides stopped them.

Freddy Tubbs showed his choppers.

"Lads! Lads!" He said crooking his finger in the direction of the two men closest to him. "The easy way." He whispered pointing to the Extremely Flammable signs plastered all over the front of the building. Two men came forward with Molotov cocktails. He took them out and reverently lit them in turn, handing them out to eager hands.

Their ends flared.

He grinned lopsidedly.

"Sautéed nig-nog anyone?"

******

"If yuh want my opinion, someting is just not right." Chief Cudjoe flexed the muscles of his mouth like a goldfish.

He said nothing more and peered at Trevor through the wafer screen.

The younger Rasta man sat cross legged on the course brown material of his kaya mat, his thoughts a dirty pool of confusing mind pictures. At his back was the open window of his apartment, with its curtains fluttering in the mild breeze. Trevor breathed evenly hoping to find some rhythm that would help him to relax as he tried to put some of the pieces together in this five dimensional puzzle.

"Are yuh keeping a watch on developments?" Trevor asked.

"Watching an planning, son." The old man answered, leaning forward like he was trapped in the confines of the monitor.

It was always a weird sensation as the Jamaican countryside was digitally thrown into his lounge.

Bush on one side and concrete on the other, all separated by thousands of miles.

Throw-weh district was right on the fringes of the Cockpit country five miles from Accompong. It was a one public phone type of town and consisted mainly of Maroons, fore bearers of the original African freedom fighters who fought the Ttyranny of English colonialist. But over the years it became one of the many communities formed on the island that had welcomed the way of life that Ras Tafari offered. Trevor was born here, grew up, took on the Lion's mane from his parents and became an independent man, right there. He knew the people intimately and could imagine not just their shock when the Nation decided to establish an office in their district but their amusement.

The Nation only showed its interest or presence in this back water town, when it came to purchase its crops, three times a year. Chief Cudjoe was not taken in by their well-sounding platitudes and told Trevor in no uncertain terms. The old goat was a man of his own heart. He trusted no one, maybe that's why he wanted Trevor as his successor.

The elder cleared his throat as if preparing his speech.

"Them ah survey deep inside the hills. Say dem looking more land to plant and build on. And they are asking questions, nuff unnecessary questions." His voice sounded like a corn husk on a grater. "Deh Nation decide to set up office so them can have a man on the spot at all times, overseeing tings. More like having people to spy on we. You have people from deh Ministry of Agriculture, yuh have engineers from South Africa, yuh have man from Public Works. Yuh nuh ask the people what they want, them just say, is for the good of the district. Most of the community give thanks, them can't read between the lines but me..." He shook his bedraggled head. "...Me, uneasy. Dem a play fool feh catch wise, son. That's why I have all Jah damn one a dem watched."

"Play fool feh catch wise," Trevor grabbed on to his wondering mind. "Elder, just make sure the Dread, knows about dem movements. Mek sure him understan what is happening and let him guide yuh. We will talk."

The old man nodded.

He sprang up from his sitting position, the ole time saying sparking something in him as he glared at the files on the monitor.

So many question marks. Now, conveniently in his absence, they were invading his district. Patriarch Yamu was preparing for his uncontested ordination as Negusa Negas. They were in Thro-Weh District for a reason. The furrows in his forehead deepened. He just couldn't say for certain what that reason was. Again he had to work in the darkness, have faith and be guided by the Dread and his gift. Even the files in the dead man's PDA posed more questions than answers. The words from the dead Spear man haunted him: Dis conspiracy yah run through deh entire Nation an dis proves it.

There was something he had missed, something amongst all this data that had eluded him. A connection that would link all these seemingly unrelated facts and would point a finger to Yamu. It was there, hidden, he was sure, he just needed to pay more attention.

"Play Video file AX1." Trevor ordered.

The dead man's legacy, flickered on the screen. Images and sounds of men in military style training filled his room. Shooting ranges, hand to hand combat training, obstacle courses, ordinance training and more. The veiled man addressing the congregation of killers. The one with the distinctive gold ring shaped like the sacred ganja leaf.

A man sly enough to scramble his voice signature, so he couldn't be matched.

******

The sound of running water woke him.

Asim rose from his prone position on the bed, an invisible shroud of pain clung to him like a suit of clothing. As he moved, he could feel the mounds of swellings all over him. He fell back onto the pillars his muscles tense and his eyes unfocused, as they roamed in the dimness. He tried to lift himself by placing his weight on his arm but collapsed back into the softness of his bed.

His shoulder was on fire.

He only relaxed when he realised, he was in his bedroom. The pictures of his recent shave with death formed slowly in his head.

How the raas, did he get up here? He lifted the sheets. They were spotted with blood from his gashes. Clean and naked too? He thought. Could he have really been in a fit state to take a fresh after the punishment he had just taken?

He didn't think so.

The running water in his bathroom seemed to say something else.

The bastards had blown up the building, he remembered. He also remembered being submerged in cold water swimming for his life, upriver, as gunshots fired around him. What happened after that was a blank.

The recollections caused every scratch and bruise on his body to light up like beacons of pain, making him simply lay back groaning for a moment, not caring how or why.

He lifted himself off the propped up pillows again and was about to painfully pull himself out of the bed, when he saw a breathtaking outline step out of the bathroom, fully clothed.

"Princess!" He croaked.

Shit!

Now he remembered he was supposed to have met Yasmeen here and realised who had improved his sorry assed state.

She swayed over to him.

Christ, this gal was beautiful, in that light or any other light for that matter.

He breathed deeply as if her scent would help the pain he was feeling. She sat on the bed beside him and planted a kiss on his forehead.

Her lips were unbelievably warm.

"How are you feeling?" Her voice was a whisper.

"After seeing you, babe, I'm getting better, much better." He grinned, looking under the sheets at his nakedness. "I'm just vexed that you didn't wake me up when you were sponging me down."

She shook her head. Even in his weakened state he was a charmer, or was that bull-shitter? Yasmeen traced her finger along his jaw line then playfully slapped him.

"This is not funny, Asim." Her voice raised an octave. "You scared me half to death. Seeing you lying there asleep in front of the door, bloodied, your clothes wet and torn, I thought you were badly hurt..." She swallowed nervously and glared at him, shaking slightly. "Never do that again, you hear me? Never."

"It won't happen again, princess. I promise."

"Good," she said. "I called the hospital as a precaution anyway and they're sending over an ambulance for you."

"Nuh need for that babe, I'm fi..." Her fingers were covering his mouth before he could finish.

"Don't bother. It's already done, you're going to be checked out." She pursed her lips. "What happened to you tonight?" She demanded, her lips curled in annoyance.

Asim smiled weakly, his fingers stroking the strands of her hair.

He manoeuvred but she was having none of it.

"You haven't answered my question yet." She said calmly.

"Because it's nothing, trust mi." He grimaced as the twinges in his back also joined in with the symphony of pain he was already forced to experience.

"Asim!"

"Okay, okay just relax, princess, I'll explain."

Just enough to stop you asking any more questions.

He circled her waist with his arms pulling her closer to him on the bed and explained how his scheduled war games with his mates had got a bit competitive.

"How can ten grown men trying to shoot each other with paint balls, in a broken down industrial estate and then nearly bleeding to death be considered as fun?"

"Boys will be boys, baby. And I couldn't let them win with my army rep. No way."

She nodded but even with his gentle kisses to her neck, her instincts were saying he was lying. For a man who seemed to have a more regimental approach to his time a spur of the moment romp with his mates did not fit in with his personality.

He was hiding something and Fatima was the reason, she knew it.

"You are telling me the truth, aren't you?" She turned to face him, probing for his reaction, focusing her eyes into his. Asim realised he would lose this confrontation of wills. He purposely interrupted her steady gaze by taking her hands and kissing her palms, his answer directed to the cotton covers.

"Would I lie to you?" The tone of his voice noticeable lowered.

To protect me from whatever you're doing, of course you would, she thought.

He moaned again and stretched out on her lap.

"Princess."

"Yes."

"I know you're worried about me, but don't be, mi safe."

He squeezed her waist, his voice drifted and Yasmeen felt his body go progressively limp. He was fast asleep.

******

"You couldn't have chosen a more appropriate place for us both to die." Ricardo stated matter-of-factly, allowing the Mercedes autopilot to manoeuvre them into the beer garden. The thoughtful nod of Asim's head in the seat beside him, hid his sense of shared apprehension.

If you didn't know the history of this place it would seem to be a normal enough neighbourhood. The streets were painfully clean, the houses middle class and more hoverjeeps were parked in driveways than was normal for an area like this. But there was nothing normal about Rushlands.

He had never seen so many checkpoints, Neighbourhood Watch Pods and CCTV cameras in any one network of streets in his life. Luckily for them the pub was situated outside of the residential area and so the security presence was less intense.

Asim looked around and shook his head.

"Yuh think I want to be here when I could be chillin at home? Believe me, Ric, this is the last place I want to be. But for what I've got to say and how I want to say it, I'm bound to be here."

The Mercedes parked itself while Ricardo folded his arms over his chest defensively and watched it with new found interest.

"I hope the risk is worth it."

Asim nodded.

The danger involved in what they were planning to do came into sharp perspective and with it the infamous history of the locale. The whole framework of race relations in London changed right here.

Ricardo remembered his outrage, when the news was made public three years ago.

The Apartheid Communities the electronic papers plastered all over their front pages. And so began a media frenzy the likes of which he had not seen since eco-terrorists tried to contaminate the London water supply. The information leaked to Fleet Street from an unknown source implicated members of a far-right group within the Progressive Party. Their actions had remained secret for some years until they felt the need to cease theorising and implement plans that would improve the country's flagging fortunes. Six experimental neighbourhoods were created around the United Kingdom, that as a policy barred ethnic minorities and people below a certain financial level. To add insult to injury, the project had been partially financed by a billionaire separatist rumoured to be a member of the Broeder ruling body.

Riots broke out across the country and anti-government sentiment ran high. What stood out was seeing the disgraced MPs telling the country, with pompous airs as if they were some type of pioneers the reasons for the social experiments. And their high expectations that the taxpayers would judge their models on the results not the methods.

And the people did express their feelings.

Raised to the ground or abandoned due to intimidation, only two of these prototype communities remained. One was a self contained fortress in the midlands, the other was the Rushland Manor and they were parked in the heart of it.

The urge to put a flame to the quaint white houses and the obscenely neat and manicured lawns, was strong.

Ricardo looked over to his partner and sighed.

"If you don't feel comfortable with this." His voice boomed hollowly, "Now's your chance to say, because when you step out the car there's no turning back."

Asim nodded, still looking outside.

"I know." He said.

Ricardo twisted in his seat uncomfortably.

"Well, if you have made your decision, let's make sure we stick to the plan. I'm here to support you, remember that. If there's any signs of a situation developing that you cannot handle, use your transmitter to alert me. And, brother, deliver your message as quickly and clearly as you can and leave. No theatrics and, most importantly, no violence."

"It's covered, man." Asim said, smiling grimly.

And with that Ricardo repeated the code for his car radio which he switched on and automatically tuned into BBC 1Xtra digital frequency.

"Test!" Ricardo said.

Asim responded by pressing a small transmitter attached to his belt and the corresponding high pitch screech bled into the channel's transmission.

"Good." Ricardo replied.

They synchronised watches.

"Fifteen minutes max." Asim said, twisting his cap backwards.

"Max." Ricardo replied just as Asim disappeared out of the car.

As he pushed his way through the old fashioned saloon swing doors, the scene that met him was reminiscent of how the traditional English pub used to be. The smell of stale beer, the tacky tunes from fruit machines, the boisterous laughter and the bartenders welcoming, 'What will it be mate?' Forming that cozy atmosphere of your local.

His wake up call to harsh reality was as shattering as a brick through a plate glass window. But expected. A silent wave of shock and incredulity washed over the punters as Asim headed for the bar, it seemed as if the eyes of the entire pub followed him. While his situational awareness was sharp and any movement out of the ordinary would spark action, his attention was focused on the layout of the interior. Closed circuit television was set at all four corners sweeping the entire floor plan with the bar situated centrally. Well-worn seating skirted the perimeter in small intimate cubicles, one in particular caught his attention.

Plan B.

Drinkers gagged on their brown ales.

It was one of the most intense walks he'd ever had to take. Walking wilfully into an ambush and knowing you were firmly between the cross hairs of a sniper's rifle came close. He somehow preferred the certainty of that threat than the uncertainty of this situation. The stakes mounted to a level he could appreciate when he reached the counter.

He leaned on the bar and was met by a head shake and sardonic grin. The grizzly bar man came over, the rest of the staff at a respectable scowling distance. Asim looked deep into his facial hair, screwed and ordered a ginger beer on the rocks.

Moments later, as expected, he was told to 'fuck off'.

******

"Your car." He stabbed at the glass with his fingers. "Move your fucking car!"

The man's hard knuckles rapped repeatedly on the driver's side while he tried to look into the parked car for some activity. The man in his late forties, who was dressed like a twenty-year-old - with more gold around his neck than a prospector - obviously hated being ignored.

The Mercedes had responded to his approach with the photo chromatic glass darkening. He just couldn't understand what else the words 'staff parking' could mean and had stood watching the cunt reverse into his space without a care in the world.

He swore some more.

By this he was adamant he was going to make an example of the pillock parked comfortably in his space. He paused, realising his ranting was pointless. And with a stylish swing of his head, he looked over to where he had left his Jaguar, doors open, engine idling and thought of something very naughty.

Ricardo could see him clearly. The man had put his face inches away from the windshield and every word he screamed left condensation marks that quickly evaporated. At first Ricardo had thought it was funny and didn't bother to turn on the external speakers to hear what he was saying, instead he tried to lip read. The trickles of verbal abuse he understood changed his opinions on the man's intent. He now wanted to shut him up as he continued to rant but no subtle method came to mind. Frowning Ricardo tried to ignore him by turning up the music and closing his eyes but the man continued to rave.

A few moment's silence later.

Ricardo opened his eyes again to see what he was up to, he realised the man had stormed off. He slumped back into his seat relieved.

It was short lived.

The man returned and this time he was swinging a rusting crowbar.

Damn! Ricardo swore. He thought of his paint work, his health and then something snapped.

Ricardo reached inside his glove compartment and carefully placed his shades over his eyes. Closing the compartment slowly he stepped out of the unit. Suddenly his motor seemed too small for him, as he stood a towering six feet three inches of Ray Ban'd malevolence. He made a three hundred and sixty degrees sweep with his eyes and was content he was not seen.

The streams of abuse stopped abruptly and so did the wild posturing. The man stepped away from the shadow cast by the African's height. His facial expressions shot through every variation of shock the human repertoire had at its disposal.

Smiling falsely, Ricardo seemed to calm the man's apprehensions for a fraction of a second.

The distraction gave him enough time to walk over and clamp his five fingers over the hand still holding the crow bar.

Overcoming his initial shock, Jack-the-lad then crazily decided to put up a struggle. Ricardo growled his frustration, easily twisting the bar from his hand and allowing it to fall to the ground with a hollow clank. They eyed each other for seconds, the man's lower lip quivering the last morsel of machismo gone and the inevitable about to happen. Dragged towards him with his massive hands, Ricardo slammed his huge fist flush to his jaw. There was a dull whack that sounded even more painful the second time around. Ricardo then caught the limp body before it hit the ground and bungled it like a jointed mannequin into the back of the car. He quickly looked around to see if the fracas had been witnessed by anybody else. Satisfied it was all clear, he got back behind the wheel, reverently took his Ray Bans off, closed the door and waited.

******

"We don't serve your kind around here, mate." The bar man leaned over his counter and said it without a hint of animosity. He was simply stating the facts. "Look around you, sunshine, you're the only nigger here." He grinned amiably. "I know you must have taken a wrong turning. So listen carefully. This is Rushlands, mate, you want Brixton - it's that way." He pointed his fleshy pink fingers to the door.

Asim ignored his good advice. "Fair enough." He said and backed up. Nothing he didn't expect.

The stares remained intense and the murmurs would soon become vocal protests then who could tell what course of action some hothead would try. Nodding to himself, he thought that is exactly what he wanted.

Asim reversed into the vacant seat just behind him. On the edge of his vision he could see some men standing up from their pints and heading over to where he had been, their eyes never leaving him. Asim could feel plan B becoming more of a certainty. He snuggled his back into the cracked leather and complimented himself on an excellent choice of position. He could see what was happening in front of him and on both sides clearly. His back was against the brickwork, so that was covered. He waited, aggravating the drinkers even further as he reached for a hip flask and took a swig from it, smiling.

The kind of smile a man gave when he was certain. Certain he knew something they didn't.

"Why are you doing this?

The question had come from a woman who had approached him. Asim had seen her coming, reckoned she was no threat but did not think she was going to talk to him amidst the tension. She was a very elegant looking woman, tanned, blonde, middle aged and definitely out of place in an establishment like this. He did not answer her as it felt somewhat rhetorical and watched her swirling what could have been a gin and tonic in her hands, moving closer to his table, her grey eyes warm.

"I'd leave before they hurt you."

Asim looked at her quizzically.

"We're not all alike, you know." Her voice was refined silky smooth. "Go, please." She said softly.

"Thanks for the thought." Asim said. "But I'll be cool."

She shook her head in defeat and walked away.

That was the cue for the likely lads who had congregated around the bar to approach him. Now finally he had someone's attention.

The five men came up to what must have been, three paces away from his table, the criss-cross pattern of their shadows failing to intimidate him. The spokesman, barrel chested, bristled haired and resembling an Action man doll, started what sounded like a threat he had prepared earlier.

"Are you deaf, dumb and fucking stupid, nigger? This is a European gaff and we're proud of that. Arnold gave you a chance to leave peacefully. Me, I want to break your bleeding neck."

"When I'm ready, you can try." Asim said cooly.

"I don't give a fuck about you, wanker." He burst out. "You're having a laugh, right?"

A few punters hearing the outburst quickly finished their pints and left. A medium built man, wearing a Ben Sherman shirt, arrogantly stepped out of the group's comfort zone and then dearly wished he hadn't.

Asim sprang forward and viciously slapped Ben Sherman across the jaw twice in a blur of knuckles and fingers. So swift was the attack, the sluggish message from the victim's brain to his legs hadn't reached in time before Asim grabbed him by the neck, dragged him backwards and slammed his head down on the table. It bounced back up with a sharp whack and with it an idea, as Asim sighted the glinting crescent in his ear.

He went with the flow.

Threading the index finger of one hand into the man's earring and with the other hand grabbing a fistfull of coarse black hair, Asim pulled.

The man screamed as the twin pains of the ring tearing into the flesh of his earlobe and the hairs of his head being ripped out of the roots, made his senses explode.

Calmly, Asim sat down with his newly-acquired charge, once or twice yanking the ring for obedience, each tug cutting a bloody trail closer to tearing his lobe in half. He swore and whimpered but Asim ignored him, keeping his face squashed to the table.

One of the likely lads slung out a shock baton from under his coat and made a move. But Asim had already released his grip on Ben Sherman's hair and with his free hand took out the Equaliser from his jacket, slamming it down in front of him.

The men stopped like a pile-up on the M97.

"Yes, gentlemen, it is strange looking but real, trust mi. It's also licensed, loaded and equipped with state-of-the-art sound suppressing technology, just so we don't frighten off the punters."

They looked at the gun and then back at him. Their eyes seemed to be saying their worst nightmare had just materialised before them.

Asim's smirk widened then he laughed in their faces.

"Don't tell me, I know what yuh thinking?" He teased. "You're saying can this black bwoy be for real? And if he is, has he got the balls, the will or even the skill to take down a few of us before we bum rush him, right? Well..."

The Equaliser hummed as Asim expertly charged the weapon, chambered a plasma round and pointed its dangerous end in the direction of the likely lads.

"... That question has no simple answer. You'll just have to try me an si."

No one moved.

"Phhuck yoooth."

Asim looked down at the only man who was showing some degree of fight and he was still under the heel of his hand, his face pressed to the table. Sighing, he pushed the gun's barrel into his mouth, forcing it. Ben Sherman's defiance immediately became pleas for mercy.

He now had their undivided attention.

"Wicked," Asim said. "We have an understanding at last. I'll make this short 'n' sweet and I won't repeat myself. Tell Reggie Thorndike that I've got a score to settle with him."

The passenger door of the Mercedes flew open and Asim's grim features darkened the interior.

He slid in and Ricardo looked him up and down as if checking for damage.

"Mission accomplished."

Asim nodded his head, the Ghanaian relaxed somewhat.

"No casualties."

"None." Asim grunted almost regretfully. "Who's that?"

He casually jerked his thumb to the figure lying on the back seat.

"Oh him," Ricardo said with a tone of unconcern. "That gentleman wanted to get into his parking space."

Asim peered over at the man's light breathing and bloody nose.

"Was that all?"

"He didn't say, 'please'." Ricardo started the engine.

"Raas!" Asim said, laughing.

The Mercedes pulled away in haste.

******

Obviously something heavy had just gone down.

Yasmeen was dropped off by an evil looking Rasta man in a darkened Isuzu Jeep. Another younger Dread walked her over the pavement and into the coffee shop.

They sat parked near the kerb.

Asim had been waiting no more than ten minutes having travelled across town leaving some pressing communications at Zulu Securities to be dealt with.

This was much more important.

They sat in a busy cafe on Kensington High Street, only able to partially see through the plate glass window covered in foam. From one side to the next a Cleanbot was briskly slurping its way through the bubbles leaving a trail of gleaming window behind it.

Asim was ordering, another black coffee while Yasmeen sat, her attention had just left the window and was now concentrated into the depth of her herbal tea.

The message had been one laced with panic, Asim recalled, now Yasmeen seemed calm.

She stirred the contents of her herbal tea once and nervously stirred it again.

The slurping of coffee and the clink of cutlery made Yasmeen look up, Asim sat and turned in his seat to face her.

She spoke before he could voice his concern.

"Someone shot the building's concierge last night and broke into my flat." She said cooly. "I'm really scared, Asim." He wondered why her cry for help sounded like being scared was some sort of weakness.

Asim's eyelids shuttered as he lay the palms of his hands flat on the table.

"What!"

His fingers closed like a spring trap, crunching the table cloth together.

"Yuh all right." His hand reached out to touch hers.

"I'm fine." She said. "I came home to find the place overrun by Met-1, my place ransacked, my walls daubed in red paint. Threats or messages, I don't know which. Quoted from the Bible, the book of Apocalypse, everywhere."

At that instant Asim's mind started to backtrack rapidly. Baldwin had confessed, "Your sister was a message to someone else, boss. It wasn't personal."

Someone else, Asim thought.

Yasmeen?

Jesas Christ!

She was the target.

The connection was made with such force and sense of

certainty, his chair rocked back nearly toppling him over. His mental processes went into warp drive. He stood up, paced outside turned and walked back in again.

A message being sent by whom and why?

Yasmeen eyed him curiously. He didn't sit, he just looked at her.

"I'm sorry, babe," he reached over to touch her hand, again. "But this is some serious shit."

"Don't you think I know that." She said softly.

"What did Met-1 think?"

She shrugged.

"What they think, doesn't matter. Whoever these people are they want me dead."

Asim couldn't shake the feeling Yasmeen knew more than she was saying.

That would make two of them.

"Anyway, I'm staying by my friend for the time being just until I can secure the flat and the Met have finished their investigations."

"You're staying with me." Asim said flatly.

She smiled.

"I couldn't, it just wouldn't be... proper."

"Fuck propa. You are in serious danger. Tell your friend 'thanks but no thanks'. We'll collect your things tomorrow and you're staying by me."

"Asim, I can't..." She protested.

"No arguments, Yasmeen man." He growled. "I have the space, if you find it impossible to live too close to a baalhead. We won't have to meet, the house is big enough."

"Stop it Asim, you know it's not like that..."

"My place set up like a bunker, it won't be so easy to breach." He paused as if he wanted to grab onto his wondering train of thought. "Let people think what the fuck they want. I don't give a shit. If they haven't sussed how I feel about you by now. This will open their eyes."

Yasmeen saw the tautness of the muscles of his face, a tick of nerves spread across an eyebrow.

"No more reasons why you can't. Just trust mi."

******

What could Yasmeen have done to attract such unwanted attention?

Her personal files revealed nothing new. Most of Yasmeen's life in England had been ordinary and uneventful up to this point. So the question that begged to be asked was what had happened in Ethiopia. What had happened to make a country girl-Yasmeen's mother - leave the land of her birth with a young baby, to a foreign land?

What was so important that men, half a world away would want her offspring dead? Who was the cause of this and if it wasn't her mother, who else was there?

Yasmeen would be kept in the dark until he knew more. In the mean time he had to keep her safe, without drawing too much attention to what he was doing.

Living with Yasmeen had been the most pleasurable time he'd had for years. She was everything he could hope for.

Stop beating around the bush bwoy, and Just call it what it is. Love.

It was a daily revelation of how special a woman she was. Now he understood why the Rasta man saw their women as queens. Yasmeen was a fiercely independent woman, yet still she'd cook for him and pamper him. Asim had protested that she didn't have to do that but she went ahead anyway.

"Why shouldn't I?" Yasmeen had said. "I like pampering you."

All of this came to him as he lay in the aromatic hot water. Yasmeen sleeping soundly in his bed and him secretly yearning for her, wondering how long he could control the fire burning inside.

The thought of how he would deal with being at such close quarters to her had not crossed his mind. An exercise in self-control.

There was one consolation from the emotional punishment he was facing and that was he had realised something very important, indeed.

He wanted her, badly.

******

The next day was his birthday. Birthdays had never been a big deal for him, the passing of time, that was all and if he was drunk enough, he'd consider the merits of having thirty-four years of experience behind him. The less fuss was made about it the better in his mind.

Sometimes it took something as mundane, as a birthday to make you realise your blessings. It seemed he had been counting so many of them lately. The day ended well and that made him even more eager to relax. It was funny how the warehouse had suddenly filled with warmth and was more appealing - no disrespect to House.

The reason was obvious.

His Porsche pulled up into his garage and parked beside Yasmeen's Mercedes. He ascended the spiral stairs up to the main porch, the glass partition slid open letting him in.

House did not greet him, unusually. His apprehension remaining, his senses switched to warrior mode.

"Yasmeen!" He called out uncertainly, his eyes checking out the place. Everything seemed in order.

She called out to him.

His shoulders slumped with the relief.

"I'm in here."

Slowly, he walked through the open bedroom door.

Asim stood there stunned into silence.

His once familiar room had now been transformed into what could have easily been some bedouin tent in the deserts of the Emirates. Silks were draped from the ceiling and walls, the bed was brimming full of pillows, aromatic candles surrounded the base, providing the only light in the otherwise dark room. But the surreal picture was completed by something even more beautiful to behold.

Maaan! He was certain his heart had stopped beating.

Yasmeen was laying across the bed, her hair loose around her face, stretched out like some exotic wild animal.

"Jesas!" Asim whispered. Except for being wrapped in a gossamer thin fabric she was naked. His manhood threatened to free itself from the constraints of his trousers. What he had imagined was nothing like this.

"Happy birthday." She said, her voice silky and her hands stretched towards him.

Asim stepped closer and took it, hugging her close. They kissed deeply, her breasts taut against his chest and his tongue searching out hers desperately. Wanting to feel more, to explore her more, he hesitantly broke from the kiss and trailed his tongue down to her chest until his lips were on the silken material. The shadowy haze of her breasts was too inviting and his mouth took to her stiff nipples in turn leaving glistening smears of saliva over the area. She shuddered and the loosely draped material fell around her ankles.

His eyes drank in her beauty, hungrily.

Sweet and sensual like warmed dark chocolate on an awaiting tongue.

Smooth dark skin shone as the candlelight flickered from his movements. Wide-eyed he stared at her large breasts and nipples, like a fruit he had been forbidden to taste until now. Her hips curved seamlessly into beautifully toned thighs which framed her dark pubic mound that was glistening from her excitement. He went to his knees, wrapped his arms around her waist and kissed her stomach. His nails traced a path along her buttocks and, as his fingers gently spread them apart, the heat and her moistness surprised him. Asim's tongue continued to explore, he reached her pierced navel, his tongue pulling on the gold ring, and then he probed lower. She shuddered, the moans leaving her lips out of her control.

"I'm yours if you want me."

He wanted to laugh out and shout out 'of course I want yuh', but instead he swept her up into his arms and gently placed her into the centre of the bed. She unbuttoned his shirt, letting it fall to one side, undid his jeans and he took over, sliding them down and off.

Yasmeen spread her legs, throwing her head back propped comfortably by her own hands, her swollen labia glistening with her juices, inviting him in. He reached into his G-string, his fingers not quite able to surround his swollen member, and started to tease it into her. The bulbous head of his gland purposely stimulating her clitoris and the lips of her vagina. Nudging forward but never sinking in too deeply. She grabbed him, searching for his mouth, wanting him inside her but he persisted to tease. She whispered something he did not understand, Amharic maybe, as she nibbled on his ear and continued to excite him with her hot breath and gasps. Then without warning he sank his cock deep into her. She shrieked out his name, hugging him tightly.

"Again," she pleaded. "But deeper this time, deeeeeper."

He complied, but not for long.

Interrupting a woman's climax as she reached her peak drove some women mad and others simply wild. Yasmeen was definitely in the latter group.

Kneeling, she waved him on the bed behind her. As he did so, she moved onto all fours and with her delectable backside facing him, he stretched over her back.

He started kissing from her backside to her neck, every feathery caress causing a response like hot brands along her spine. Yasmeen's mind was a haze of sexual excitement.

His weight on her back was reassuring as his hands cupped her breasts and continued to nibble at the back of her neck. Asim's nose flared with his harsh breathing, sucking in the fresh aroma from her hair.

"You excite me." He whispered hoarsely in her ear. She twisted her neck around the distant smile remained and their lips met again. This time he sucked tenderly on her lips and for long moments their tongues breathlessly battled for supremacy.

Yasmeen took control. She reached behind her, fingers grasping his seed and massaging them. Asim let out a gasp. The pads of her fingers gently moved along the length of his member, squeezing in places and then softly prodding the swollen glands of his penis. He did not think it could become more erect but it did. Ignoring Asim's groaning she started guiding his manhood into her. Moistening the tip with high strokes on her slick centre, she then placed it in herself, its thickness spreading her wide open.

It was her time to gasp. She arched her back like a cat, Asim's left hand was massaging her smooth flat stomach and his right hand on her shoulder as he slowly eased into her. The sensuousness of her tight core was incredible. His strokes were becoming more urgent, his penis evoking sensations she had thought forgotten. The tempo of thrusting rose a notch as did the slurping sound of his brisk entry. His own control he knew was on the verge of collapse at any moment and he didn't care.

She collapsed on her stomach, keeping her bottom raised. Asim kept hammering into her pleasure centre.

Yasmeen was meeting his strokes with expert flicks of her hips. Gritting his teeth, the hand he used to brace himself with, slid over her perspiring shoulder. She stretched forward her fingers gripping the sheets, clawing at them.

He continued to slide in and out of her.

Her spasm came from the tip of her toes and started to vibrate up her legs but she was not quite there.

He held on.

Her shuddering became more violent.

"Kabir la amlak!" She screamed, her body tensing as if a surge of electricity had shot through her. Slowly relaxing, Yasmeen held him inside her, Ahi movements continuing to make her tingle.

He abandoned all control.

Asim's explosion came mere seconds after that, with a loud drawling grunt of satisfaction.

Moments later they lay silently in the stillness, the tide of sensations ebbing pleasantly away. They were so close together as if they wanted to merge, sweat dripping off their bodies and both on a high no mind stimulating-machine could ever induce.

This was much more than physical. And they both knew it.

AUGUST 17, THE DAY OF ASCENSION AND THE BIRTHDAY OF THE PROPHET MARCUS MOSIAH GARVEY

Asim eyed the digital numbers flashing weakly on his timepiece.

"One twenty-two. Plenty time." He decided.

Looking out from the parking space on Hume Street, he watched the smooth droning of the cars as the volume of the traffic slowly increased and with it the cloying smells of the cars low-emission fuels.

Putting his hand in his pockets, he walked through the enclosures automated barricades and jogged over the zebra crossing into a blurry haze of cool shadow thrown by a lone oak tree. Turning right up Charles Street and flanked on both sides by office buildings that seemed like they had been sculpted from gigantic glaciers. He made his way against the flow of scatty brained pedestrians and office types, vying for the walkway and cannoning their way through slouches like him, not as obsessed with time as they were.

He reached for his shades.

"Shit!"

His fingers immediately recognised the absence of his Equaliser under his arm.

Old habits die hard. Even when locking it away had been a conscious decision, it had become second nature to him. The Baldwin affair had rekindled dangerous instincts that he had acted on but at the same time he needed to keep things in perspective. This was a day out with kids, in the safe confines of the Museum of Ancient African History.

Zygote had profiled her as best he could, from sources he had dug up from Ethiopia and at home. There were no secrets, nothing about her that would warrant intimidation or murder.

He hoped his threat to Reggie Thorndike would do the trick.

But if that didn't, it was all just a matter of time. They would get closer, covering their trail, readying themselves for the kill and he would be there, waiting.

For now he had to maintain the pretence of normalcy and what could be more normal than this. It was a great excuse to be with her and keep her under close scrutiny at the same time.

Or more to the point, he was watching over Yasmeen, Akilla and ten other kids from Haile Selassie Saturday School. Not exactly what Asim would have planned but as much as he wanted her to himself, he was willing to share her for the day. A very special day in Ras Tafari history, he was told and this was her treat to the children. On the eve of the ordination of their first world leader, the symbolic high priest, Negusa Negas. Yasmeen had arranged this for the children as her small offering to the worldwide celebration of Ascension - The election of Negusa Negas.

He saw Yasmeen on a balcony just to his right in deep discussion with the redheaded Rasta man he was introduced to at Finsbury Park. He smiled at his sense of dress. It reminded him of his old jungle warfare instructor in Malaysia.

He let his attention drift elsewhere and allowed his security consultant mould to slide into place, just for the hell of it.

Asim shook his head, dismally.

Security arrangements for the exhibits was a total fuck-up.

The more expensive pieces were protected by shatterproof glass casing and the lesser valuables surrounded by sonic nets.

That was passable.

The larger displays though, were rigged with ancient devices that seemed to have come with the building three hundred years ago. Then there was the human element.

He hadn't witnessed one security guard patrolling his immediate area since he entered. Where were they?

A Zulu Securities consultation officer would call them in the morning, they needed help.

He made a mental note and then thought of something

devious.

"Praises," Trevor said, his brows furrowed. "Well today is the day."

Yasmeen nodded, her smile was forced almost painful.

Trevor shook his locks and held her with his stare. "I need to explain a few tings to you, sista..."

His words were lost, because just as he started speaking she felt a gentle kiss on her neck and strong arms wrap around her waist. She wondered how she hadn't heard him approach.

"You're too tense," Asim said grinning broadly. "Relax nuh."

Trevor stood forward from his leaning position on the rails.

"You remember brother Ras Trevor, from the concert." She nodded in Trevor's direction. "My... *friend*, Asim."

"Light and levity." Asim parroted one of Yasmeen's many greetings.

"One blood, rude bwoy!" Trevor responded, his eyebrow raised and head bowed slightly as he clasped hands with the baalhead. Both men's grips were strong and uncompromising and they both came to the same immediate conclusions about each other.

Warriors!

"You were about to tell me something, Trevor."

"Not important, sista." He said quickly.

I man won't leave you an inch.

"Are you sure, it seemed urgent."

"It all right." He said, showing a half-formed smile. "I will wonder around the place, learn some new tricks."

I man will be in deh background a watch an a wait.

"We can reason, later."

"Don't leave because a me, boss." Asim placed his hand on Trevor's shoulder. "Just relax. You might learn the fine art of keeping a herd a pickney under control."

Yasmeen planted her elbow in his side and said, "Why not?"

The Rasta man thought about it for only a moment.
Better business.

"All right then, sista Yasmeen, so what you have planned?"

Yasmeen locked arms with both men.

"Ask no questions, gentlemen, just follow me."

******

Trevor stood enthralled by an augmented reality image of His Imperial Majesty Haile Selassie I. Ras Tafari himself, dressed in his royal finery and seated on his throne breathed steadily, the merest smile on his lips while looking out to an imaginary court. The illusion of life couldn't be more compelling.

"King of kings." Trevor murmured.

And as if he was confirming his words, the lights dimmed.

The children in a boisterous mood paid little attention. The Rasta man wasn't concerned either as he was delighted by the exhibits.

Asim would have done the same, if he hadn't followed Trevor's lead and broken from the group. Leaving Yasmeen, the class teacher and the kids to continue their adventure, unburdened by his adult questions. He was in the Ethiopian brush land watching the animatronic desert creatures when he heard the exclamation of 'fuck me!' and the stifled conversation of panic. A guard who had been stationed to his right for the last thirty minutes, near a flight of wrought iron stairs, was leaning threateningly over it, with the mobile in his hands and forcing his words into it, as if it had caused him offence.

That was a minute ago.

Realising his voice was rising beyond normal conversation and being carried in the subdued silence, he nervously looked around. Asim's eyes met with his. The guard smiled weakly, struggling to wipe the expression of terror off his face. Failing he dashed into the adjoining chamber.

Asim leaned off the post.

By then Yasmeen and the children had moved further away

from where he had left them, their high-pitched voices raised in laughter as someone poked fun at one of the historical figures.

Another guard from the other side of the hall disappeared too.

Asim's gaze met Trevor's. They regarded each other tensely from opposite sides of the hall.

Asim looked around and tried to dispel his discomfort. But something was on the fringes of his awareness which was making him nervous. What was it? His eyes slowly ran up the walls to the ceiling. There.

The background hum had stopped. Overhead the roving surveillance cameras that scurried about on the ceiling observing the patrons movements, had all frozen in place.

Malfunction? Maybe.

No such thing as coincidences, he reminded himself.

He drew his eyes away from the ceiling and quickly peered over to his daughter laughing amongst the other children. Yasmeen turned and waved.

The serene picture jolted him into action. Alarm bells in his head were going crazy. Surveillance dead, the electrics shorting, rent-a-cops panicking. His intuition was a six-sense not to be fucked with and he had learned the hard way to trust it with his life.

Asim was walking over to the children before he even knew what his plan of action would be, only knowing he had to be closer to them as he viewed the exits and entrances expectantly.

Trevor stayed put. This was much more than paranoia. The children listened to a story being told. Taking up position behind them, Asim mustered as much cheerfulness as he could and interrupted Yasmeen in mid-sentence.

"Guess what?" He piped. "I've got something I want you kids to see. You're not going to believe dis."

Yasmeen shot him a confused stare and shrugged in the children's direction. Luckily Akilla and her over-excited friends swayed the decision, demanding to know what was this surprise that couldn't wait.

With no idea what he was going to do or say, he led the way.

His only concern was wanting the children to be as close to an emergency exit as possible without frightening them. After all, he had been wrong before.

He hoped this was one of those few times.

Herding the group into the far corner of the building, Yasmeen protesting, he finally bungled everyone beside a set of emergency doors. Then he stood there. His mind. Went. Blank.

Yasmeen cleared her throat, impatiently.

Bare seconds from that point, her mobile started to bleep.

Asim's disquiet amplified ten fold.

Shaking her head and thinking what next, Yasmeen walked away from the protests of the children. Unclipping it from her jacket, she slipped it onto her ear and pulled the telescopic mike to her lips.

"Yes."

"We have a Priority red situation, Miss." A frantic voice screamed at her. "Casualties on two levels," his voice hissed from interference. "Priority red...!" The line buzzed and died with a stream of sharp electrical crackles.

The lights dimmed in slow pulses.

Yasmeen looked up and made some quick adjustments to the frequency and tried again.

The emergency lines were all dead.

Frowning, she looked over to Asim huddled with the children protectively. He was desperately calling her over. What was going on?

Her frown deepened. Then thirty pounds of plastic explosives detonated in the adjoining room, demolishing the separating wall in a flash and propelling with it an expanding cloud of bellowing dust.

Moments later screams and moans all around, Asim raised his head and shook it. He was on all fours, breathing heavily, his head throbbing and his eyes straining to see through the dust and debris. It was deathly quite, no alarm bells, no voices in distress just the intermittent showers of dust particles from the ceiling to the floor. He jumped up first, broken glass and masonry crunching under his feet as he scrambled over to the children. They were fine but still huddled together and covered with fragments of fire-resistant ceiling tiles. Akilla was whimpering in the arms of one of her classmates. Asim lowered his head as the relief swept over him.

"Getting everybody safely out is priority. Can we use the emergency exits near by?" Asim shouted.

Yasmeen shook her head. "They can't... be opened manually." She finally managed, her voice husky. "The entire system is intuitive, reacting to differing environmental changes. It controls light levels," She swallowed, trying to lubricate her throat. "Heating levels, power and air-circulation. It has to think there's an emergency before it kicks in."

"Dis is an emergency." Asim said flatly.

"The intelligence core, the brain that controls all of the museum's systems must have been corrupted. The emergency exits should have opened by now."

"Obviously, things are not going as planned." Asim shook his head. "I'll check things out. Stay out a sight till I get back," he said. "And keep the youts, as quite as possible."

Then he was gone.

The adjoining room was belching dark smoke and the wails of people in distress was piercing through the bubble of incredulity he was in. Three Japanese girls came dashing into the Ethiopian hall, their clothes stained in dark soot and blood obviously disoriented and in shock.

Asim was about to sprint forward when he heard someone calling him. He lifted his eyes to his left and saw Trevor appearing from behind an animatronic nomadic herdsman. Dressed for war.

His hair was loose around his face and he wore only a string vest and slacks torn at the knee. He gripped two 'baby machetes' in both fists and was cursing like a sailor.

"They're on deh roof, town man," Trevor's eyes rose to the ceiling, his grating patois intense.

Asim looked up. The vast circular glass roof which naturally lighted a portion of the constructed environment of the Ethiopia hall was dotted by vague figures, moving around its edges and then suddenly moving out of view. Like the shadow of a huge bird of prey a hoverjeep banked away from the building. Trevor with agitated hand movements, signalled him to back away. This Asim did. And as he shielded his eyes, he knew what was about to follow. The circular sky light flashed red, followed by a high-pitched whine as it shattered. A shower of glass hit the sand on the desert display and with it dangling ropes.

Men soon followed, faces blackened, locks tied back.

Their weapons gleaming and their intentions wicked.

Asim needed to see nothing more.

It nah go happen, not again.

He would despatch them 'raas' with maximum disrespect if he had to.

Preparation.

That's what he had to do now.

Prepare.

And if he was to stand a chance of survival, he would have to think smart.

Quickly he edged around a virtual boulder and saw Trevor atop a virtual hill. The Rasta man was swearing at the top of his voice just before he let fly one of his knives.

It was an impossible throw, fuelled with anger and desperation. But as it whistled through the air, defying the odds, it found its target, sinking itself deep into the thigh of the last locks man, swinging down to earth. The man bellowed, his first disastrous reaction was to let go of the rope and grab at his wound. He plummeted thirty feet, bouncing off a hard plastic rock and then lying there, his muscles twitching.

Looking back up to congratulate him, Trevor had disappeared.

Pam-Pam! Bad bwoy.

It was a pity Asim was not as well-equipped as his friend-in-arms. His Equaliser was snugly tucked away at home, where it could do the least damage.

He looked to the main entrance leading into the Ethiopia Hall. Men with weapons were stationed there.

No way out.

Others had abseiled in from the roof, were meticulously searching the hall.

Jesas, Yasmeen and the kids.

Weapons fire, startled him.

The sounds were coming from Trevor's last location and the uncertain way the rounds were being 'let off' said they were trying to flush him out into the open.

Something told him they would have their hands full.

Asim on the other hand still needed a tool.

Improvise, boss, he told himself. Improvise!

He marshalled his thoughts desperately and headed towards a display based on the ancient civilisation of Kemite.

Stalking the vast maze, like a madman, he ran through a throne room, occupied by a pharaoh and his subjects. He reached for a sword held by a burly guard in sandals. The image rippled as his fingers passed through it.

Shit. A hologram.

Hesitating for a moment, uncertain of what was virtual or reality, he dived to the floor and made his way on his stomach. Just to his left, his probing fingers happened on a cold, smooth solid. It was a 'real' glass display case with an array of ceremonial swords and spears. He crawled forward until he was right beside it, then checking he hadn't been spotted he propped his back against the glass column and applied pressure. It resisted him only partially and Asim tensed some more and heaved. Grunting it swayed and then toppled, crashing to the floor. His eager hands dove into the fragmented case pulling out the ancient weapons which his Ethiopian brothers had not used in centuries. He slung a throwing axe over his shoulder and decided against it. Too cumbersome.

Pulling out the short spear he discarded that too and took a sword with him instead. A bow and quiver full of arrows made his eyes light up. He grabbed them and sprinted for cover.

Asim tried to make the widest sweep of the hall as was possible without skirting too close to the wall. He stopped when he was near one of the exits to an adjoining room and made sure he hadn't been seen. Slowly he advanced to the centre of the exhibition hall his every sense attuned, filtering out the shouting at the distance and the sporadic gun fire and only concentrating on the sounds and smells close by him. He was on his stomach crawling forward, just about to break through a clump of dense artificial foliage, when heard the voices approach his position.

He froze.

Inches from his extended finger, an army issue boot planted itself there.

His free hand touched the hilt of his sword and he prayed again that he was concealed properly by the synthetic bushes.

One of the two men gave a situation report, sounding out of breath.

"The British Library, Windsor Library, British Museum and the Museum of Mankind have all been successfully breached. Teams Philistine, Sodom, Abel and Zion are ready."

"Tell dem feh gwan." The older man ordered.

The dread with a communication rig slung around his shoulder, delivered a coded transmission on some obscure bandwidth.

"What of deh girl?" The elder dread asked.

"Every section covered. She is not there."

"Wha bout her office?" He sucked hard on a spliff.

"Nuthin!"

"Then she is here. Search every crevice of the Ethiopia Hall an when yuh find her, kill her." He checked his timepiece. "We have ten minutes."

The foot soldier grunted and sprinted off. The other man took one last pull on his weed and killed it.

He followed close behind.

******

Keeping the children calm and quite was difficult. Yasmeen tried to allay their fears as best she could.

"It's going to be all right," she whispered hoarsely. "When

uncle Asim gets back, we'll all leave here together. I promise."

She heard the footfalls heading in their direction from the other side of the display.

Asim!

She jumped up. But there was no one there.

Yasmeen spun back to the children, her lips puckered in confusion and saw what at first sight seemed like convection currents carrying a cloud of black soot towards them.

They took human form.

The first shadow stepped out into the light. Yasmeen backed up, her mouth open and a stunned look in her eyes. Shuffling away from the image before her, she slammed into someone else.

A warm solid someone.

She spun around horrified. The scream stuck in her throat as a massive hand clamped over her mouth and jaw. As their eyes met she realised she was face to face with the black heart man.

Locks tied back and greasy, eyes piercing and a large gun pointing at her chest.

"Glad mi find yuh, sister Yasmeen, deh Spear was getting impatient."

******

The flames were spreading rapidly as Asim wormed his way back to Yasmeen and the children. Dropping to his stomach again, he eased his way through artificial shrubland. Then froze.

Desperate cries from the children.

Jesas!

His daughter's screams.

Don't hurt them, he repeated with every step he took.

Please God, don't let them get hurt.

His sword drawn.

Don't give in to yuh fear, boss, think.

A blur of movement to his left.

His momentum unchecked, he could do nothing to swerve out of harm's way.

A savage parting of the air to his right side then an exploding warmth engulfing his back. As if he was caught in slow motion he felt his shoulder muscle split open then his senses suddenly kick back into hi-gear and a wave of pain engulfing him.

A delicate kiss by the keen edge of a blade.

Blood spurted from the wound and Asim bit down hard to stifle a scream. His world tilted for a moment from the sudden nervous shock. He stumbled away giving himself distance, his left hand clamped to his bloody back as he whirled violently, his right hand pointing his sword at the man in black standing a few paces away.

The locks man sized him up carefully.

Smirking he lifted the gun strap from around his neck and dropped the automatic to the floor. Then he kicked it into the gloom. He did the same with his bloodied dagger.

He bowed respectfully, his eyes never leaving Asim's.

Mano e Mano, Asim concluded.

Fair enough.

With deliberate exaggeration he pulled a gleaming cutlass that was strapped to his back. Dispensing with any further pleasantries, he came at Asim like a furious lion. His blade flashing from left to right and his movements so quick, they seemed to be caught in the beams of a strobe light. Asim bared his teeth and staggered back, feeling the fear bordering on desperation as he barred his assailant's slashes, every swipe making the difference between his survival or death.

Their blades whistled through the air, Asim blocking his advances and feeling the pain with every strike of metal. The dreadlocks tested him. He attacked low and to the right but the ex-soldier read it and fanned the assault away with a clash of his sword.

The locks man tried again. Attacking down the centre this time, a practised move he performed with blistering speed, swinging his machete on both sides and then thrusting to his opponent's solar plexus. Asim kept his composure well, only just side-stepping the blade.

Frustrated, the dreadlocks struck and struck again, each stroke weakening the baalhead and bringing him closer to him.

His smug smile disappeared when Asim used the fist gripping the sword as a battering ram. Delivering two blistering blows, once to the jaw and another to his neck.

Staggering back two steps, and daubing blood from a gash on his cheek, the natty let out a scream like a wild animal and furiously dashed at him again. He made a diagonal swipe, expecting to catch Asim unawares and part him from his shoulder to his waist. The baalhead brushed his advance away easily but lost his footing and stumbled backwards. The sword fell out of his hand and clattered away. The locks man grinned, lunging at him with the point of his blade, sensing the inevitable kill but still the baalhead rolled away from him. He kept slashing, kept chopping, but the bwoy was quick, his sense of survival acute.

Anger took control of his concentration and Asim took advantage. Instead of doing what was expected of him and continue to scramble towards his sword, he shot across to his assailant and swept his feet from under him.

While he was regaining his footing, Asim exploded backwards across the floor, using his feet like pistons and skidding for some distance before he rolled to his right. Just a finger's length from the sword.

He could hear the clamouring and curses behind him as his adversary regained his footing and charged again mindlessly. Weakly, Asim propped himself on his knees, swung his sword up and across and then brought it down in a wide arc.

Metal sliced flesh and parted bone.

The dreadlocks fell, gripping one knee cut to the cartilage and pressing his free hand to a deep gash in his chest. Unable to stop the arterial spurts of blood, he clamped his hand over the wound and bellowed out for help.

Asim's dark features towered over him.

"I ought to kill yuh pussyclaat now, but I won't. That will be entertainment for me later, turf bwoy. In the mean time be my guest and scream as much as yuh like."

Asim struck him once with the back of his fist and staggered off.

His chest heaving from the exertion, the wound to his back stymied by the adrenaline pumping through his system, he turned towards the exhibit.

He took no more than two steps before a vibration of metal above startled him.

No!

Asim stepped back and looked up.

Another figure dropped in front of him, from the roof above, as silently as a ninja. Slowly, the man lifted himself from his crouched position and cautiously approached him.

Noooo!

Asim's scream of frustration and anger, could only be heard in the caverns of his own mind as he charged through the smoke, ignoring the pain, wanting only to get to the children.

He slashed out at the new threat, but his assailant was quicker, fresher and more agile.

Jumping back from the attack, the man smiled without retaliating.

Smiling?

"Easy, town man."

Asim's grimace melted in a wave of relief.

Trevor looked at him smugly.

The Rasta man had lost his clothes and was now decked out in the outfits of one of the invading locks men. They didn't speak, there was no need to. Asim pointed to the exhibit, lifting his three fingers and made a slashing motion to his throat with his hand.

Trevor nodded.

He jerked his thumb right and Trevor took his point without a question.

The smoke was getting denser by the minute, Asim stifled a cough and took his position. The squeals drifting up on the updraft were edged with absolute childish terror.

It was now or never, his cue to move.

Yasmeen stared into the unfeeling eyes of the wicked, pointing his gun at the children, and then lowered her head again her long black natty falling around her face.

"Please, just let the kids go." Her voice was a harsh murmur. "Can't you see they're frightened?"

An elbow slammed into the back of her head.

"Who deh bomboclaat a ask yuh? It better them frighten than dem dead."

She blacked out for a moment, finding herself on her elbows. Slowly her vision swam back into focus and she managed to drag herself back into a kneeling position. Any thoughts she may have harboured of struggling had died.

"Please let them go." she slurred. "I'm begging you."

The men laughed

Vaguely, she felt the cold metal pressed hard at her temple and the disconcerting presence of the man behind her. The chill hands of panic and fear massaged her insides and she struggled for control, trying to garner some inner calm. Nauseous and weak she swayed forward, the pressure of grit and stones hurting her knees.

She toppled.

But was grabbed by her neck before she fell forward, the man behind roughly pulled her upright. He spoke into her ear, his breath hot and rancid.

"What yuh tink yuh doing? Pretty gal like you."

"Why me?" She asked weakly, her voice unable to muster much more volume.

"You're special, yuh nevah know dat? Jus like your old man. An you come with a healthy price on yuh head, too. I need no other reason."

Like my father?

More questions, she would never have the answers to.

The images of Miriam, her work, Akilla and Asim flitted across her mind's eye. Her life had been good. Shuddering, tears streaming down her cheeks. For the children. She consoled herself. Her fingers reaching for the gold cashew nut slung around her neck, rubbing it gently she recited Psalm 23.

Her executioner spoke into his mobile.

Yea though I walk through the valley of the shadow of death.

He smiled and nodded.

I will fear no evil.

He charged his weapon.

For thou art with me thy rod and thy staff will comfort me.

Opening her eyes to see the children for the last time her vision fogged with tears.

Thou preparest a table before me in the presence of mine enemies.

She looked away from them, unable to handle the tidal wave of terror. A terror that was so all-embracing Yasmeen began seeing things.

There was an outline of a shaggy head, briefly hidden by the smoke. Red locks and a cheeky grin. Then it was gone. Her prayers ended abruptly.

"Natty Palmer!!!"

The man with the gun to Yasmeen's head froze when he heard his name screamed out loud. It was the voice of his sparring partner, Ray-I. In pain. His attention shifted for a mere moment and Yasmeen used the opportunity to uncertainly stand and face him.

"What deh fuck yuh think yuh doing, gal?"

By this, the muzzle of his weapon was pressed firmly against her forehead instead of her temple.

"Just making sure you don't miss," she said.

The brethren's screams were getting louder. The dreadlocks with his gun trained on her was struggling with the decision to stay put or go investigate. Yasmeen's stare was unnerving him as well, he looked away.

"Look into my goddamn eyes when you pull the trigger, boy." Yasmeen dared.

The man hesitated, confused under pressure.

"Not so easy, face to face, is it?" she whispered.

He shook his head as if he was clearing the cobwebs and snarled, lashing out with the gun, sending Yasmeen twisting to the floor.

"Fuck dis."

Cooly kneeling beside her, he pointed the weapon to her head and wrapped his finger around the trigger.

Asim absorbed the whole picture in one snapshot.

A dreadlocks had his back to him with a gun to Yasmeen's head as she lay on the ground, all the children were on the floor at the other end, covered by another two men.

He locked into autopilot. Three quick steps and he was directly behind the first 'bwoy'. The other two aimed at Asim who had already kneeled behind the first man, shielding himself, while he dragged him up by the scruff of his neck and twisted the gun from his hand.

The weapon discharged harmlessly into the ceiling.

"You need to be quicker than that, pussy," Asim hissed.

A professional would have taken out both him and his shield but after due consideration these 'raases' were no pro's. The dread in the arm lock struggled, Asim kissed his teeth heaved backwards and jerked. There was a discernible crack as his spinal chord fractured. The body went limp and folded. Asim fell with it, in the fashion of some dance macabre, his own finger replacing the dead man's around the trigger.

As the tiles rose up to meet him, he squeezed off two rounds in the direction of the other two Spear men.

One sizzled wide, shattering a plastic panel above one man's head. While the luckier of the two saw his chest exploding and felt the momentum fling his body against the wall. Eyes wide with surprise or shock, he left a filthy crimson mark as he slid down on his backside.

Trying to scurry from underneath the corpse, Asim swung his weapon a fraction to his right, already taking aim on the third man and bracing himself for some return fire.

Shit, he'd gone!

Then Trevor stepped cooly out from behind the exhibit, droplets of scarlet dripping from his big knife and splashing to the floor. He wiped the blade on his trousers and nodded casually.

Asim heaved the body off him and stood up.

"Let's leave this place, now." He barked, rousing the children from their crouching positions on the floor. The flames were licking just beyond the display and the heat even at that distance was becoming unbearable. Asim lifted Yasmeen up from her knees, kissing her while he did so. The children huddled around them shocked and confused. Akilla had broken from the group and attached herself to her father's leg. The horror she had seen reducing her to fits of sobbing. The smoke was becoming unbearable and the automatic fire doors had still not opened.

THE CITY OF SHASHEMANE, ETHIOPIA.

"Soon it will be time." Yamu muttered. "Jah will be done."

He spoke to the masses as if they were before him. But the visuals he was staring at were being transmitted to his private meditation cubicle, deep in the Tabernacle of the Conquering Lion.

He could feel the crowds intensity as they gathered outside in the square, the hum of their excitement rising into the African skies. This was his spiritual home, the golden city.

Shashemane was set in the middle of a rift valley, the tail of the Ahmar Mountains stretching to the east, lake Awasa and Shala close by. Today it was the focus of a pilgrimage unheard of in Ethiopia's history. They had travelled not just from Addis Ababa but from across the globe.

They were here to witness his rising up.

While the sun sunk into the mountains, Shashemane lived up to its name for a few moments longer, the last rays transforming the roof tops into slabs of the precious metal. Date palms stood even higher swaying with the brisk breezes while the unofficial capital, held its breath like all its citizens. Thousands of the Ras Tafari and Ethiopian Orthodox family waited with Muslim and Christian as the Ceremony of Ascension continued behind closed doors.

The final prophecy was to be fulfilled and the atmosphere surrounding the graceful spires of the Tabernacle was charged with energy.

Yamu had been given the privacy to meditate on the task he

was to face. There was no need for that. He was born for this. He knew what he had to do, he had visualised this occasion a hundred times before and it held no mystery to him. His focus was elsewhere. He looked keenly at the message that was being decoded on a terminal in his chambers. He smiled hungrily.

All four Babylonian repositories of African treasures in London had been successfully raided and a large collection of these invaluable pieces would be returned to their grateful owners.

And grateful they would be. Some of these artifacts had much more than historic significance - literally the symbols of nationhood for some.

Already he was making history and lasting partnerships.

The raising of Negusa Negas was two hours away.

He held his eyes level as the text scrolled slowly across the screen.

His niece was dead.

He shook his head with feigned regret.

There was no other way. You should have stayed buried, brother.

Yamu's eyes flicked over the twenty-four-hour clock. He smiled, again. Soon no living person would be able to challenge his title.

Very soon.

COCKPIT COUNTRY, TRELAWNY, JAMAICA.

The killing team had advanced through the thick undergrowth of the Trelawny bush in excellent time. They had traversed streams, hacked their way through mangrove swamps, following their guide who led them on an intersecting route to a roughly trodden footpath leading directly to the target. Their cover as engineers working in Thro-Weh District, had allowed them to carry out initial reconnaissance by jetcopters, making them comfortable with the lie of the land. This was not the standard incursion into enemy territory. The target was non-military and, from their intelligence, unable to respond to an assault on the scale they were planning. Orders maintained they proceed with extreme caution and leave no trace the target ever existed. They dug into their positions, certain no surprises lay in wait, but wary nonetheless.

Exotic birds cawed and hooted, up in the canopy of leaves above their heads.

Fifteen minutes before the assault would commence, Sergeant Katz scanned the terrain with his binoculars, still not satisfied.

It was clear.

Small animals foraging for food, heat signatures of birds and reptiles. No trip wires, no hidden snares. Clear.

He looked back at his men, so well blended into the surroundings, the eyes he could see showed relief they had reached the killing ground undetected.

They wanted just to finish the job and go. It was a harsh land but not too dissimilar from portions of New South Africa, a terrain they were very familiar with indeed.

The Rasta community was something else entirely.

They were peaceful but carried an underlying threat he couldn't quite figure.

He wanted to be sure.

The shooters waited patiently nibbling on wild okras and bamboo shoots. Their eyes and weapons never left the camouflaged building in the distance for a moment.

In three minutes, the Dread was about to be reminded that the Brotherhood never forgot to repay old debts.

SOMEWHERE BELOW MUSEUM OF ANCIENT AFRICAN HISTORY.
Yasmeen threw the switch on the Master Control unit.

The bomb shelter lit up, accompanied by the computer melody of systems in operation. Information streams were being sent out, bypassing the faulty main core upstairs and allowing the fire prevention protocols to come into play.

Overhead they could hear the alarm bells and the groaning of emergency exits opening.

Raas late, Asim thought. But Yasmeen's thoughts were ones of thanks.

The old World War II bomb shelter had been kept functionally intact by the civil engineers as part of the original features of the listed building.

"I'll help keep the youts occupied." Asim said, the slump of his shoulders showing how drained he was.

"Bettah business." Trevor said, waiting until Asim was out of earshot. "I need to talk to yuh in private anyway."

Yasmeen's eyebrows formed a puzzled 'V'.

"Nuff tings yuh need to know." Trevor continued in a bass tone that was supposed to be a whisper. "An is near time for me to tell yuh."

"Tell me what?"

Trevor produced a reassuring smile and checked a timepiece he had hidden in his jacket.

"Soon it will be all over, for the good or deh bad. Then you will overstand, everyting."

COCKPIT COUNTRY, TRELAWNY, JAMAICA.

The men advanced cautiously.

Fine spears of light stabbed into the soft soil, revealing a break in the canopy of trees above their heads. The thatch house was illuminated like a precious prize. A prize they were about to raise to the ground. Slowly they came closer.

Firstly, they would secure the perimeter, then a three-man team would go in, eliminate the old man, set explosive charges, detonate them and disappear.

A hundred metres from the objective. Their eyes peeled, their other senses reaching out to detect anything out of the ordinary.

They kept moving.

Sergeant Katz, signalled the elimination team to move in with a slice of his finger. The men dashed forward. Open and shut, he thought. Fifty meters from the objective. The team leader stopped dead in his tracks.

He cocked his head and listened to whatever jungle instincts men like him possessed. The hairs at the back of his neck rose as his ears strained to distinguish some present danger. A bird chirped and the wild flutter of some large insect far, far away and then so, so... close.

Pain!

It was sudden and explosive as his hand instinctively flew to his neck and blood burst from the wound as he fell sideways. Sergeant Katz stiffened in front of a dead-an-wake bush, hearing and seeing nothing but his captain collapsing in a spray of scarlet.

Then the environment suddenly came alive.

Men fell out of trees, shrubs nearby suddenly became muscular forms covered in camouflage war paint, bodies partially buried in moist mud rose up with weapons at the ready like militant zombies, all with long matted hair and bushes seemingly growing out of what little clothing they were wearing.

The mercenaries who resisted, paid with their lives and the others, wisely threw down their weapons and surrendered.

The Rasta men caked in mud and foliage stood silently watching armed with catapults, Bows, crossbows and machetes. The old maroon traditions had not been forgotten.

A heavy jawed, grey-haired Rasta stepped forward and pointed his blood splattered cutlass to a young mercenary with communication equipment on his back.

"You, young bwoy!" He said. "Step forward." Hesitantly he did. "A want you feh pass on dis message to yuh boss." The old dread placed the sharp edge of the blade to the young mans fore head. "Tell dem deh mission accomplish. Nuthin more nuthin less."

BOMB SHELTER UNDER MUSEUM, LONDON.

He's alive?

Yasmeen could barely think straight.

Was that what Trevor said?

Yuh father is still alive.

The statement repeated itself in her head like an echo and then came the emotions of disbelief, joy and apprehension, all rolled into one.

Trevor wouldn't dare lie much less joke under these circumstances.

His expressionless demeanour said he was serious.

How in Jah's name?

Trevor checked his time piece again like his revelation was nothing of major consequence.

Asim had just walked into the end of their conversation, his face flushed from loss of blood.

He looked at Trevor and then at Yasmeen.

"Yuh father's dead, right," he said picking up the thread of conversation. She squeezed his hand, her lips pursed tightly and looked at Trevor, still uncertain.

"You could be wrong?" She was clutching at straws.

"I know exactly what I know. You think him dead and that was what your Mama had to tell yuh. It was all about protection. But your father is alive, sista. Alive an well. Ready to lead, as he did in the past." Yasmeen's vague look received an understanding hug from Trevor.

She asked.

"He led you in the past?"

"It will all become clear, sista Yasmeen." He smiled. "By the way. The Dread seh if we pull through, he wants his only daughter to have this."

The Dread?

Yasmeen burst into a spate of questions of which Trevor shook his head to them and gave her instead what was in his hands.

Her eyes filled with tears as she clenched her fingers over what had been given to her. The knuckles of her fist whitening with the pressure, she was exerting.

Then ever so slowly, she opened them like a flower caught in bloom, a dry seed lay unsubstantially in her trembling hands. It was nothing more fantastic than a shrivelled cashew seed punctured by what seemed like an old shoe lace but its significance to her was immeasurable. She gently touched the other half of the whole, slung around her neck on a gold chain.

The two parts fit perfectly.

The memories rushed back with such force she held onto Asim for support. Her mother had given it to her when she was three years old, her father wore the other half before he supposedly died and it was the only tangible memento that her father ever lived. Miriam would always say:

"Your father made me promise him, never to make you forget."

The cashew seed was to be that constant reminder of the love of a father who had died when she was a child and who had just been resurrected like a latter day Lazarus.

TABERNACLE OF THE CONQUERING LION, SHASHEMANE.
The old man hobbled up to the guards who stood protecting the perimeter around a huge wrought iron gate that led into the Tabernacles forecourt. One guard, a burly Ethiopian with long curly hair, looked down at the bent figure approaching him with a walking stick and then looked out to the sea of humanity he had appeared from, wondering how he had managed to make it through. The old man had passed through security personnel further up and had produced a verification chip that needed okaying at his terminal. The guard's naturally inquisitive mind had wondered why he wore the robes of a Rasta patriarch but his choice of entry and his timing was all wrong. Just a late arrival. The Ethiopian's suspicions were forgotten as the man offered his hand and they clasped. A strong handshake, a warm infectious smile and soul searching eyes that seemed to look inside you. He liked him for some unknown reason and anyway his pass cleared.

The elder from Jamaica hurriedly made his way into the Tabernacle.

"Weep not: Behold the Lion of Tribe of Judah, the root of David, hath prevailed to open the book, and to loose the seven seals thereof."

The patriarch paused for dramatic effect only. "Centuries after these words were set down in the Bible, Ras Tafari was crowned Emperor of Ethiopia. Taking the name of Haile Selassie I, King of Kings, Lord of Lords, Conquering Lion of the tribe of Judah. He became the 225th ruler of the 2000-year-old Solomonic Dynasty. Today in memory of the prophet we begin another great period in our history."

The elders from both the Ethiopian Orthodox Church and the Nation of Ras Tafari sat in silence as the presiding patriarch completed his litany.

Outside thousands of the faithful were becoming impatient.

Excitement that couldn't be hidden even amongst the wizened eyes of the assembled. A momentous occasion was coming to a close and the only man who could lead the world wide Rasta faith was on his knees and being sanctified by the incense smoke from the swinging urns of the two supporting altar boys. Flickering torches were set on poles surrounding the circular hall, the harsh looking seats, rising in levels like an amphitheatre filled with orthodoxy and Rasta decision makers. The prophet, Bob Marley provided the reverent atmosphere, that sometime later, was replaced by words of Thanksgiving.

"Glory and praise, and Majesty, and honour, and supplications be unto the Holy trinity for Iver and Iver."

It was now time for the presiding Father to face his brothers and sisters for the symbolic question of acceptance for the first ever Negusa Negas.

The Rasta Father was a scrawny man, with large intense eyes, shrouded by bushy brows, his stringy locks fell limply around his pencil thin face and he was blessed with a voice that made him speak with a power that seemed to come from someone else.

"You have been elected by Jah through we the leaders of the Nation and our Mother the Ethiopian Orthodox Church. The Redemption Prophecy told all the faithful of your arrival, not by name but simply by deed. You will become the defender of the faith and Jah-Jah has decided through we the Fathers." He cleared his throat. "For the history books, let us hear your final words."

The I's of agreement rang out all around as a unanimous vote was needed for Patriarch Yamu to ascend.

He had his eyes closed and his hands clasped to his chest while still on his knees. He felt a warmth prickling the crown of his head. As the "I's" continued to boom from the mouths of the elders, Yamu's grand plans of racial conflict blossomed undisturbed.

A new order, Iyah!

Seconds passed and then the unspeakable was said.

"No sah!" Blurted from the mouth of a patriarch from New South Africa. It took mere seconds for that response to sink in and outrage to flare up. Victory for Yamu seemed less certain because another Nay! blurted out, then another and another.

Yamu's eyes sprang open as the murmurs of confusion rose to a deafening crescendo. The orderly ceremony immediately descended into chaos. The presiding Father had lost all control, his calls for calm went unheeded. Shouting and derision spread like a bush fire.

Just as quickly the pandemonium subsided.

Yamu jumped to his feet screaming something at the top of his voice, trying to regain the focus that had since departed.

In horror he realised the new focal point of the gathered was an old man hobbling down the aisle that split the amphitheatre in two.

There was hushed silence. Then the whispers. Next came the voices raised in incredulity and lastly the astonished recognition.

The Dread was seething with anger.

He stopped in his tracks and pointed his ginep walking stick at his brother in the distance. Yamu's face darkened, his sulphurous eyes slid across his brothers face with a contempt that was destroying his judgement.

"Joshua!!!" He bellowed. "Dis is my time."

The Dread stood his ground.

"Surprised to see me alive, mi know." He hung his head and shook it feeling the disgrace, his brother was incapable of. "You're not fit to even walk past dis holy house, much less hold the mantle of Negas. Mi Bredda, yuh have blood on yuh hands."

The chants of the Dreads name resounded off the walls, struggling against the voices of popular opinion until they too relinquished and his name became the dominant cry.

A dead man walking.

The prophet.

Yamu's eyes were darting around in his head like a cornered animal. His lips contorted, the aura of calm gone. Stripped of its mask the face of Yamu radiated evil.

Him still alive. Alive! Them all fail me, every Jah damn one a dem, fail me!

The patriarch's shock quickly became one consuming thought blazing through his head.

Him not taking what is mine. I will finish deh job, myself.

Scrambling to his feet, Yamu burst forward.

Deacons and ceremonial guards tried to hold him back but he flung them to one side.

He headed towards a forest of candle stands, his fingers embracing the cold metal of one and then pulling it towards him.

He paused as if some internal power supply had suddenly depleted and fixed Joshua with a stare that had just teetered over the edge of sanity.

Reanimating, he frantically broke off the soft wax of his make shift weapon, revealing the sharp protruding spokes. His eyes were filled with rage or madness, a bloodcurdling scream leaving his twisted lips.

"Negusa Negas is mine!"

Joshua shook his head and whispered," Forgive mi Father."

Slowly twisting the handle of his ginep walking stick, he pulled a keen blade from it.

Forgive mi Father.

He flung the scabbard to the floor in defiance.

It must end.

******

EPILOGUE

London, Three weeks after the museum fire.

The numbers flashed weakly on the tissue thin watch face.

He had to imagine his old Team completing their job and merging with the shadows thrown by the building because no one including him would see them disappearing into the Soho night.

Satisfied he nodded his head, the illumination from the streets dancing over the dark skin of his scalp.

The Porsche was parked on a double yellow line, facing the Blue Note. He had been there no more than a minute and a half. The laser lights were bright and hypnotic announcing to the entire West End that they're open for business. The pleasures hidden inside would be attracting the wild life very soon.

But before that, he awaited his own grand performance.

He glanced at the digits again and looked unconcerned at the hungry-eyed traffic wardens scouting vehicles for removal. He watched an unlucky motorist have his engine block surgically removed from his car for a parking violation.

Secure, Asim winked at the female warden looking his way.

He wouldn't fall victim to their zealous execution of duty tonight because he had no intention of leaving his car.

"One minute and counting." He murmured to himself and started the Porsche's engines, just as a dark coated warden flapped over.

He kissed his teeth and engaged the car's reverse program. The Porsche backed up, sensors sounding as it neared another car's bumper, locked right automatically and pulled out. As he took control of the steering wheel, he heard the initial deep rumble and wound down the window, poking his head out. The Blue Note lit up like a star with an ear splitting shriek. The building belched smoke, electrics sparked and the foundations shook.

A precision implosion if he had ever seen one.

The superstructure was left standing but the interior was completely gutted.

Asim straightened his jacket and peered at the smouldering ruin.

That was for putting the life of my family in danger, pussyhole. And Mr. Thorndike, if you ever do bounce back from this little disaster and clock on I was the cause. I will give you two options, peace or war. Either way I'll be waiting for yuh bloodclaat.

In the resulting panic he drove off.

Yasmeen looked so helpless as Asim approached her sitting on the bench over looking the shimmering Thames. So much had happened. It was no wonder she was deep in thought.

The image of sadness disappeared as she looked up to see him coming towards her. Those hazel eyes brightened and she raised her head, the indomitable inner strength returning.

Earlier that day they had put Trevor on an Air Jamaica flight home. Yasmeen had been through a lot with him so it was quite emotional. Even Asim had bonded with the coarse Rasta man in the few life threatening hours they had shared. He had cleared up the gaps in the puzzle as he had promised but still it was an incredible story.

Her father had remained hidden in Thro-weh District for many years protected by the maroons and presumed dead to the world. Maybe he would have remained dead if not for the threat on his daughter and the title of Negusa Negas.

How he knew what had been developing in England with Yasmeen, the plot against his life by his brother and sending Trevor over to keep her safe was anybody's guess.

The old man was an enigma who now held the mantle, uncontested. But even with his influence, there was the constant threat of the Spear and others in the flock who believed in violence to elicit change. And with a den of influential friends who shared the bounty of stolen treasures, their reach would be extensive.

The worst was yet to come.

The South African connection was still murky. Trevor guessed the alliance between the Spear and the Broeders - was simply a shared hatred for the Dread, going back many years.

What Asim knew for certain was they had left his sister comatose, tried to kill him and his woman and he would not forget it. He had his own theories and in time he would channel that information to the right people.

For now, he had to be in a state of constant preparedness and any hope for a normal existence was gone. He had craved to be just another Mr. Joe Public but destiny had other plans for him. His only consolation was, he had found a woman like no other and his family was intact, a little wiser and stronger.

"I thought you weren't coming?" Yasmeen said standing up.

Asim feigned a look of hurt and then smiled. He held her and they kissed deeply remaining in a warm embrace for a while.

"Apologies, princess," he said. "Some buddies of mine from South Africa dropped into the offices without an invitation. After a chat and a few drinks, I couldn't leave without pointing them in the right direction for a party. I know they'll be bombing up London town, t'night."

"I bet." She smiled her red lips turning ruby as the light from a hover vehicle caught it. They held hands and walked along the Waterloo promenade for a distance.

"How's Fatima?" She asked.

"No better, no worse, but we have a specialist interested in looking at her case. Lets hope."

"Lets hope." Yasmeen said.

Then Asim asked.

"How do you feel about meeting your father for the first time?"

She shrugged.

"I'm not sure. I'm frightened and excited all at once. I owe him so much but wish I didn't have to fly all the way to Ethiopia. The images of running for our lives still frighten me, even now. But if that's what it takes."

"It can do nothing but good, princess. Relax, rediscover yuh roots."

They stopped and leaned on the railing watching the speed boats skim across the water's surface. Asim turned his head around to watch her.

"How are you going to break our situation to the old bwoy?"

"Gently." She said with a smile.

"I might need time to grow a descent looking 'natty' though." He rubbed his hands over his bald dome and she laughed.

His grin disappeared quickly.

"I don't have to remind you that it's going to be rough on all fronts. People won't forget about Yamu and what he stood for. Some maniacs are going to blame you and your father for his death. The threat on both your lives could never go away. Can you deal with dat?"

Yasmeen turned to face him.

"Will you be here with me?"

Asim nodded.

"Like yuh shadow."

She kissed him on the forehead.

Ignoring his pounding heart, he leaned over and spoke directly in her ear, his voice soft.

"Lets go back to your place and..." He stopped himself in mid-sentence, a question forming. "I've never been home with you since everything that happened, have I."

"To my Flat." She corrected. "And no, you haven't. Is this your subtle way of getting an invitation?"

"Maybe."

"It's no palace."

Asim shook his head.

"Let me be deh judge of that. I want to see you on a different vibe, tonight. Really relaxed. You know what I mean." He winked.

"And..." A smile parted her lips.

"Sample some more ital cuisine?"

"And..." She prompted, her voice nearly a whisper. "Okay!" He braced his chest with mock confidence. "Lets test out the difference between my good old fashion bedspring and the magnetic suspension on your bed."

Yasmeen glared at him for long seconds and slowly shook her head. Unable to maintain that look of seriousness, she let loose a fit of laughter that danced across the sparkling waters of the Thames.

She was still giggling as they walked off hand in hand.

Asim stopped, looked at her and took a mental snapshot of the moment. Making sure he captured Yasmeen's laughter and his feeling of completeness and stored it away for safe keeping.

He had an uncomfortable sense of certainty he would need it, in the months to come.

End